I0724605

RULES, SCHMULES!

BECCA SEYMOUR

RAINBOW TREE PUBLISHING

ALSO BY BECCA SEYMOUR

Zone Defense

No Take Backs | No More Secrets | No Wrong Moves

Fast Break

Rules, Schmules! | Facts, Smacts!

True-Blue

Let Me Show You | I've Got You | Becoming Us | Thinking It Over | Always For You | It's Not You | Our First & Last

Outback Boys

Stumble | Bounce | Wobble

Stand-Alone Contemporary

Not Used To Cute | High Alert | Realigned | Amalgamated

Urban Fantasy Romance

Thicker Than Water

RULES, SCHMULES!

BECCA SEYMOUR

RAINBOW TREE PUBLISHING

RULES, SCHMULES! Copyright © 2022 by Becca Seymour

All rights reserved.

All rights reserved. No part of this book may be used or reproduced in any written, electronic, recorded, or photocopied format without the express permission from the author or publisher as allowed under the terms and conditions with which it was purchased or as strictly permitted by applicable copyright law. Any unauthorized distribution, circulation or use of this text may be a direct infringement of the author's rights, and those responsible may be liable in law accordingly. Thank you for respecting the work of this author.

RULES, SCHMULES! is a work of fiction. All names, characters, events and places found therein are either from the author's imagination or used fictitiously. Any similarity to persons alive or dead, actual events, locations, or organizations is entirely coincidental and not intended by the author.

COVER DESIGN: BOOKSMITH DESIGN

EDITORS: HOT TREE™ EDITING

E-BOOK ISBN: 978-1-922679-25-3

PAPERBACK ISBN: 978-1-922679-26-0

AUTHOR'S NOTE

Rules, Schmules! is set in Georgia and uses both fictional and real locations and references. The basketball league in both the Zone Defense and Fast Break world is called the League, not the NBA. While I loosely followed the NBA structure, I created my own league and team names, my own competition names, and took liberties to make my fun, low-angst world work.

CHAPTER 1
RULE 8: NO GETTING WASTED DURING THE SEASON

DEAN

Switching colleges the summer before my junior year sucked hairy balls. You know, the kind with hair that is wiry, rough to touch, and escapes too easily so gets caught between your teeth? Yeah, those ones.

But heading to Brixham University in a small-ass town not too far out of Atlanta was a necessary evil. Not that I'm overly dramatic with the whole "evil" concept, but still, back in LA, I'd been comfortable, happy with my classes, my friends, and close enough to my kid brother to keep an eye on him but have my freedom.

Three weeks at my new school, and it's a struggle to feel settled. That hasn't stopped me from dressing and behaving however I wish. Screw that. What it does mean is I'm rolling my eyes so often I'm worried about RSI in my eyeballs. Not that anyone has come out and said anything derogatory, but since I grew up in a blip of a community not so dissimilar to this one, I hate to admit I expect some sort of homophobic derision.

So yeah, feeling like I have to stay on guard sucks those furry balls.

But at least I have Lester and Simone, my two newfound friends I've been lucky enough to attach myself to. There's also my mom and my brother, Zeke, the two people I love most in the world and the reason I left LA in the first place. There wasn't a chance I couldn't be close by to Zeke.

"Did you read the email from Professor Henderson about the group project?" Simone speaks into her handheld mirror while applying extra eyeliner.

I squint at the bright blue she's penciling on, not quite sure it's her color, but with the way she blinks and grins at her reflection, she's clearly happy, so I sensibly keep my mouth shut. "I did," I grumble. "Does he usually add such limitations?"

"He did something similar last year, so I suppose, yeah."

"And we really can't request who we're grouped with?"

Simone shakes her head, her platinum-blonde curls bouncing with the movement. "Nope. He's a little old-school. We just have to suck it up."

"Figured." While the group project doesn't sound overly complicated, the class is big and filled with such a range of students that the likelihood of me being stuck with at least one person who's a pain in the ass, if not a slacker or possibly an asshole, is high.

It's hard to not embrace the negative Nelly in me, but with my reluctant, albeit sensible move to be closer to my mom and my fifteen-year-old brother, being super upbeat seems impossible. Sure, I make an effort, honest, but I can't be "on" all the time, you know?

Not that I blame either of them for the move; it was my choice, after all. And Mom being evicted from their rental as the owners were selling was hardly her choice. What neither Zeke nor I expected was her to move halfway across the country for a new job and more affordable accommodation. I understand, though.

But more than that, and the truth of my move, is affording to live in LA, and attend school there, became exponentially more difficult. Adulting is hard, people. For real. Making the sensible decisions, not being in a mountain of debt when the reality is post-college I'll have a shitty teacher's salary, well, yeah… moving ended up being the logical thing to do.

Doesn't mean I can't pout or kick the sand about the change, though.

I am super grateful Brixham U offered me a partial scholarship—something I never had in LA. Plus they were awesome about transferring my credits. I seriously lucked out.

But the last couple of months with the move have been stressful, and finally with Zeke settled, I'm able to allow myself a few moments of feeling sorry for myself for leaving my friends and my regular hookups behind.

Yeah, yeah, I'm all woe is me, and these are totally first world problems.

"You may be grouped with someone great, Dean." Simone eyes me and bobs her thick brows, adding, "Or someone hot."

I snort. Chance would be a fine thing. I may have noticed a sexy guy or five on campus, but I have a terrible weakness for athletes. And in my experience, jocks don't take kindly to being crushed on by five-foot-seven twinks who wear mascara and like to top. Such a jock is my unicorn. Add in a guy who's genuinely smart and, heaven forbid, has a sense of humor, and perhaps I need to think of something more fantastical than a unicorn to compare my ideal man to.

A griffin maybe. Or a dragon.

"Come on. Let's pack up, drop our bags in my room, and head to Jack's party." Simone puts away her mirror and indicates for me to get my ass into gear.

"A couple of drinks would help me relax," I admit, pushing aside my athlete fantasies. I know better than to dive headfirst into such impossible dreams.

"That's the spirit. Did you tell your mom you're going to be MIA tonight?"

"Yeah." And don't I feel and sound like a dork with that answer? I set about packing away my laptop and handwritten notes. "I managed to catch up with her this morning before her shift at the hospital." With my mom doing extra shifts as a nurse at the hospital in the slightly larger town about twenty miles away from campus, I've tried my hardest to select courses that will give me enough time to easily commute and spend with Zeke so he's not home alone too often.

A few weeks in, and it's working so far. It's still a shock to the system no longer living on campus and having the freedom of my own space, but not spending the extra cash is a blessing. Plus there's the reassurance of seeing Zeke for myself and making sure he really is as okay as he professes to be.

"Remind me if there's a reason this Jack is having a party again." I have no idea who Jack is. While Brixham U is nowhere near the size of my old college, it's a big enough place to get lost in. Well, for maybe ten minutes before you spot someone you've seen at least once before.

"It's Friday night." She follows up with a wink and stands.

I chuckle as we leave the quiet library together. Unsurprisingly, it's all but empty since it's close to nine on a Friday night. Stepping outside into the dark, I peer up, marveling at the stars not made invisible by smog or light.

"You're doing it again." Amusement lifts Simone's words.

"And I'm not sorry." I grin, not looking away from the inky blackness and twinkling stars. "This is one thing I love about being out here. Far enough away from the city not to be doused in fumes."

"Hey," she jeers, nudging me. "*One* thing? I know it's only been a few weeks, but I better rank high on that list of yours."

I pull my attention away from the sky and to her,

still smiling. "You do. You may even rank number one if you make sure a red cup is in my hand within the next forty minutes."

"Done." With a tug on my arm, she leads the way to the small house she shares with a couple of other students just off campus. Once there, I wash up, put on a fresh spray of deodorant, and after a swipe of mascara, I call myself done.

I'm not in the mood to get dressed up. My jeans, slim-fit tee, and hoodie featuring a small rainbow and stating boldly Queer AF are good enough. While I like my eyes to pop a little, beyond a hilarious array of T-shirts and hoodies, I live in my jeans and Converse.

Despite Simone's questionable eye makeup choices, she's fairly low-key too so doesn't take long to get ready, and with ten minutes to spare, we're at Jack's, where she fills a Solo cup with beer, places it in my hand, taps her own against mine, and winks. "And relax," she orders.

I take a healthy gulp and sigh contently at the crisp flavor. I'm far from a big drinker, mostly because never in a million years growing up could I get away with passing for older than I was. It meant I relied heavily on my friends and parties just like this to give me a taste and help me unwind enough that, for just a little while, I can behave like a twenty-one-year-old.

"You finished that fast." Simone draws my focus to her wide eyes. A frown pulls her brows low. "You okay?"

"Yeah. Was just thirsty," I lie, not even realizing I downed the drink, too lost in my woe-is-me thoughts. "I'm going to get another. You want one?"

She studies me for a beat. "Yeah, sure. I'll just wait over there. I see my friend Tammy." I follow her line of sight so I'll know where to find her among the growing crowd.

"Sounds good." I head off, reminding myself to sip the next drink. I have work tomorrow at the diner. Locating the beer, I smile at a pretty blonde who's pouring a drink from the keg.

"You having one?" she asks, her gaze floating down to take in the writing on my hoodie before she makes eye contact again.

"Yeah. Well, two actually."

She nods and passes me the filled cup. "Take this, and I'll get you one more."

"You sure?"

"Absolutely." She pours away. "You're the guy who recently transferred from LA, right? Lester's friend?"

My brows lift in surprise. "You know Lester?"
She chuckles. "I'm his cousin."

"Oh wow, this really is a small town," I tease. "Please tell me there's a whole clan of you on campus so I can make hilariously bad jokes and tease Lester mercilessly."

She passes me another filled cup, grinning. "Afraid not. Just the two of us. Name's Lana."

I nod at her in greeting. "Dean." I tilt my head. "What gave me away that I'm Lester's friend? My dreamy good looks and wicked dress sense?"

She chuckles. "Well, that, and Lester was showing me a couple of photos of his art project, and we swiped through to a few of you guys."

"Lester does like selfies."

She laughs loudly. "Right. His phone's practically a permanent extension of his hand. Are you—"

Her words are cut off by loud shouts and laughter as a group of guys pours into the house. I angle to observe them, taking in their laughter, their clothes, their physiques.

Basketball players.

I can sniff out an athlete and identify their sport with a 95 percent accuracy. Legit, I tested myself both in high school and college.

"Looks like the Bears won their game."

I return my attention to Lana. "Basketball?"

"Yeah."

I give myself a mental pat on the back. At this

rate, my accuracy rating is going to rise. Turning my attention back to the incoming players, I take my fill like the sucker for sexy forearms and built biceps I am. Damn, there are fine specimens on the team. I also know the season doesn't officially start for another month, so I'm assuming they're having friendly games with other colleges in the state.

"You follow basketball?" Lana draws my attention back to her.

"Go Eagles!" I smirk.

She chuckles again. "I'm a Pandas fan myself, but I can understand the draw to the Eagles." Her wink is less than subtle.

With a snort, I nod. "Right. Don't get me wrong, I genuinely love the game, but Minnesota knows how to seduce the hot-as-Hades players to join their team. I suppose it makes up for the less-than-stellar couple of years and the injuries they've been having."

"I often take in a school game if ever you're up for it. The team was away today, but they're at home next Thursday if you want to come. It's only against the Marlins and not for points, but it should still be a decent game."

I force myself to focus on Lana rather than take my fill of the eye candy who've since spilled through the house, some heading in our direction, no doubt seeking a drink. "I'd like that, thanks. Simone and

Lester aren't sports fan—" I grunt and lurch forward, my drink sloshing and spilling on my hoodie. "Fuck."

"Shit, sorry, man."

Scowling, I shift my gaze to the six-foot-whatever beast of a guy peering down at me and not looking overly apologetic at all. I offer a tight smile and fight hard to keep my mouth shut. I refuse to say it's okay, as hello, beer on my awesome hoodie, but there's no point challenging him. Turning my back on the guy, I focus on Lana and roll my eyes.

"Hey, I said I was sorry. No need to be a dick."

With my stomach plummeting, I shake my head. Hearing murmured words, I refuse to look back. My buzz is already on the way to being ruined.

"What?" the same voice says, clearly responding to the lower voice with words I can't catch. "Whatever, man. I just need a beer and then I can get away from guys with sticks up their asses."

Heat hits my cheeks, and my gaze connects with Lana's. Her brows shoot high as her focus drifts from me to the people behind me. When a toned arm appears over my shoulder, reaching for the stack of cups before me, I snap, "The fuck. Rude much?" I spin on my heels and am greeted with a gray T-shirt straining over a broad chest not concealed by the unzipped college hoodie he's wearing. The guy lifts his hands immediately, palms open.

"Sorry. Just trying to get a cup so I can get a drink and shut my friend up."

"By being in my space?" I finally meet his gaze after a slow trail up to the face. Holy shit, he's fucking handsome and has the prettiest deep brown eyes I've ever seen. Rather than panting, I manage to keep my scowl in place.

I know guys like this, thinking they can do whatever they want with no consequences.

He shrugs, nothing but sarcasm in his voice when he says, "Sorry. I just thought you'd want my friend, who bumped into you by total accident, by the way, out of your hair. I was trying to be a good guy."

I quirk my brow, if only to give myself an extra moment to not start salivating or rubbing up on the man. While he's behaving like an arrogant jerk like most players I've known over the years, it doesn't mean he's not devastatingly gorgeous. "Perhaps next time use your words. If that's at all possible for that pea-sized jock brain of yours," I sass, my bitchiness front and center, having no patience for anyone using either their size or status to behave like an asshat.

Surprise registers on his features for the briefest of moments before he narrows his gaze. "No need to be a jerk about it."

In response, I turn my back to him, pour myself a fresh drink, and indicate to Lana I'm leaving.

She nods, her expression startled and still bouncing from me and then over my shoulder. "Dean, hold up. I'll come."

I smile, no longer quite sure if the guy and his clumsy friend are who I'll be supporting if I take in a basketball game. I turn, the guy with the pretty eyes still in my space. "You wanna move so I can leave you to get a drink you so desperately want, please?" Proud as punch I remembered my manners, I even add a tight smile.

He takes a step back, narrowed eyes drifting down to my hoodie before meeting my gaze. "Nice hoodie."

I clench my jaw, certain he's being a sarcastic prick, and leave to find Simone.

As soon as we're out of earshot, Lana grabs my arm and leans in. "Holy shit, that was Kieran Kendall."

"I have no idea who that is."

"He's the Bears' captain, their star player."

I snort. "Figures. It explains why he thinks he can be rude, leaning over me like that." While I'm not the shortest guy in the world, I've been told more than once, often loudly, that I'm petite and cute. Sounds nice, right? Those descriptors? Yeah, they can be, unless it's with dripping derision, as though being a little shorter than average is something I should be ashamed of. Screw that, fuck you very much.

I'm perfectly compact and just the right side of fabulous. I promise I'm not completely egotistical either. But seriously, ego is my armor, as well as my long lashes and my snippy mouth.

We stop near a wall and angle to take in the rest of the room.

"He's usually really decent and down-to-earth. I've never known him like that before."

I sigh. It seems I have a gift for bringing out the asshole in people. "Lucky me." I hate that I'm shaken and frustrated. What's also pissing me off? How freakin' hot the guy is.

She nudges me. "Don't sweat it. Focus on having a few drinks and having a good night."

"Now *that* I can do." I bring my red cup to my mouth and take a large gulp, peering around to track down Simone. I need to unwind after that encounter. Maybe I overreacted—probably... maybe—but defensive, remember?

Kieran Kendall isn't someone I need to be worried about. We clearly don't run in the same circles. Nor can I imagine being in any of the same classes. Athletes are known for general studies, right? Shh, I know I'm being totally judgmental, but the dude deserves it. I can begrudgingly admire him from afar when he's on the court. Well, if he proves he really is a god on the basketball court. Admittedly, I'm interested to see for myself if that's true. Purely for my love of the game, of course.

CHAPTER 2
RULE 3 SECTION B: NO CRUSHING ON COLLEGE GUYS

KIERAN

THE BROWN-HAIRED GUY IS AS CUTE AS A BUTTON WITH a bite like a rattlesnake. And hell if I can't take my eyes off him as he walks away. That doesn't mean he isn't a complete douche. Talk about overreaction.

Tyron, my buddy who spilled the guy's drink, is a fun guy, though admittedly only to those he knows well. But he can flip like a switch, which probably didn't help that whole exchange, but still, it had been an accident.

"Drink this and keep out of trouble. Remember we're meeting at nine in the morning, so do not get wasted or Coach will have you running drills all morning."

Tyron rolls his eyes as he takes the Solo cup off

me. "Are you mistaking me for Bentley, who can't handle his drink?"

I grin, thinking about all the times Bentley has found himself in compromising positions. "I don't think there's ever a chance of mistaking you for Bentley, Tyron." The guys are as different as oil and water. They share the same skin color, but that's where their similarities end. "Come on, let's go and find somewhere to sit."

His brows shoot high, but rather than make the comment that I'm sure is on the tip of his tongue, he presses his lips together and heads toward the patio. We've been to this house a few times over the past two years, and the patio, complete with heaters, is my preferred spot. Everyone on the team knows that.

Once outside, I relax in the fresh Georgia evening, relieved it's a few decibels quieter out here. I loosen up more seeing Leon already looking comfortable on the outdoor furniture, clearly staking a claim for us. The guys, my team, can be a real pain in my ass at times, but when they do shit like this, look out for me this way, I have to admit, I get the feels something fierce.

I give him a chin lift when I sit next to him and kick out my legs, settling my feet on the small wooden table positioned in the center of the sofas and chairs. "Good game tonight." I angle my cup for him to tap his own against.

"Back atcha, Kieran. This season, man, I can feel it."

I bob my head, feeling the exact same thing. It will be freakin' everything if we make it to the championship game. That's sounds a tad preemptive, since the season hasn't officially started, but I want this for us so bad.

Last year we got close but fell at the last hurdle. "We keep playing hard, working our asses off, we're in with a good chance." There's nothing more that I want to do than agree and big our team up, but no way am I going to jinx us. "You not partying tonight?"

Leon shakes his head. "Nope. Thought I'd come and hang with the grown-ups."

I snort. "I think you're sitting in the wrong place if that's the case."

"I'm good right here. Just need to unwind after the game, then I plan to head home in maybe an hour." He kicks up his feet, and they settle next to mine. "How about you? Not feeling the need to mix it up and let your hair down?" He bounces his brows for good measure.

"Let's get through the season; then we can talk about me letting my hair down." I take a sip of my beer, appreciating that it's not piss warm, and glance toward the open patio doors, my gaze snagging on the cute douche from earlier. A wide grin stretches across his face as he focuses on the blonde standing next to him. Laughter follows, and I wonder what it sounds like. With his sharp tongue and his fiery attitude, I don't expect it to be light or tinkling.

When he speaks, his free hand moves around, super animated. I'm captivated and would love a taste of the twink. I don't want to examine this too closely, as he's so not the sort of guy I usually hook up with. Based on his hoodie, there's a chance I wouldn't get shot down immediately, especially as, when the occasion calls for it, I've talked a few guys onto their knees.

But never in a place like this. Never at school.

"Kieran, you hear what I said?"

My focus snaps to Sammy, not realizing he'd joined us. "Sorry, man. Zoned out there."

"Going through all the plays, right? Right there with you. We won, but man, those two three-pointers should have been ours. Perhaps we need to run them tomorrow at practice?"

I nod, not correcting him that my mind was on the twink rather than plays. I can't quite believe it myself, and I'm sure my team wouldn't either if I told them the truth.

I have a handful of hard-and-fast rules since coming to college—though in truth, I had them in high school too. The third rule on my list is no dating or getting distracted by hot guys. That means quick blowies have been all I've allowed, certainly not with anyone who'd even hint at a relationship. And only on the very rare occasion I'm away from school.

I won't get distracted by ass.

My team thinks it's weird. Not me receiving the occasional blowie by a willing mouth, but the fact I'm firm in not finding a boyfriend or even willing to go on a single date. Screw that.

Being out to my team and being their captain is already a hell of a thing. I feel that pressure and the weight on my shoulders every day, and that's just with my team, who are my brothers and supportive to a fault. The rest of the world, not so much.

Going pro after college, which is absolutely my ambition, I'll be going back in the closet.

And I have a hundred and one reasons why that's the best thing for me. No one else walks in my shoes, and while the thought of stepping back inside sucks, when I do go pro, I want to be known as a kickass player, not the only out queer causing a stir.

"Fair enough, but when you're ready, hit me up and I'll go to that bar in Atlanta we went to last year," he offers, complete with bouncing brows.

I chuckle, not only at his ridiculous gesture but at the memory of the night. As far as I know, every one of my teammates is straight, yet five of them had all but dragged me to the gay bar with the mission of me getting off, complaining I was being uptight and needed to dump my load in a willing mouth.

Paints a pretty picture, right?

My friends aren't the most poetic of guys, or the classiest, but they're good men.

Obviously I happily obliged and found the willing mouth of a bear, who is absolutely the type of guy I fantasize about. The thought draws my attention back to the windows, and the twink. Still animated, he's waving at someone while talking. While I can't see it from here, I noticed earlier he's wearing some sort of makeup around his eyes. That mascara shit women usually put on their eyelashes. On him, it looks sexy and drew my attention immediately to his large brown eyes.

"Who you looking at?"

Tyron's voice pulls my attention away, and before I can come up with some bullshit, he's angling to look in the same direction I was. When he turns back at me, he lifts his brows high.

"What?" I aim for innocence, but the narrowing eyes means he's not buying it.

"That's the dick with a stick shoved so far up his ass, I'm not sure he can bend over."

The guys around us laugh, question in their gazes.

"You can't be thinking of hitting on the guy." Tyron's brows pull together.

"I'm not thinking of hitting on anyone," I answer quickly. "You know I have a no-campus rule." Admittedly, that's a sub-rule of number three on my list.

My sexuality isn't common knowledge, nor do I plan for it to be. It was important to me to come out and be honest with my team. Sure, it could have backfired, and I'm beyond grateful it hasn't. I needed them to trust me to make the right calls, offer support, and to know I had their backs. Coming out to them was one of the ways I achieved that.

Tyron bobs his head. All the guys understand—or at least as much as straight guys can—my need to stay under the radar with my personal life. "Thank fuck for that. Dude's an asshat. You don't need that drama in your life."

While I agree fully that I don't need drama, and nod, it doesn't stop me from being curious about the guy. "You know who he is?"

Tyron shrugs and shakes his head. I gaze around at my friends, and they follow suit, not having a clue.

I certainly haven't seen him around campus. Considering it's not a huge campus, that's a little surprising. Though I tend to focus on my team, getting through my classes, and not searching for potential hookups.

I do not need that carrot dangled in front of me.

As I return my attention to the twink, our gazes catch. I freeze at the connection, taken aback by his deep frown, sneer, and shake of his head before he speaks, looks away, and then shifts from his spot.

Well, if that's not confirmation the guy is a serious jerk, then I'm the principal dancer in a ballet. Okay, maybe that's an odd comparison, but trust me, my mom signed me up for ballet lessons when I was a kid, and I majorly sucked, to the point where the teacher turned pale when she saw me enter the room.

"Who wants another drink?" Sammy cuts through my annoyed confusion at the guy's reaction to me.

I shake my head, despite really wanting to drink myself out of the weird funk that look put me in. "I'm finishing this, then going to head out."

Rather than the guys ribbing me, a couple say they'll be leaving at the same time, while the others nod in simple acceptance. I ease back against the soft cushion of the couch, grateful for my friends and that they know me so well.

When Sammy heads off to grab a few more beers,

I angle to focus on Leon. "We still heading to your place tomorrow night to watch the highlights?"

"You know it. Just make sure Tyron doesn't take care of the ordering. I swear to god, if my pizza arrives stinking like fish, there's finally going to be a beatdown."

A handful of chips land on Leon's chest as the words "Screw you, man. Anchovies are the best" come from Tyron. "And I'd like to see you try to beat my ass. Maybe I'll organize some ladders or a forklift or some shit to give you a fighting chance." A teasing grin stretches across his lips, and the guys and I laugh.

Leon is the "short" guy of the team. At five eleven, he's received ribbing from day one, all with a side serving of love.

"You want me to start looking down on you, all you need to do is get on your knees," Leon shoots back in challenge.

I snort and almost spit out the dregs of my drink.

Tyron, however, is shocked speechless, his mouth opening and closing, making us all laugh even harder.

"On that note, as much as I'm loving all this man-on-man love, I'm going to head out before I see anything that requires me bleaching my retinas." I stand and throw my empty cup in the bin beside us.

Tyron, finally finding his voice, eases back a little too casually in his chair, saying, "Don't sweat it. Leon wouldn't know what to do with all of this." He gestures down his body, and I smirk. He's seriously fit and good-looking. Not my type. He needs reining in far too much for me to find him truly attractive, plus there's the whole him being straight thing.

Another sub-rule of number three is no hooking up or crushing on straight guys, especially those just looking to experiment.

Before Leon can respond, I cut through their testosterone-filled flirting, as that's totally what it is, which honestly, isn't that unusual for the guys in our team. I'm not sure if I'm blessed or cursed at their comfort at flirting with men and talking about one-upping each other in the bedroom. "I need my hearing too and can't handle any more without earplugs. I'm out." I eye the group. "Do not be late for tomorrow's meet."

They all dutifully bob their heads, Raphael and Brad standing and joining me to head out.

We make our way inside to exit through the front, and I take in the party. I look beyond the girls dancing, the few couples making out on couches, and the beer pong tournament going on in the kitchen, searching for the guy from earlier. I spot him near the door and am unable to resist taking my fill.

When my gaze lands on his tight butt, I swallow hard, just imagining how sexy it would look sans clothes.

I grunt, running into Brad, who paused. "Fuck. What did you—" I look over his shoulder and figure the reason out for myself, seeing Lexi stagger. "Shit. I've got her."

Brad steps out of my way, and I make a beeline for Tyron's twin sister. Clearly wasted, she stumbles into the wall. A couple of guys are around her, and if I don't get her out of here and away from them, Tyron will cause some shit.

Without speaking, I step to her side and put my arm around her. It takes her a beat to look up and focus.

"Hey, Key. You gonna get me a drink?"

"That'd be a no. I'm heading out, and you're coming with me."

Her face scrunches. "I want another drink."

"Water's all you need. Come on, Lex. Tyron's outside."

When she rolls her eyes, she sways the other way, so I tighten my hold on her. I then focus on the guys she's with, shooting them the stink eye. "You know whose sister this is?"

One of the guys folds his arms, a brow arching high. "The fuck do I care?"

I release a humorless snort. "Tyron Channing. You know him?"

The cocky guy loses some of his arrogance, his shoulders tensing a little.

"Yeah, thought you might." I jerk my head in a fuck-off motion, and lucky for them, they do so immediately. While Tyron is one of the best friends a guy could ask for, he's intimidating as fuck. Well, unless you're a cute brown-haired twink who's afraid of no one, apparently.

Without further difficulty, I ease Lexi around. She seems to have lost the will to argue. Angling back to make sure Raphael and Brad are with me, I give them a chin lift. Holding Tyron's sister close to my side to make sure she gets out of here safely, I continue toward the exit, making one more cursory sweep, my gaze snagging once again on the cute guy. His brown eyes are directed my way from just a few feet away, and for the first time, derision isn't directed at me.

And then his gaze is gone, pulled away to whatever his blonde-haired friend is saying, and I'm left wondering if I'll ever see him again. He's piqued my interest far too much.

CHAPTER 3
RULE 2: MAINTAIN A 3.5 GPA

DEAN

I'VE BEEN UP SINCE FIVE SO I COULD GET TO MY JOB AT the diner, work a few hours, then make it to my 10:00 a.m. class. These mornings are always a rush, but I need the cash. It seems like someone is smiling down on me, though, since I find a parking spot on campus without driving around for ten minutes. It means I'm early to meet Simone before Lit 129.

By the time she gets to me, I have my head stuck in a paperback I picked up at a flea market, and admittedly, I'm a little resentful that I have to use my bookmark.

"Got yourself some sophisticated reading there, huh?" A saucy smile follows, one that is impossible not to laugh at.

"You daring to diss a quality YA novel?"

Her grin is wide, contagious. "Me? Never."

I stand and join her as we enter the large lecture theater. "Usual?" I ask, 'cause yes, even though we're only four weeks into the year, we've staked our claim on seats. Five rows from the back, on the end so we can head out quickly, usually missing the bustle.

She bobs her head, and I notice a fresh strip of pink in her blonde hair. "Get bored last night?"

"You know it." She pulls at the bright-pink strands and eyes them as we sit.

"It's cute."

"Right! It totally paid off. I had three compliments this morning already. Even snagged a number when grabbing a coffee."

My brows shoot high. "You go, Simone. Hope the lucky individual was appropriately hot and looked like they had a decent amount of brain cells to keep you riveted."

By her shrug and cat-that-ate-the-canary smile, I'm assuming the former is covered, though there's no guarantee of the latter.

Professor Henderson's signature *War of the Worlds* theme tune—you know, the old one from ancient times better known as the '70s—plays, signaling the start of the lecture. Even though the man is pretty ancient himself and has set an assignment I'm not looking forward to, I like his quirky style.

The theater quickly settles, and then he's straight into his lecture, breaking down the symbolic connotations that are common identifiers of early-twentieth-century literature. I'm typing frantically and am grateful my high school taught touch typing.

Seriously, best skill ever.

My fingers hover over the keys however many pages of notes in when Professor Henderson breaks down the dreaded group assignment in more detail.

"Check your emails now. There you will find a link to a private group that's been assigned to your group of five for the assignment." He waits a beat while everyone focuses on their phones, tablets, or laptops, checking their mail. "By tomorrow, you should have engaged in a chat with your fellow group members and arranged a time to meet…"

My gut clenches, truly hating the very idea of relying on others to help me get my grades. Tuning the professor out, I focus on the chat, which is already pinging. There are no names attached, just student IDs.

BBan12390: Hi. Can we do a preliminary meet after class? 5 mins tops.

YKris13239: Can do. Not got class till 1.

KKen15648: 5 mins. Sure.

BBan12390: Great.

SWen19456: K. Only 5 mins as I have a work shift after class.

BBan12390: Just be good to do a quick schedule check.

I hold back my groan and force myself to respond, knowing I have no choice but to participate. I suppose I'm a little relieved that this BBan12390 is kicking things off and seems keen. I fire off a response with my ID, DWhit16574.

Me: That's fine. Where's good?

SWen19456: My shift is at the library, so outside would be ideal for me. :)

Four thumbs-up follow.

KKen15648: We going to coordinate? All wear red or a rose in our lapels or something?

I snicker at the dorky response.

Me: Make it a rose between your teeth, just to be sure. :P

Three laughing emojis appear, and then I'm brought to reality with an elbow in my side.

"What?" I glance at her.

"Who's in your group?" she whispers as I notice Professor Henderson still talking.

I tune in for the barest of moments to make sure I haven't missed anything. Fortunately, he's just clarifying all the assignment details that are on the intranet.

"No idea yet. They're willing to at least meet, so I have everything crossed."

"That's good. I already have someone who hasn't joined my group yet." A roll of her eyes follows. "If I get a waster, I swear I'm going to lose my shit."

Before I can respond, there's movement around us. Everyone's packing things away, so I grab my laptop and shove it into my bag. "I'm going to meet my group now at the library. Want to caffeinate after?"

"As if I'd ever say no. I'll meet you at Barney's."

She waves me off, and I make my way toward the library, feeling a fraction more positive about this assignment.

It's literally a two-minute stroll to the library, giving me just enough time to enjoy the sunshine. While it's not quite the warmth of LA in autumn, and I don't go anywhere without a jacket or a hoodie, I take any opportunity I can get to absorb some vitamin D.

As soon as I spot the library, I seek out the group I'm meeting. Of course, there's more than one cluster of students hanging out, but seeing three students standing together without speaking, I figure it's them. There's that awkwardness between them normal for strangers.

"Hey, Professor's Henderson's class?" I ask as I close in.

"Yeah, that's us. I'm Sarah. I'm the one who works at the library."

I smile in greeting and try to get a read on her. With what looks to be dyed-black hair, she's sporting two quirky pigtails. Her backpack is fit to burst at her feet, and she looks every ounce the adorkable librarian nerd.

"I'm Dean." Turning my attention to the guy at her right, I smile.

"Bobby." He offers me a nod and a shy smile.

"Yasmin," the last person in our group offers. "Thanks so much for meeting up. We're just waiting for the last person."

A crunch of gravel grabs my attention, and I turn to see who it is. My eyes spring open, and I peer up, and up some more, as Kieran Kendall steps next to me. "Lit 129?" He's smiling, tone easygoing. "Name's Kieran."

Yasmin is the one to answer. Once she's shared our names, she asks, "Shall we just grab a seat inside and work out at least the next couple of times we can meet properly?"

I hear the responses, but I'm still reeling from Kieran standing next to me. It's been just a week since the party. And holy boner, he's even hotter in the daylight.

As if he can hear me thinking how hot he is, his focus drops. From the widening of his eyes, it's clear he recognizes me. Just as I'm about to at least attempt a smile, trying to start afresh, his mouth tightens, and I swear he actually grinds his back teeth.

What a cockhead.

Me, being the special soul I am, shoot one arched and perfectly manicured brow up high. You better believe there's challenge in that brow lift.

Kieran stares at me for a beat before he turns away, nods, and then follows the group inside.

I follow behind, actively avoiding looking at the basketball player's ass. It seriously is a crying shame that such a fine specimen of man has the personality of a chair. One with a wonky leg and that's super uncomfortable on your ass.

I jerk my head back. Thinking about asses is not

where I want my mind to go, especially when my traitorous gaze drifts there, admiring the firm globes obvious in his butt-hugging jeans.

When I reach the small table, there's one seat left between Bobby and Kieran. I sit, doggedly avoiding eye contact with the man on my right.

"So commitments, schedules? If we can share emails too, that'd be great. There's some research we can split and then come back together to share before we tackle the assignment head-on. Does that sound okay?" With her iPad in hand, Yasmin gazes around our group, and despite my inability to breathe properly or comprehend the fact that I'm going to have to work with Kieran, at least a couple members of the group seem on the ball.

I've yet to make up my mind about Bobby. Even though he's the guy who suggested we meet, which I quickly deduced from the student IDs, he seems super shy. Though saying that, since Kieran arrived, I haven't said anything.

Releasing a silent sigh, I pull myself together.

So what if the asshole from Friday is here. So what if he's so hot, I'm struggling to not melt at his side. Does he tick my unicorn boxes? Well, some of them, but since I'm sure he's a wankstain from our interaction at the party, I've mentally put a big fat cross through his name.

It turns out that only two of us work, which causes a few scheduling issues, well, that alongside the plethora of different classes we take. Of course Kieran has the biggest issues. While I know athletes train hard and have regular games, I can't help but wonder how his team gets schoolwork done with the commitments he's listing.

I notice his apologetic grimace when he vetoes another possible time. The only thing that's making me believe his sincerity is the short exchange on Friday night when I watched him help that girl out.

It doesn't mean I think he's worth my energy, though.

"Okay, how about a working lunch at two next Tuesday? I've got an hour, and that should give us time for the preliminary research, right?" Kieran's tone is light and breezy, casual even, almost like he's doing us a favor by giving us his valuable time.

I clamp down my thoughts, more than aware I'm reacting to this guy. In truth, he's done nothing wrong, but with how my body's responding to him every time he shifts and I inhale his body spray, mixed with his own natural scent, I need to believe he's as awful as I decided last Friday.

Unreasonable? Sure. But I need to protect myself and teach my cock that getting a chubby around him is all levels of not okay.

"I can do that time and date."

You see, I can be magnanimous when I want to be. And since I'm forced to work with the guy, I'll be civilized.

There are head bobs around the table, and more than one of us exhales in relief to get at least a single date agreed on.

"Do we want to decide who's researching what? Make our preference, or do you just want to divide the tasks, Yasmin, and we can get this done quicker?" I'm banking on the latter, more than happy to be told what to do if it means I can get out of here.

It doesn't take long to agree that Yasmin can go ahead and decide. "I'll email you each your research focus now I have your emails. Thanks." Her smile is bright, her relief mirroring my own that this initial meeting went off without a hitch. Hell, maybe I'm wrong and she's struggling to concentrate being in the same proximity as Kieran Kendall too.

I'm totally judging here, but I imagine Yasmin is the sort of girl Kendall would totally go for—long blonde hair, pretty blue eyes, and a sweet smile. Except after our brief discussion, there seems nothing vapid about her. A relief for me and our group project, but no doubt a bummer for jocks wanting a quick hookup and piece of dumbed-down eye candy on their arm.

Me? Judgmental?

I know. I completely suck and should be ashamed of myself, and I totally know better, especially after spending so much time on the receiving end of so much judgment. But hey, I never once said the snide in me wasn't alive and well.

It's not my best characteristic, and I usually don't share such bitchiness aloud. I do try to at least pretend to be a decent human being. Having been the secret hookup of a basketball player for six months of high school doesn't always help me rein in that not-so-pleasant trait of mine either.

"Fabulous." I stand before anyone else does, smiling at the other three members of the group. "Thanks for this. I'll see you next week." With a slightly dorky—okay, a completely uncool—wave, I hightail it out of there. I have another lecture soon, but I really need that caffeine fix with Simone.

When I'm just a few feet away from the library, my name is called from behind me. I freeze, having already committed that voice to memory.

Don't judge, as it's seriously delectable. I could happily relax to the sound, perhaps while he read a novel aloud or something. Though likely I'd be simply jacking off to his voice, ideally while my name escaped from him in short gasps. Yeah, that's where my mind is already at. So much for avoiding fantasizing about the man.

I turn, remembering I'm playing nice. I wait for him in silence, though, a little tense, wondering what he has to say to me.

When he stops in front of me, he has a smile fixed in place, and he's rubbing the back of his neck. I force myself to not glance down and eye the sliver of skin peeking between his shirt and jeans. "About the other week."

I lift my brows, waiting for him to continue.

"Tyron spilling the drink on you really was an accident. He meant it when he said he was sorry."

I press my lips together, needing to let that night go. Tyron hadn't seemed sorry to me, but I can be the bigger person here. "Okay."

His brow furrows, as if taken aback by my response. "Okay…" He drags the word out. "So I understand why you'd be pissed having beer spilled on your hoodie, but it was a party, you know. Shit happens. But yeah, he's really a good guy and didn't mean anything by it."

As far as apologies go—though was that even an apology—it's not the greatest. All it does is raise my hackles. "Honestly," I say, unable to stop myself, "I get that, and it's beer, so it washed out—"

"Great, so, like, we're okay then? No hard feelings? It's just you seemed really pissed off and it just seemed a little, I don't know, excessive or something."

My mouth is still clamped shut from when he cut me off, but… yeah… he really said those words. Blood boils under my skin, searing my veins. The need to unleash on this arrogant asshole has me vibrating.

"So great. I'll see you next week." A wide yeah-I'm-so-pleased-we-chatted-about-this-and-you-realized-I'm-a-god smile appears on his face, and then he turns and jogs off.

Literally. Jogs. Off.

Without a backward glance.

And I'm sure he's thinking that what he said wasn't insulting as fuck and that we're new best friends or some shit.

Fuck coffee. Is it too early for a shot?

CHAPTER 4
RULE 1 SECTION E: PLAY LIKE IT'S THE PLAYOFFS

KIERAN

THERE'S NOTHING LIKE A HOME GAME TO GET MY adrenaline pumping. Not only are we having a killer preseason, but my courses seem decent, and I haven't jerked off once to thoughts of Dean.

Okay, there was once, but I had no control over that. He sabotaged my sex dream, and Matthew Daddario morphed into Dean Whittaker. The name that I didn't spend too much time looking at in the group email exchange.

But my point is, while the guy is cute, I know I can resist the pull. Sure, I've only chatted with him the once outside the library a couple of days ago, but it was enough to remind me why rule three exists and why it's so important.

Our winning streak preseason and our great season last year have been achieved because I've had no distractions. Not that I'm saying it's all because of me, as my team is kickass, but my rules have been working, and I'm not going to break them anytime soon.

"Yo, Key."

I turn to look at Tyron who's standing in front of his locker. Dressed for tonight's game, he looks every bit the intimidating player he is. There's something about the deep blue of our uniform, complete with the Brixham Bears logo, that looks almost sleek to the point of deadly on the guy.

That may also have something to do with the scowl he regularly wears in public. At the house, not so much. He's actually a joker at heart but plays up his intimidation whenever he can.

"What's up?"

He smirks. "I bet you two shots there are at least four floppers tonight from Calderston."

I snort. "No way am I taking that bet. You know Calderston players are notorious floppers. Hell, fart in one of their players' directions, and I guarantee he's going to act like it's a gale force wind and he goes down grabbing his arm."

The locker room erupts in laughter. Every single

player on our team knows I'm right too. There's nothing like fake-as-fuck ballers. It seriously pisses me off.

Tyron's still smirking when Coach Maple enters the locker room, hollering for our attention. He does his usual spiel, reminding us of a few plays, then calls me over. "Shakespeare."

"Yeah, Coach?" I'm pointedly avoiding any reaction to my nickname here. It's not one I would have picked for myself, but apparently, my double degree in literature and business ends up with names that compare me to a dead dude who wrote so many sonnets it would be impossible to read them all in a lifetime.

Before you react, yes, I know the Bard was awesome in his time. There's even a couple of plays I legit enjoyed, but I'm not Will's biggest fan.

"You watch the Lockerman kid out there. You spent time going over his plays?"

I nod. That was my mission this last week. Lockerman moved to Calderston College at the end of last year, at the start of the final semester. Since he's a former West Coast player, I've never come across him before. The guy has some serious skills as point guard.

"Yeah. I've already spoken to Bentley and Leon.

Got them watching replays." I know it seems a bit much, but in four weeks we'll be seeing Calderston when the season starts. Tonight is about letting them know we're the team to watch out for.

Coach claps me on the arm. "All right, kid, go lead your team out and show the Wildcats what a real team looks like."

Immediately, my adrenalin spikes, and I call out to my team. "All in, Bears."

We huddle together, all twelve of us.

Tension vibrates around our tight circle. Some of the guys are bouncing a little on the balls of their feet, while some are still and silent. Tyron, as always when it comes to basketball, is nothing but intense and focused.

"Fire up, kick ass, play ball, and let's show Calderston what a real team looks like. You got me?"

The team shouts, "Yeah!"

"We gonna play?"

"Yeah!"

"We gonna win?"

"Fuck yeah!"

"Absolutely we are," I fire out, this time with a grin. I squeeze Tyron's neck. "Let's go, Bears."

We head out, the not-quite-full arena bursting into cheers when our feet hit the court. There's seriously nothing like the buzz of playing at home, especially as our supporters are so vocal. It doesn't even matter that this is a no-points game, not to our fans.

After ten minutes of warm-up, going through our usual passes and shots while Calderston does the same at the other end of the court, we're called together to start the game.

I give the arena a cursory glance, ignoring the cameras and film crews. There aren't many here, as this is just a friendly game. Almost two-thirds of our three-thousand-seat stadium is filled. Sure, it's smaller than some colleges, but all that means is the spectators aren't as hazy.

And that's made super clear when my gaze snags on a pair of brown eyes belonging to none other than Dean Whittaker. Surprise flitters through me. I know better than to believe in stereotypes, but Dean doesn't look like the sort of guy who's into basketball.

Without even considering the reasons why, I send the guy a chin lift. I stare for a second longer, just long enough to see his eyes widen and red flush his cheeks, and then I'm joining my team and shutting myself down from any and all distractions.

Every game matters.

But fuck, the thought of winning when Dean's

here, just five rows from the court, has my body vibrating with renewed energy.

I shake the thought off, eyes on Howard, our center.

And then there's no time to think about anything beyond getting the ball through the hoop.

We have first possession, Howard receiving the ball from Tyron. Leon's immediately available and gets his hands on leather before I step in. I'm aiming for a layup but am blocked. I'm back immediately, managing to reposition before I turn, shoot, and get our first three points.

Like every game, there's no time to celebrate. No pauses. No breaks.

It's what I love about the game. The pace, the speed, the absolute intensity of every second.

The game rushes on by, and we're holding our own and managing to not roll our eyes too much at the floppers. I'm relieved I didn't take up Tyron on his bet. I would have lost.

By halftime, I'm dragging a towel across my face, clearing the sweat from my eyes, and listening intently to Coach. We're up 30–24, which is too close for my liking.

With just twenty minutes to go, I want at least a ten-point separation between us.

"Leon, focus on Lockerman." My voice is low and

filled with an intensity that vibrates through me. Lockerman is seriously everywhere. But what I noticed is he plays a clean game, not like so many of the floppers on his team.

"On it."

And I know he will. Leon on a mission is a beautiful thing. I swear he's the feisty chihuahua of us all. I swallow my grin at the thought and love how so many opposing players underestimate him. He's fierce when he needs to be.

We break, and I scoot down to tighten my laces. Once I finish, I stand and look directly ahead, realizing I'm in front of Dean.

His gaze is on me once again, and I find it difficult to pull away. I tilt my head, thinking something's different. That's when I spot the scarf he's now wearing.

Bears paraphernalia looks good on him, and I can't help but wonder what he'd look like wearing my number.

Oh fuck no. There's no way I'm going there. Not only would doing so go against my carefully constructed rules, but even though we had a decent conversation the other day and he accepted what I had to say so easily and without any of his previous snark, he's not even my type.

Maybe if I keep telling myself that, I'll start to believe it.

But fuck, it's as if my eye has a mind of its own. I swear I've been possessed as, like the fucking horndog dickhead that I am, I wink at the guy.

Way to be subtle and stay under the radar, Kendall.

Fuckwit.

Refusing to see how he reacts, I glance away, only to find Tyron at my side, a scowl on his face.

"Should I be worried?"

"No." I can't make eye contact with him as I speak, but I have no choice when he steps in front of me.

"Eyes on the ball."

I stand up straighter, swallowing back my frustration—at myself rather than my best friend. "Always." A firm nod follows, and Tyron claps me on the shoulder.

"Let's go win this thing."

"Fucking A."

He steps away, and we return to the court, focused, and prepare to put this game to bed.

It takes ten minutes to gain the advantage points I'm happy with. It takes the final ten minutes of Calderston battling and pushing, but Leon does his job like a pro. Tyron makes an impressive as hell splash, and I bring it on, making it fucking rain.

By the time the buzzer sounds, I'm flying. Every shot I took found its target, with Sammy dropping dimes like he was playing the slots. I tug him close, wrapping my arms around the small forward. "Your assists, man…" I pat him hard and pull away grinning. "You're a fucking legend."

Bright-eyed and covered in sweat, Sammy smirks. "You know it. Nice shots there, Key."

We head toward the sideline. "Couldn't have done it without you."

By the time we reach Coach, he's already talking to a reporter, a camera in his face. He spots me, and I know my job.

It's not hard to fix my smile, my adrenaline still pumping, and my emotions soaring.

Do I like camera time like this?

Not especially, but I'm the captain, and win or lose, I'm expected to say a few words, reflect on the game. And with my ambition to be drafted, I'm determined to do the best job I can.

"Congratulations today," the interviewer starts, mic held out before me. "I'm sure this makes you feel good as we draw closer to the start of the season."

"Yeah, absolutely. The team has some good players. We had to really push hard to stay ahead. But it's good to be challenged. It makes us all stay on top of the game. The Bears were tight, and we found our stride and worked like a team should."

"After today are you encouraged about facing last year's conference winners for your first game of the season?"

"We play a tight game and play to win. We'll continue to bring our A game. We'll be bringing our all, our focus and talent when we're in Birmingham." I nod, hoping that's the last question.

It seems like the interviewer is going easy on me. "Congratulations."

I hold back my relieved sigh, say, "Thanks so much," and hightail it out of there.

The locker room is loud when I arrive, the guys hyped up and looking to celebrate.

We're heading to a party tonight, pretty much the norm after a win, especially as we're trying to make the most of the downtime before the season kicks off in a couple of weeks. I'm not sure where we're going. Sammy is usually the one taking control of such things, and he'll let me know.

Tomorrow is an easy day. My first class isn't until two in the afternoon, and while we have training, we don't start till ten. Our next game is on Monday before we have a week off, and then it's our Friday game against Birmingham.

I plan to make the most of tonight. Maybe even

allow myself more than one drink. You know, live it large… a little. I snort at myself, understanding why the guys equally respect my decisions while mocking me and comparing me to an old man.

But with just two seasons to go before entering the draft—all being well—I'm determined to stay on course.

I shower while shooting the shit with the handful of guys freshening up, then get dressed, ready to be directed by Sammy to where we're heading.

As always when we leave, it's a little crazy with fans asking for autographs, something I'll never tire of or quite believe. I make a beeline to the local families with young kids, signing a few shirts and caps. I also hand out the few pre-signed photos that the college distributed to us a couple of weeks ago.

Once we're done, we make our way toward the party. Tyron is paying attention to his phone, somehow managing not to walk into a streetlight, and I'm shooting the shit with my housemates, going over the game.

"Holy shit."

All our attention shifts to Tyron, and I'm confused that his focus is solely on me.

"What is it?" I ask, wondering why he's staring at me so intently.

After a quick glance around, he says, "Tim Delaware has just come out."

With a slam that almost has me stumbling, my heart whacks against my chest and doesn't give up.

"This is fucking awesome," Tyron continues. His fingers fly across the screen, and Leon leans over to see what he's doing. Meanwhile, I can barely hear myself think from the sound of my pulse in my head.

"Nice," Leon says, and I flick my gaze to him. When he makes eye contact with me, I'm sure his smile softens a little. "He's tweeting, offering his congrats and support."

I swallow hard, because of course my best friend is doing that. When I came out to him and my teammates, they were fucking epic. I have no other way to describe their reaction.

"He's the second out player in baseball," I say a little breathlessly. My chest constricts, wishing someone could do the same in the League. Fuck, I'd consider giving my left nut in exchange for a pro basketball player to come out.

No hiding. The chance to be my authentic self.

I like to think I could be the second out player in basketball—obviously that's all dependent on me getting drafted. But the first in basketball? Fuck no. Just the thought makes me nauseous.

Tyron tucks his phone away and swings his arm

over my shoulder. "One day, Key." He squeezes tight before releasing, and my love for this guy springs to life.

I simply nod, not trusting the emotion in my voice, while my head is wondering *what if* and going through the possibilities of a different future.

By the time we arrive at the party, my heart's calmer, but I need a drink. I consider getting wasted, but I won't. Not when we're in season. It would go against one of the many rules I put in place when I figured I could possibly go all the way to the League. That doesn't mean I won't have a few drinks. My nerves really need them.

There's plenty of students around, but it's nowhere near as crazy as a weekend get-together. I'm relieved, appreciating that whoever's party this is, they seem to be selective about who they're letting in tonight, and while there's music playing, I'm not going to be deafened.

Shit, I really do sound like an old dude.

"You drinking tonight?" Tyron falls into step beside me.

"Thought I might have a few. Not enough to give me a hangover, but I feel like celebrating."

He taps his shoulder against mine. "You need me, you just let me know."

I angle to look at him as we head straight for the

kitchen. Tyron is armed with a pack of beer and dumps it on the counter, snagging us each one. "Thanks." I take it off him and ask, "You planning on something tonight?" From his earlier words, it sounded like he was on a mission or something.

"Angie's coming."

"That right?" Tyron has been crushing on the girl in his biology class since freshman year. He's never done anything about said crush, so I'm wondering what's different tonight.

"She split up with her boyfriend last week."

Concern has my brows lifting. "You're not getting into rebound territory there, right?" Usually I wouldn't say anything, but I know Tyron genuinely likes the girl.

"No plans on that. Just thought I'd be a friend." The grin on his face is the goofiest I've seen perhaps ever.

I raise my beer, and he taps his against it. "Go do that then. You need me, the same goes. Come find me."

With a chin lift, he glances around and then leaves me.

Alone in the crowd, I take a moment to try to decompress. That lasts barely five seconds before a shot is shoved into my hand by Sammy.

I down it immediately, earning me a surprised

chuckle. "Yeah, yeah." I roll my eyes at him. "Thanks."

"Another?"

I hesitate, but the shot was easy and sweet. Sure, the fumes tickled my nose, but one or two more will take the edge off that I'm looking for. I nod and accept another, knocking it back, followed by a third.

"And that's me done."

"Good man." Sammy smirks at me before saying, "There's a sofa in the room out back."

"Cheers, Sammy." With the small buzz warming my stomach, my shoulders ease, and I make my way out in search of the sofa, hoping I can get my ass comfortable and kick back and relax, maybe have a decent conversation.

The sofa is facing away from the door. It's already occupied by a guy, but there's space next to him. The TV is playing tonight's preseason College League Basketball highlights. Chilling out and looking at footage sounds ideal to me.

I step around the couch. "You mind if I join you?" I'm already angling to sit, the words honestly just courtesy rather than really asking for permission. As my ass hits the cushioned sofa, I turn to look at the guy, only to freeze.

My breath legit catches, eyes widening. "Dean." The word escapes far too breathily, and I'm wondering if it's too late to simply make an excuse, stand, and run away.

He's even sexier this close.

In the library, we may have sat next to each other, but I'd been focused on the meeting. Even when I spoke to him afterward, my mission had been on clearing the air rather than truly appreciating just how attractive he is.

His cheekbones could cut glass. They're all defined and draw even more focus to his pouty mouth. I've never thought that about a man before. Usually I wonder if a guy's mouth is fuckable, and while I absolutely can imagine the same with Dean, he has lips just begging to be kissed and nipped at.

And I realize I've been staring at Dean for an uncomfortable amount of time, literally eye fucking him and taking in his features. Warning bells blast loudly in my head, but that buzz of alcohol grows a little louder, trying to override the blare.

"You're here." I don't even bother cringing at how inarticulate I am. My words do earn me an eyebrow lift and a slight smile. Which is bad, so bad, as once more my focus is on the slight sheen of his lips. "Are you wearing lip gloss?" I'm impressed I remember the name, and I'm also wondering if it's flavored.

Even in my buzzed state, I notice the stiffening of

his shoulders. "Why?" There's clear challenge in that one word.

"It looks nice… your lips do."

I need to shut up and back away, but with the surprise lighting up his features—his widening eyes, the slight flush to his cheeks—I'm held captive.

"O-kay…"

My hand has a mind of its own as it reaches out and tugs lightly on the scarf he's still wearing. I smile, really liking that he ended up wearing the school colors. "You enjoy the game?"

"Yeah. You guys played well. Twenty-eight points and five rebounds is pretty impressive."

Holy shit. I hold on to the neck of my beer, using it as a focal point so I don't humiliate myself and pop a boner. "You know your basketball?"

He chuckles, and rather than close my eyes to absorb the sound, my gaze doesn't waver. It's deep and has a carefree cadence to it. Not what I expected, but mesmerizing.

The warning siren goes off again, but fuck, he knows basketball, as in legit *knows* the sport.

"I rarely missed a game growing up, not when I was out in LA."

"You transferred, right?"

"At the beginning of the school year."

"A little different, I expect… LA to here."

His smile is wry. "It sure is."

"You're okay, though, happy with the move?" I ease back more fully on the couch and turn into him so I can see his expression. He watches me reposition myself, and while he doesn't mirror my movement, some tension leaves his shoulders.

And when he says, "It's been an adjustment, but classes are okay," he seems more relaxed.

I take a pull of my beer. This time, he follows suit, though chugs back a couple more mouthfuls than I do.

"Dude, shot time!"

Sammy appears in the doorway, a smirk on his lips and a glint of amusement in his gaze. There's also question there, as he knows I don't drink much during the season. When I nod my acceptance, there's a flicker of surprise, followed by a smile. He eyes Dean at my side and hands him a shot. I see the question in the way he's taking the both of us in, but Sammy doesn't say a word. Fuck, maybe he should. Here I am, sitting cozily with a guy I can't get off my mind, and for the first time ever I'm thinking about how stupid my rules are.

Instead, Sammy raises his cup, throws me a wink, and the three of us take the shot.

And why do I do it?

Do you not see the man at my side? Yep, I need a

shot to have the balls to either get up and leave or stay. I haven't decided which one yet.

The alcohol is fiery, not the sugary sweetness of the previous ones I had. I wince, and Dean laughs. My gaze snaps to his, but rather than amusement directed at me, he's wearing a similar expression.

"Holy flying dicks, what is that shit?"

I snort at his word choice, and Sammy joins in.

"It's called dregs of society. My own concoction." Obviously delighted with his shit mixture, Sammy bobs his brows at me. "You want another?"

Since my throat's on fire and my chest is warm, I'm convinced one more will lay me out. I'm just relaxed and together enough to shake my head.

"Hell no, but thanks for clearing my sinuses," Dean jests at my side.

I turn to face him, liking him like this. While it was a very different version of the guy beside me that first caught my attention, and there's something about his snark that gets me hard, I like this softer, more relaxed version.

"Later, losers." Sammy leaves, but not before winking at me and closing the door behind him.

And there goes my cock again. I should check to see if there's a lock on the door.

"Have you had much to drink?"

Dean tilts his head at me, his gaze roaming my

face. I swallow hard at the attention, liking his focus on me. Just when I don't think he'll answer, he shrugs. "Enough to take me to my happy place, not enough I'll be throwing up."

Without breaking eye contact, I nod and try to figure out exactly what I'm doing here. I like to think I'm a man who's always in control and uses the head on top of my shoulders, not the one straining against my jeans. But when his gaze darts to my mouth and his tongue peeks out, wetting his bottom lips, I react.

I'm running on instinct.

And need.

And that big what-if.

And my cock is cheering me on when I take hold of him and drag him toward me. I have just enough time to see his brows shoot high before my mouth is on his.

Relief, confusion, and desire sweep through me, heating my veins. I absorb each feeling, reveling in the sensation, my pulse going crazy.

When I brush my tongue against his, a jet of fire surges through me. I react immediately, tugging Dean on to my lap. He clings to my shoulders, and I wrap my arms around his back, keeping him close, loving the press of his chest against mine.

He's so much smaller than I am. Compact.

Though rather than tallying the differences, I hold tighter, my brain fogging in lust.

And then he grinds. Steel touching steel with a rub of rough denim in the way.

Gasping, I pull back, a heavy groan escaping. "Fuck." The single word is breathy, almost like a grunt.

And my mouth's back on his, chasing his kisses, needing the connection, needing his tongue so far in my mouth I can suck on it, wanting that as a precursor to what I want to do to his cock.

His whimpers are addictive. His movements steady, controlled, and I can't help but wonder how he's not only holding me captive but how he's so together when it feels like I'm spiraling out of control.

It's no use.

I need more.

Specifically, I need to taste him.

Effortlessly, I push him away. There's a flash of emotion on his face, his expression turning guarded.

"Stand up." My voice is so gruff I hardly recognize it. "I want to suck you off."

His reaction is immediate, as is my grin at his enthusiasm. And that he hasn't said a word, which should perhaps freak me out…? Hell, at this point, I don't give a damn.

The world could be on fire, but I only have one thing on my mind, and it's not saving the world, not when the spark between us is combustible.

Screw that.

All I care about is seeing, touching, and tasting him.

Words are overrated anyway, especially when he unzips his jeans and tugs out his cock.

I groan. He's fucking perfect. Long and slender, enough for me to really get my lips around and show him how great my mouth is.

What is it with my desperation and absolute need to taste him? Hell if I know, but I'm too wired to question it. Too horny to see anything other than his dick.

I scoot forward, relieved the couch is low so I don't have to strain to get a taste.

Just before I take him in my mouth, I cup his denim-covered ass. I'm met with trembling muscles, his silent reaction zapping me with a new hit of desire.

Without using a hand, I nudge his cock with my nose and inhale. Another desperate groan escapes me at his scent, pulling a new reaction from him as he grips my hair.

The sensation is heady as fuck. I love being controlled, even though I rarely let it happen, never trusting or building a connection with anyone enough to have the many itches I have finally be scratched.

Dean, though…

I shake off the thought. Instead, I lap at his cock and angle around until I find purchase.

With my mouth wrapped around him, I go to town and don't stop until he's a quivering mess, grunting and groaning like I'm the fucking master at giving head. And hell if my gag reflex isn't getting a workout.

I take him deep, nose in his pubes, and pause, swallowing a couple of times for good measure. And finally I get his words.

"Holy… nngh…"

Well, sort of. They're good starting words, considering how much I'm clearly blowing his mind. I ease back and work on my suction, ignoring my own aching dick that's hard enough to give Thor's hammer a run for its money. And then he truly gives me what I've been waiting for.

My name.

"Kieran… holy… so good… gonna…"

I double down, not sure I've been so focused on giving head in my life. But I want to make this everything. Want this moment to be burned in both our memories, as I know it can never happen again.

Gripping his ass cheeks, I squeeze and encourage him to fuck my mouth.

The taste of precum is more potent. He jerks, his hips erratic. The hold on my hair intensifies, enough to have my eyes stinging, but I refuse to back off.

My balls draw up to my stomach as the tingles behind my eyeballs intensify. My scalp is on fire, magnifying every sound, every movement, and each sensation threatens to unravel me any second.

And then he comes. Warm jets hit the roof of my mouth and the back of my throat, and I squeeze my eyes shut, dick throbbing, and I'm shooting my load in my pants like I'm fifteen years old.

"The fuck?"

The voice is a punch to my gut. I scramble away, wincing at the audible pop as I release Dean's half-flaccid dick, and drop my hands.

The door shuts. *When the hell did it even open?*

Dean rushes to tuck himself away, but my eyes aren't on him.

I glance around Dean and am both relieved and humiliated that Tyron is standing in the room.

"For fuck's sake, Kieran, I could have been any-fucking-one." His brows are pulled down so low, I can barely see his eyes.

With my reaction a little delayed by the booze and

the crash of adrenaline, I wipe my mouth, uncomfortably aware that I've jizzed in my pants.

I scoot back, unable to look at Dean, who's since put his cock away but is standing rigid. He's also moved from in front of me and is looking toward Tyron. I bend forward, elbows on my knees and head in my hands. "Shit. I didn't think." My words are slower than they were fifteen minutes ago. Whether it's from sucking Dean off or the shots fully hitting me, I have no idea.

"Fuck, are you wasted?"

Having the nerve to glance up, I wince at Tyron's expression. The frown and his stance make it clear he's battling with concern and annoyance. I know the latter's on my behalf, though. He's looking out for me.

"Is he drunk? What's he had?" The words he shoots Dean's way are hard, on the edge of accusatory.

I still can't look at Dean, and while that makes me feel shit, regret is already weighing me down.

"How the fuck should I know?" Dean's voice is tight, defiance in every syllable. "He's only had one shot and his beer since being here."

Tyron's gaze narrows. "Who gave him the shot?"

Despite my wooziness and how exhausted I feel, I

know completely where he's going with this. "Sammy," I say. "I've only had four shots and a beer."

"And no food."

My mouth twitches at my friend's concern, but now is not the time or the place for smirks. I definitely don't have any energy to joke about this or brush it aside.

"You need to get the fuck out of here. Come on." He shakes his head, grumbling, "Rules, man. You forgot your fucking rules."

As I stand, Tyron's "For fuck's sake. I can't even —" has me grimacing. Heat rushes to my cheeks, and I totally feel like I've been caught by my mom. I tug out my tee, which is barely long enough to cover the mess. "I've got my coat," I say absently, thinking I can at least carry that in front of me before we leave.

Movement to my side catches my attention, and I sigh, knowing Dean is looking at me. Shit, I'm a prize asshole.

As hot as this was, it should never have happened.

I find the balls to look at him. His arms are folded across his chest, and his face is blank. I have no idea how he's managing that—I'm kind of envious—but I wish I could get a read on him. Hell, I'd prefer it if he was spitting mad, considering how much of a jackass I've been since I swallowed his cum.

"Uhm… I have to go. I have practice tomorrow." The words are lame, not quite as slurred or gruff, but still pathetic. "I'll see you around."

An arched brow is shot my way. "As in, next week." While his face is carefully neutral, there's clear derision in his tone. But since I deserve it, I nod while mentally punching myself.

Dean is not a faceless, nameless hookup I'll never see again.

Fuck my life.

"You best be going, since your rottweiler is waiting for you."

I will not get hard. It really is the snark that riles me up and gets a reaction from me. Even though I'm spent, and humiliation sings in my bones, my limp dick stirs.

"Yeah. Okay. See you next week."

Somehow I don't run, but I do pause when Tyron says, "Listen, he's not publicly out—"

"I'm not in the habit of going around and forcing jocks out of the closet." Steel is in every word.

I glance back at Dean, and for the first time since this clusterfuck, I can read a glimmer of emotion. Whether it's at the implication of Tyron's words or not, I have no idea. Our gazes connect, much like they did when I was on the court, and a tightness squeezes my chest.

I refuse to put a name to the emotion trying to punch its way out, threatening to destroy my carefully organized world.

Wordlessly, I look away and tug on Tyron's arm. I need to get out of here, and actually get Tyron to lead the way so no one sees the cum patch staining my jeans.

But what I really need to do is fall unconscious and try to wipe tonight from my memory.

CHAPTER 5
RULE 3 SECTION D: NO STRAIGHT GUYS

DEAN

"Come on, Zeke, you're gonna make me late."

My slow-ass brother is something akin to a sloth in the morning. At the weekends, I couldn't care less, but when he's going to make me late for class unless he hauls ass, I want to shake some speed into the kid.

When he enters the kitchen, he's midway rolling his eyes at me. "I didn't say I needed a ride."

"Yet without one, you'd be late too, wiseass."

Another eye roll follows, but when he walks past me, picking up his backpack on the way, he knocks his shoulder into mine. It's a light tap. This is teenager speak for "I love you really. You're not so bad. I could do worse."

While my mom is incredible, and we have a good

relationship, Zeke is the one person I'll do anything for. Need a new kidney? I'd already be flat on the operating table. Need me to turn my life upside down to make sure he's happy? Well, yeah, I already did that, and while I sulk at times, I have no regrets.

Plus, this town and school aren't so bad. And Mom finally seems to be getting ahead, so soon, hopefully, she won't have to be working herself to the bone.

"You got your training gear?"

He bobs his head, and I take in his overstuffed backpack.

"Please tell me you washed your gear since last time?"

He snorts in my general direction as he pulls open the door to head to my rust bucket. "I'd have my ass handed to me if I didn't. Coach Milton is a hard-ass."

I grin, thinking about just how hard Zeke's delicious basketball coach's ass is. The man is especially divine, and it should come as no surprise to any of you that I feel this way. You know my weakness for jocks.

I slam on the brakes on that train of thought, refusing to think about last Thursday and another fine specimen of jock. I can't. Well, not without getting a chub while becoming so livid I wish I could shoot lasers out of my eyes.

"You still taking me to the next home game?" Zeke glances over at me as he gets into the front seat, and I nod. He was seriously pissed when he found out I took in a game and didn't take him.

Zeke is a talented player. At fifteen, he already has four inches on me. I'm just relieved there's still a semblance of his baby face visible. Our genes went in completely opposite directions; not that surprising since we have different dads. The only thing that marks us as brothers, apart from our on-point wit, is our eyes. They're the same shape and shade as our mom's.

And that's where the similarities stop.

"It's next Friday, right?"

He knows exactly when it is, since it's the first official game of the season in CLB. I assume he's laying it on thick so there's no chance of me forgetting.

Chance would be a fine thing. I hold back my snort.

"Yeah," I answer as I start the engine. The Bears had an away game yesterday, which they'd won. Had I been checking scores before last Thursday? Nope. Though admittedly it was a kick-ass game, and that's the only reason I bought a Bears jersey at the weekend.

It's nothing to do with receiving the best blowie

of my life. You know, the one I can't tell anyone about, as I wasn't lying to the rottweiler about not outing anyone.

"You head home straight after practice today, okay?" I don't have to look to know he's once again rolling his delinquent eyes at me. "I'm serious," I say, the mind reader in me kicking in. "Get your homework done. Your basketball schedule is going to be ridiculous from next month, and there's no way you'll be getting into college if you start slacking off and your grades drop." Before he can bite back, I add, "With or without an athletics scholarship."

The deep sigh of my younger brother, who's clearly over being told what to do, fills the cab of my car. "Fine, but I want hot dogs at the game. Your treat."

Relief settles in my shoulders. "Deal."

At the school, I'm gifted with a chin lift before he leaves the car. A quick check of the time tells me I should make it to my first class with just enough time to spare. I may even be able to grab a to-go coffee first.

Something tells me I'm going to need it before my working lunch with my study group.

Sᴡᴇᴀᴛʏ ᴘᴀʟᴍs ᴀʀᴇ ɢʀᴏss.

It's five minutes before meeting the Lit 129 group, and my heart is beating overtime. Seeing Kieran again is going to be a test of my restraint.

The smartass in me wants to flirt and make him super uncomfortable, but that would also make me a prize prick. I also want to ignore him and not give him a moment of my attention.

There's no denying that as soon as the rottweiler entered the room last week, I felt like shit—Kieran's reaction going a long way to making me feel that way. The thing is there's no point questioning any of it. He's not out, so of course he freaked. Though it was the rottweiler who made it clear that "publicly" was the word of the day. So at least he knew. Maybe his family does too? His friends? I have no clue. And then he started going on about breaking *his*—as in Kieran's—rules…. Who the hell knows what that's about?

So here I am, about to meet at the picnic bench over by the IT block, lunch in hand, paper bag threatening to go soggy with my sweaty palms, battling to settle on a single emotion or even knowing how to react.

I suppose there's only one way to find out.

I turn the corner and realize I'm the last one to arrive. Great. Fixing a smile, I head toward the group. There's one spot left open for me, which of course is directly opposite Kieran, but I don't hesitate.

Screw that.

I'm made of tougher stuff.

Having embraced my twink identity when I was sixteen, and with hours of practice turning insults into a part of me that I embrace and love, I'm no stranger to hostility or acting up or out. Not that it can't be exhausting. Heck, it's the reason I didn't pursue drama. Putting on a performance in everyday life was a drain, so studying it as well would have pushed me over the edge.

"Hey, how's everyone?" I glance around the group, receiving nods, smiles, and general one-word responses. Kieran's gaze is noticeably absent. He's staring hard at his laptop. "Excellent. Should we get started?"

We get to discussing the analysis and our general findings. Even Kieran joins in every now and then, but his responses are limited, and he's doggedly refusing to look in my direction.

With our task title "As the English language evolves, so do stylistic conventions for literature. Select four different examples of published pieces from four different centuries and prepare an analytical multimodal presentation of the evolution and

language and its significance to your texts of choice"
—anyone else glaze over with that title? It wasn't just
me, right?—the possibilities had been limitless. Yet
our individual tasks this past week had been to find
ideal examples to bring to the table, as well as additional research into said stylistic conventions.

We throw around ideas, and I snort more than
once as our discussion gets slightly ridiculous. It's
reassuringly refreshing that the members of the
group have personalities and decent senses of
humor.

Bobby's warming up too. He's grinning as he
talks about the merits of *Irene Iddesleigh.*

If you've never heard of the book, don't waste
your time researching it. For real. Don't. And if you
go ahead and ignore me and look it up anyway, I
dare you to have a read. Just don't blame me if your
eyes bleed or you hurt yourself with laughing so
hard. And if you pee your pants, that's on you. I'm
not responsible for dry-cleaning bills.

I throw a potato chip at him, joining in with his
laughter after the no-longer shy guy quotes a line
from the book that's so cringeworthy, I almost choke
on my sandwich.

He carries on after swallowing the salted chip.
"Just seven days and I shall be fettered with chains of
dragging dislike and disappointment! Only seven

days and thus shall end my cherished hopes, my girlish pride, my most ardent wish, but, alas! not my love! Seven days more shall see my own darling Os—"

"You know, those *Os* totally stand for orgasms," I offer to a chorus of laughter. Except Kieran's. I look toward him as the other three members of the group become increasingly silly about making sex the common theme we focus on in the assignment.

I grin, despite looking at Kieran—my group is so not what I expected. "You don't agree?" I call him out, aware I'm potentially poking the bear. Ha! *Bear…*

His gaze snaps to mine. Pink stains his cheeks, and he looks anything but relaxed and happy.

"There a problem?" My voice is low, and I lean forward for good measure, trying to make sure I'm not overheard. I don't want to cause any discord in the group, but if he's going to be a turd and just sit here silently brooding, he needs to get over himself.

The movement of his jaw drags my attention to his mouth, and I wish I couldn't remember how hot our kisses were. Before I roll my eyes and dismiss him, he finally speaks. "I'm busy. Literally, I'm lucky to have two free hours a day to work on assignments, so whatever this flirting bullshit you have going on with Bobby, do it in your own time. I'm here to work, get a good grade, and this"—his brows lift high—"is stopping me from doing just that."

I'm honest to god startled. Not only by his outburst but his accusation of me "flirting" with Bobby. I've been super friendly; that's it. Okay, Bobby's kinda cute, but not the sort of guy I go for. He's far too nice and not up his own ass to be on my radar. But there's also the fact that he—the illustrious captain of the basketball team—has better things to be doing.

Fuck, don't we all.

I narrow my gaze on him, ready to tell him to fuck off and stop being an arrogant prick. Sure, we're having fun, but we're still working, and I know getting to know this group will make us work better together.

Before I can bite, Yasmin interrupts. "Okay, so all joking aside, we have three of our choices." She's smiling when I turn my focus to her, and I think she's completely unaware of the tension set to explode between Kieran and me. "How about we circle back to *Maurice* by Forster for our final book?"

"That's fine by me," Kieran is quick to say, no doubt eager to get out of here. And I can't help but wonder if he's even heard of the book, let alone read it and sees the irony in the selection.

Bobby and Sarah agree, which just leaves me.

"Yeah, sure." Hell, it should be interesting pulling apart such an iconic queer book.

Yasmin smiles. She really is pretty, and apparently not the sort of person to turn Kieran's head like I'd originally assumed. Assuming he is gay and not another fabulous letter in the rainbow alphabet.

We chat for fifteen minutes about how we plan to fulfill the assessment criteria, and then I pause when Sarah says, "So I think we split up into a two and a three for more regular meets, our schedules allowing. That way we can bounce ideas around and don't struggle as much to find a time that suits all five of us."

Wide-eyed, my heart bounces around in my chest. I'm about to indicate I'll pair up with her, or either Yasmin or Bobby, when Bobby beats me to the punch. "I think that's a good idea. Since the three of us live so close together"—he looks at the girls. Apparently they've been chatting outside of our chat. I work hard at controlling my reaction to that news. I don't do well with feeling left out—"it probably makes sense for us to join."

His smile appears genuine when he focuses on me. "That okay with you guys?"

Well, shit on a waffle. I can hardly say no.

"Sure."

I jerk my head in the direction of Kieran, who

instantly agreed, surprised to find his attention on me. And the fucker is quirking his brow. I want to smack him and kiss him and maybe twist his nipples for good measure.

Not to be outdone, I smile, aiming for seductive and mischievous, and I push every ounce of flirtation into it. "I absolutely would love to be paired with the Bears' captain. What a treat."

A flash of what I like to think is lust or surprise, but is probably fear and irritation, appears in his gaze.

"Excellent." Yasmin claps her hands. "We've got five weeks to get this project tuned to perfection. If we can try to meet maybe in two or three weeks, but keep everything online and check regularly, that would be great."

"Sure." I nod, refusing to look away from Kieran.

"Absolutely," he says, staring me down.

Everyone starts to pack up, and I do the same. It's a little tricky, as my gaze remains locked on Kieran while I put my laptop away. Sometimes it's important to stand my ground, and since he's the asshole who did a runner on Thursday with a shitty excuse and what felt like a what-the-fuck-did-I-do apology, you can bet your ass I'm going to dig my heels in.

The other three members of our group say goodbye, leaving us alone.

"Want to give me your number so we can hook up?" Yes, totally deliberate vocab choice right there. My smile is saccharine sweet.

The blush on his cheeks is fast and adorable. It shouldn't be, because he's a wankstain, remember?

"Fine." That one word is gritted out, but I'm convinced he's breathing a little heavier. I hope he's recalling how he sucked me off so good that he came in his pants.

Without. A single. Touch.

The power of my magical cock. I can make jocks jizz without doing anything other than ramming my dick deep down their throats.

But holy BJ, that image is dangerous. There's a twinge in my jeans, and sitting here is becoming increasingly uncomfortable. I'm grateful my over-sized shirt is long enough to cover my groin.

Kieran reels off his number. Each word sounds painful, and I get sadistic pleasure from every grated number he gives me.

"Done." I smirk, punching Call on my phone. His cell rings, and I wink. "You've got my number now. If you want, you can add a nickname. Something cute. Sassy. How about One Blow?"

Apparently that's a step too far, as he shoves off the bench and grabs his bag.

"Sorry. Too soon?" It's a half-assed apology, but it

gets his attention. "How about Rule Breaker?" I quirk my brow, totally looking for a reaction. While I have no idea still what the "rules" thing is about, getting a rise from this man is surprisingly good fun.

And slightly evil.

But if I'm forced to spend time with him, I need to make my stance clear and have fun while I'm at it.

"No?" I shrug as he closes his eyes and shakes his head at me, his cheeks puffing out. "Well, just so you know, I'm going to label your number as One Shot."

Fuck, I just can't help myself. But when he looks at me, I can see I really am pushing it a step too far. I hold my hands up in a placating gesture. "I promise when we meet next time I'll behave. I'll be focused and all work." As much as it pains me, I will stick to that promise.

Not only do I want a good grade, but I've put him through enough, and I'm not a complete asshole.

He doesn't look convinced. "You going to somehow control that mouth of yours?"

I tuck my lips between my teeth and tug an imaginary zip over it. It's the only way to not respond with innuendo. I then give him a reprieve and offer, "I do know how crazy your schedule is." He lifts both brows at me. "Not yours specifically. I'm not stalking you or anything. What I mean to say is I know how grueling training and all the travel can be.

So I promise, if you're not an asshole, I'll make sure I'm not either. I want to nail this assignment."

He hesitates for a beat but takes a step back closer to the picnic table where I'm sitting. "You know basketball, really? I know the other night—" He slams his mouth shut, and I remember all too well how my knowledge of the game had surprised him.

"I know the game, have always been a fan. Plus my brother plays in high school."

"He any good?"

My smile is immediate, genuine when I think about my kid brother. "He really is. Zeke is aiming for a full-ride scholarship, and he's on a mission to go pro."

Surprise flashes through me, heating my skin when Kieran sits back down.

"That's great. How old?"

"Fifteen. He's a sophomore over at East Middleton."

Kieran nods, a tentative smile stretching his far-too mesmerizing lips. "They have a good rep."

"We only moved over the summer, so he's new to the school but got starting line straightaway."

"Impressive." A new hint of color brushes his cheeks again. "Have you… uhm… brought him to a game?"

My heart melts a little, the traitorous organ it is.

"No, but I promised him we'd go to the first game of the season. Last week was the first game I took in since being here." I can't help but add, "And you know how much I enjoyed that."

He clears his throat, gaze dipping to my mouth before he looks away, and fuck if I don't want to cheer, grab his face, and kiss the sweetness out of him.

Yeah, sweetness. I totally went there. Don't get me wrong, he's still a prize asshole, but since we're managing to have a civilized, dare I say, pleasant conversation, there's definitely some sweetness there.

"I can get you tickets if you want?"

I'm not sure which of us is more surprised, considering his wide eyes and my stuttering heart.

"I…" I scramble for words. "I don't want to take advantage—"

The shake of his head cuts me off. "Honestly, I'm happy to organize tickets for you both, especially if you're going to become fans."

I chuckle, my shoulders relaxing a little more. "Well, after last night's win, I'm almost there."

His brows practically reach his hairline as he stares at me. "You watched yesterday's game?"

"Sure did. The diner I work at stays open till late and always puts the local college game on."

I don't miss the small smile I'm sure he's trying to hide. "Okay, well, I'll text you the details."

"Thanks. I really appreciate it. I'll also let you know my work hours. If you can let me know when you're available, we'll arrange a time to meet up."

He grins and knocks the table as he stands. "It's not quite got the same ring to it as hook up, right?" Those are his parting words as he offers me an up nod I can never quite master and walks away.

Me? I'm left alone wondering how the complete one eighty of the past hour has rocked my world and left me shaken.

"I'M BEAT."

A quick glance in Kieran's direction and I see the truth of that statement in the tiredness in his gaze. Considering yesterday's game when the man was on fire and barely stopped for a breath, it's not surprising.

"I'm good to stop. You look like you could sleep."

"For at least a week." His smile is sleepy and sweetly endearing. I've been receiving a lot of these—not only in today's study session, but the one from a few days ago too. I like them a lot, probably more than I should.

"Your schedule is crazy. I'm not sure how you do it." It's admirable, something I told him in one of the many text exchanges we've had. Should we have kept our conversations strictly school related? I've no doubt the answer to protect my heart and my forever-hard cock should be yes, but damn if I can stop myself from liking the guy.

"It'll be worth it." He stretches as he yawns, and I can't help but peek at the sliver of skin on display, just below his navel. What I wouldn't give to lick a line across it before dipping lower.

I gulp hard and tear my gaze away. If he caught me, he doesn't show it. There's no cocky grin shot my way or even flushed cheeks. Heck, does it sound like I'm disappointed? If you think yes, then you're absolutely right. I love getting a reaction out of Kieran, and a sexy reaction would be even better.

Clearing my throat, I offer a small smile. "It will be. I know what it takes for players to go pro, and you, my friend, have got what it takes in spades."

A sweet flush spreads across his cheeks at my words. While it's not the flush I was hoping for a few moments ago, this will do just as well. "Thanks." The word is whisper-soft, and it takes everything in me to stop from reaching out to him and squeezing his hand.

"Just saying it as I see it. I'm not one to blow smoke up people's asses."

His brows shoot up at that and his lips twitch.

"It would interfere with the flavor of my lip gloss," I sass, earning me the laughter I enjoy hearing so much.

"Well, I wouldn't want to get in the way of you and your lip gloss."

"Sensible man."

Kieran snorts and finishes gathering his things. 'Time's almost up here anyway."

A glance at the time on my cell shows it's a little before eight. We booked out one of the study spaces in the library to ensure we could discuss the assignment without being shushed.

"What are you getting into tonight?" The question slips out unplanned, but I'm curious. I'm totally not putting the feelers out to do something else. I know Kieran's tired, but would it be so bad if we spent a little time together relaxing?

That, by the way, is totally a rhetorical question, because we all know the answer. It doesn't stop me from wishing things were different.

"Sammy's cooking tonight, so I'll eat, consider spending an hour on my business studies assignment, then the plan is to crash."

"Sammy cooks?" I know perfectly well who his

housemates are, courtesy of quickly becoming the Bears' number-one fan. "As in, doesn't just heat up a frozen meal?" The surprise in my voice is clear, enough that it gets him laughing. It stops me from asking about the idea of them eating together as a household, like a family. If that's the case, it's all levels of sweet while being equally mind-blowing.

When out in LA, I had housemates, and we all fended for ourselves. It's funny that the more I think about being in LA and comparing it to Brixham, the less I'm seeing my two years through rose-tinted glasses. It's kind of reassuring—how much I'm really starting to genuinely love my life here.

"Don't sound so surprised," he says around his chuckles. "We have a schedule and take it in turns to cook. Sometimes we'll cheat and just get cars of red sauce or something for spaghetti, but usually we cook from scratch. Our diet is important." Kieran puts the strap of his bag on his shoulder, and I do the same. "Though we do have to remind Ty sometimes and limit him to making pizzas once a month."

Okay, I'm impressed. "Wow, okay. Makes sense with all the nutritional stuff I suppose you have to pay attention to."

As he holds the door open for me, a gesture that makes my stomach fizz, he nods. "Exactly. Plus we all have budgets we have to keep too."

It makes sense. Kieran's parents aren't hurting for money, but that doesn't mean it's the same for his friends.

"How about you?" he asks. "What are you getting into tonight?"

"Pretty much the same as your night. Only flip business for a lit and sci-fi module. Oh, and mac and cheese, from a box." I bounce my brows. "Living the dream."

"Nothing wrong with mac and cheese."

The cool air hits us when we're outside, and I pause when Kieran does. Once again, there's a fizz in my stomach when I turn to face him, my gaze lifting to his. I'm beginning to think it's the only way my body knows how to react to him.

"You need me to walk you to your car?"

I quirk my brow at his words, not quite sure if I'm pissed that he thinks I need an escort, or I'm touched that he's offering. "Would you offer, I don't know, Ty the same thing?"

The pink in his cheeks is fast to appear and clear in the outdoor lighting. "I... uh..." Kieran runs a hand through his hair and scrunches his face. With a shrug, he says, "Sorry, I wasn't suggesting you need an... uhm... I don't know, escort or something."

"No?" My mouth twitches. It's endearing, right? His reaction?

"No." He shakes his head, relief evident in his gaze when he takes in my smirk. "Let me rephrase that. I'd like to walk you to your car. Is that okay?"

That fizz in my belly goes wild. I could be an ass and push him further, ask him to clarify more, hope to tease additional words and truth out of him. Instead, I nod. "Okay."

His grin is wide and totally does not take my breath away. We walk together toward the southside car park in silence, but rather than it feeling awkward, each step I take with Kieran by my side is relaxing, feels right.

All too soon, we stop by my car. Kieran places a hand on the roof and gazes around the lot. There are a couple of groups of students milling around still, some laughter amid the rustling of the trees.

"Drive home safe." He's standing close enough that his words feel intimate, but not close enough that I can feel the heat of his skin.

I bob my head. "Will do. You walk home safely, and enjoy whatever masterpiece Sammy has cooked up."

A low chuckle escapes Kieran. "Since he can cook three dishes, I'm not sure masterpiece is the right word, but thanks." He steps back as I open the car door. "Have a good night," he says as I settle in my seat.

"Yeah, you too."

He nods and closes the door. Once I've started the engine, he taps the roof of my car and I offer a dorky wave before pulling out. Unable to resist, I glance through my rearview mirror, far too happy that he's rooted in the spot, attention on my retreating tail-lights. By the time I lose sight of him, I shake my head. Kieran Kendall is a cinnamon roll wrapped up in lickable abs. He's also worryingly distracting.

My attention is diverted to my message notif-ication. There's a series of four alerts, ones that get my heart pounding. Is it him? Kieran? I know we just parted, but for the alerts to come right now, it's not just a coincidence, right?

With my heart in my throat, I will my hands to stick to my steering wheel like glue. It won't be long before I'm home and I can put myself out of my misery.

I'm all but vibrating by the time I pull up outside my house. Immediately I snatch up my phone, my grin instant when I see Kieran's name. Yes, his real name. Not the teasing nickname I may have threat-ened him with.

Kieran: I was thinking more about that lip gloss and the flavors. There can't be that many, right?

Kieran: If there are, maybe I need to get in on it.

Kieran: But I don't want anything gross.

Kieran: Smokey ass doesn't sound great. :P

Heat floods my entire body, my smile stretching so wide it's a good job I'm still in my car, so Zeke or Mom don't call me out on it.

Me: Smokey ass lip gloss… it seems like an idea I could pitch.

Me: Right along with cheesy dick… oh, the possibilities.

I don't even have to wait ten seconds before three bouncing dots appear.

Kieran: Bahahahaha! A whole new range of gloss for the discerning man. But… please don't tell me they smell too.

Me: Well, my cherry tastes and smells delicious. It's not as good as the real thing, but pretty close.

Kieran: Huh…

Me: Huh?

Kieran: I've tasted your raspberry.

My cock reacts immediately, remembering all too clearly that night when he did indeed taste me wearing my raspberry lip gloss.

Me: Blue raspberry is one of my new favorites.

Yes, I know this is so wrong and dangerous, but he started it. It would be worse if I cut him off. He'd feel like shit. I'm being a good guy here, so no rolling your eyes at me.

Kieran: Yeah?
Me: Definitely.

I smirk as I type: **That along with cinnamon roll.**

Kieran: Cinnamon roll? Any reason? Not that pastries aren't delicious.
Me: Sweet, fluffy, too good to be true... yeah, my favorite.

His reply isn't immediate, so I grab my things and exit the car. As I reach the front door, my cell pings.

Kieran: Do they have Twinkie flavors? If so, sign me up. There's nothing quite like the creamy goodness of one of those.

Holy cocking hell. My dick turns solid, and I hope like hell no one is on the other side of this door, as there's no concealing the hardness in my pants. What I need is to escape to my room and take myself in hand. Will I be imagining Kieran sucking me off? Damn straight I will.

Before I unlock the door, I fire off: **Twinkies and cinnamon rolls... now there's a combination.**

When his text comes through, my breath hitches.

Kieran: Sometimes it takes the unlikeliest of combinations to make the best flavored gloss. Risky but it could totally be worth it.

CHAPTER 6
RULE 10: MAINTAIN YOUR IMAGE

KIERAN

"SOMETHING'S LIT A FIRE UNDER YOUR ASS," TYRON says as we're dressing after our epic win. And, yes, against Birmingham. The whole locker room is buzzing after the game we played. "What gives?"

There's no holding back my grin. It's impossible not to after a 75-59 win. Plus, during my brief interview, the reporter shared the news that our team's power ranking had already jumped up four. I know it's jumping the gun, as it's the first game of the season, but I'll take it.

"Just feeling the game. Everything went right as soon as we stepped foot on the court." Which isn't a lie. What I don't share with him is how I immediately sought out the intense brown eyes of a certain guy who's gotten under my skin. And when he'd smiled, the adrenaline that had pulsed in my veins had absolutely stoked the rightness and the flames Tyron's talking about.

To be clear, I wanted to show off. Wanted to win that game, so aware Dean's eyes were on me and he'd be cheering. And come halftime when I realized he was wearing a Bears jersey with my name on it over his long-sleeved shirt, everything had become crystal clear.

I'd be winning tonight's game. There was no doubt about it.

Tyron eyeballs me, and I school my features. I haven't told him about the handful of texts I've exchanged with Dean, or the two study sessions we've had. Nor have I told him we're actually in a class together and working in a group. It'll only concern him, and he'll go into full-on dad mode on me.

"You about ready to go?" he asks, apparently giving me a free pass.

My gut clenches, as I know the words that are about to come out of my mouth are lies. "Almost. I need to just check in with Coach. Why don't you go ahead? I won't be long." I shoot him a chin lift and aim for a "there's nothing to see here" smile.

The full-on stare he shoots my way is more effective than twenty questions. But I won't back down. If I do and I tell him I texted Dean and asked him to hang around after the game before leaving, not only will he lose his shit, but it's likely he'll beat some sense into me. I don't want to be reminded of my rules. The ones I've lived by since high school. The ones I know have helped me make it to team captain, maintain my GPA, and are getting me a step closer to the draft.

My gut clenches, and I focus on rummaging through my bag rather than make eye contact with Tyron. The thing is, I don't know why Dean has got under my skin. It makes no sense. We don't even know each other all that well.

Both times we've met up, we worked our asses off. But in our texts especially, I discovered more about the man, understood a little more about his personality, and even discovered that he has a whole range of lip gloss including different flavors.

"Fine." Tyron eventually gives in, and I release a slow exhale. "I'll get the pizza ordered, but don't blame me if your ass is too slow to get a slice."

Glancing at him, I grin. "A slice? Damn, man, that's cold. I need a whole pizza after how I played tonight."

When he smirks at me and rolls his eyes, I know we're good. "I'll get Harold to guard two pieces, you know, as I'm feeling generous." He smacks my ass with his damp towel and heads out.

Guilt tries to claw up my throat, but excitement pushes past it, determined to take center stage. While I know I'm playing a dangerous game, there's a pull to Dean that I'm struggling to ignore, and whether a conscious decision or not, I've decided to follow my gut.

I'm the last one to leave. Coach is outside his office talking to someone from PR; he claps me on the back as I walk past. "Let's keep seeing plays like that, Shakespeare."

I grin. "Will do, Coach." Once I'm past him, I pull out my cell and open up the text exchange. I fire off a message letting Dean know I'm on my way.

His thumbs-up is immediate, and I pick up my pace, heading toward the side entrance where I asked him to wait. It's quieter here, and less likely the media or fans will be hanging out, especially as I dragged my feet getting ready.

The cool autumn evening air hits me when I step outside, and there's a noticeable scent of rain. A few puddles litter the ground, and since there's no moon-light, I expect it'll rain again soon.

There's plenty of streetlights lighting the pedes-trian only area, and it takes me no time at all before I'm zeroing in on Dean, who's sitting on a bench a few yards away. A tall form stands next to the bench; his brother, I assume. I return my focus to Dean, whose attention is on me. He stands and is so much shorter than his kid brother. I wonder how he feels about that.

"Hey." My grin is wide, the pleasure at seeing him impossible to hide. "Sorry I took so long."

Dean smiles back and shakes his head. "We didn't mind."

The reference to "we" reminds me to stop staring at Dean, and I turn my attention to his brother. "Zeke, right?" I stretch out a hand, and the kid seems to fumble a moment, his eyes wide and pink touching his cheeks as he clasps my hand.

"Shakespeare."

I chuckle just as Dean says, "What? Who?"

"You didn't tell me you're friends with Shake-speare Kendall." While I can hear the awe in Zeke's voice, there's accusation in there too.

Dean just looks confused. His nose wrinkles. "Well, we're not exactly—"

I cut him off, not wanting him to finish that sentence. "It's my court name," I direct to Dean, focusing instead on his "who" question.

Understanding shines in his eyes. "Of course. I've just never heard anyone call you that before."

"It tends to be the media, Coach, and some of the

guys, but usually only during a game. It's not the easiest name to roll off the tongue." With the final word, his gaze snaps to my mouth, and I can't resist shooting him a cocky grin.

"So," I turn back to Zeke, "you enjoy the game?"

He bobs his head. "It was incredible. You guys seemed everywhere, and those steals…" His brows are high. "Thanks for the tickets," he rushes to say.

"No problem. Dean says you play."

His eyes are still comically wide, and a new flush of pink spreads across his cheeks. "Yeah. Small forward."

"How's your team preparing?"

"Great. First game's next week."

"Nice. Make it to the final, and if I don't have a game, I'll come and watch."

"For real?"

I smile. "For real. Your brother will keep me informed." I return my gaze to Dean, who's staring at me as though I've grown an additional head since the conversation began.

Dean's reaction is delayed, as he seems too busy trying to figure me out. "Of course. Yeah, sure." He looks at his brother. "Kieran said *only* if he's free, okay, so don't get swept up, and don't go telling all your friends."

Zeke rolls his eyes at his brother, and I snort a laugh.

"Well, we best get going. I'm sure you've a party to get going to." There's an intensity in Dean's eyes, one that's a little similar to the night we hooked up.

I shake my head. "Not tonight. Me and most of the guys are having a night in. Pizza and watching the highlights. How about you?"

"We're heading home. I've got an early start at the diner in the morning."

"Which diner is that again?"

Before Dean can respond, Zeke helpfully says, "Aunt Pattie's in Grounder. It's on Main Street. They have the best waffles."

"Is that so?" I tilt my head, and then my gaze connects with Dean's. "One of these mornings I'll take a drive out and check out these famous waffles." My attention snaps to the bob of his Adam's apple, and I know it's time to get out of here before Zeke calls me out for eye fucking his brother.

I clear my throat. "Thanks for coming, Zeke." I shake his hand once more. "I promise if that final happens and I'm free, I'll be there."

His mouth stretches so wide, I can't help but return it.

"Dean, I'll be in touch about the assignment."

He nods, gaze darting around my face, and I

swear he can tell how much of a struggle it is not to reach out and touch him in some way. Like seriously, what the fuck! My fingers twitch at my side, acting as if I know the guy and have a right to him. I shift my hand to hold on to the strap of my bag to stop myself from doing something stupid.

"Okay. I'll speak to you soon." He tugs on his brother's jacket, gives me a wave—which if his heated cheeks are any indicator, he regrets immediately—and then all but drags his brother away.

I stay rooted to the spot and watch him leave.

It'll be good to be friends with the guy. We're working well on the assignment together, so us getting along makes a whole lot of sense. My rules can remain in place. Just because he's gay and cute and has a gorgeous dick doesn't mean I can't keep it in my pants.

I crack my neck, knowing I need to keep my resolve.

A working friendship. Yeah. We can totally do that.

Feeling more resolute—and pointedly ignoring the mocking laughter in the back of my mind—I turn and head home. I have pizza with my name on it just waiting to be inhaled.

Fortunately, I didn't have to kick anyone's ass last night. I arrived before the pizza delivery did, so was able to snag my spicy pepperoni and, like a selfish fucker, keep it to myself.

Do I feel guilty? Fuck no. My teammates are pigs and would eat two whole pizzas given the chance.

I headed to bed early without looking once at the exchange of text messages with Dean and woke up at dawn. I've just finished a run, hosed down in the shower, and now I'm starving.

Waffles sound like a pretty perfect breakfast option to me.

The thing is, how do I sneak out with no one knowing? I suppose a couple of the guys could come with me, but no way can Tyron. He'd sniff out the reason we're there in two seconds flat, and the excuse of good waffles won't cut it.

I sigh as I step into our shared and surprisingly tidy kitchen. It's amazing how clean the space can stay when my roommates aren't stumbling in at two in the morning and cooking up feasts. It even looks like someone has stuffed the multiple pizza boxes in the garbage already too.

"Where is everyone?"

Leon is sipping coffee by himself at the kitchen counter, his laptop open and textbooks littered either side.

"Sammy's gone back to bed. Tyron's meeting up with his sister for breakfast."

I bob my head, fighting hard to contain my excitement at having an easy escape. "I'm heading out too."

Rather than questioning me, Leon waves me off, his focus completely on whatever assignment he's working on. I take my leave with an extra bounce in my step, not believing my luck that it's so uncomplicated. Wonders never cease.

It doesn't take me long to head to the town where Dean works. While I'm not a local, two years here and travelling around for games so much has made me aware of my surroundings. I've actually been to this town a few times. The first was during the off-season when me and a couple of the guys were bored and took a drive to explore.

We stopped at an ice-cream store, which I have to say, took us by surprise in a small town like this. It's good gelato, and we've been back for more since that first happy find.

Seeing a spot to park, I pull in and ease down my visor. I sweep back my hair, hating the one strand that kinks and annoys the shit out of me. It keeps springing back up like the asshole it is, and I sigh at my reflection. "What the fuck are you doing here, Kendall?" My voice is enough to have me wincing, and I take a surreptitious glance around to see if anyone's spotted the crazy guy talking to his reflection.

There's only a handful of people I see, and all are thankfully minding their own business. One more quick glance at the mirror, and I huff out a breath. "Fuck it." I flip the visor up and exit my car.

Once the car's locked, I glance down the street, immediately spotting the diner.

Here goes.

I'm inside before I can continue to overthink. With a racing pulse, I search the place, hoping to catch sight of the guy who's got me tangled in knots.

"Be with you in a second, hon. Just take a seat wherever you want."

I nod my thanks at the middle-aged woman at the register while wondering if Dean works in a particular section, and if so, how the hell do I make sure I'm sitting in the right place.

There looks to be about twenty or so tables, plus stools at the long counter. It seems like a typical mom-and-pop place, a little retro and kinda quirky, and I immediately like it.

There are several tables filled, and I spy an empty booth toward the other side of the room. At least there, I'll have a decent vantage point of the comings and goings of the place.

With my destination in mind, I head on over, glancing to my right when I see the swinging door of the kitchen move. Dean appears, his ass pushing the door open. I slow down my steps and keep my attention in his direction. There's no playing coy here. No happenchance meeting.

It's gonna be obvious why I'm here, and hell if my cheeks don't heat knowing he's going to read me like a book.

And then his eyes are on me, and I pause. They widen, comically so, before a slow smile stretches across his mouth that I still remember the taste of.

"Kieran." He tilts his head to the side, and when he rakes his gaze over me, the heat in my cheeks spreads across my body like a lick of flame. "You're here."

"That I am." I quirk my brow at him, and his own blush is quick to appear.

He's fast to recover. "The waffles got you, huh?"

"You know it."

"You heading for that booth?"

"Yeah."

He's still smiling, one that's filled with disbelief and "I totally know your game." But not an inch of me is embarrassed, especially with the way his face is alight. I swear he seems happy to see me. Seriously, just look at that damn twinkle in his eye. Before this point, I thought that description was clichéd and horseshit, but it's there, as clear as day.

"Go take a seat and give me a sec." With his focus back on the table he's serving, he leaves, and I take a few seconds too long to tear my gaze away from him. It's only the sound of the cash register that has me moving.

Once seated, I unzip my hoodie, my focus trailing Dean as he works efficiently dealing with orders and topping up a few coffees. That he looks at me more than a couple of times pleases me more than perhaps it should.

Friends.

Yep, totally. I'm working toward having a positive relationship with the guy so we can ace our assignment. Plus, I am hungry, and I really do like waffles.

With a menu in hand, Dean approaches me. His face is friendly and open. There's none of the snark or hesitancy from our first couple of meetings. And while I absolutely like his snark, I like his smile more, especially when it's directed at me.

"So, you really going for the waffles?" He passes me the menu.

"Are they seriously that good?"

Did you hear that? Yeah, me too. I'm totally fucking flirting. I know, I know… when I talk to myself, I'm apparently full of shit. *Apparently* I'm a liar too.

"They really are. Add some extra crispy bacon and syrup and you won't regret it."

I lean back against the booth, holding the menu out for him. "In that case, sign me up. No need to look at the menu."

Dean takes the menu off me, his gaze connecting with mine. I have no idea what I see in its depth, but him looking at me this way is something I could get used to. "And to drink?"

Immediately my skin heats. I wish I was a guy who loved coffee. Could ask for something like a strong black coffee, but I totally don't get the coffee addiction experienced by practically every single person I know.

And why exactly am I blushing do I hear you ask? Well, because whenever I ask for what I really want to drink, I usually get ribbed until I'm ready to either punch someone or crawl away to a private corner, ideally with my hot drink.

My pink cheeks have his interest, though. Both his brows are high, and I swear there's a slight tilting of his body, as though he's leaning a little closer. No doubt it's just my animal magnetism.

Okay, I hear you laughing and feel those rolling eyes directed my way, but dude, a man has to have ambitions. And having animal magnetism is high on my list.

I expect Dean is just super curious about my pink cheeks and my weird silence as I mull everything over in my head.

"Peppermint tea, if you have any."

Eyebrows that I thought previously were high seriously weren't. Now, they're all but touching his hairline. He opens his mouth once, twice, and I expect he's going to either think I'm messing with him or the teasing will begin in three… two…

"Absolutely. We actually have a range of fruity teas, not just herbal. Pattie, the owner, is obsessed with trying different varieties. You want the menu back to take a look?"

Warmth spreads in my chest. It feels unfamiliar and kinda weird, but not at all horrible. "Thanks." My smile is slow and I'm aiming for sweet. I'm not sure I pull it off until he beams at me in response. "I'm fine with peppermint, but maybe next time."

"Next time?"

Like a doofus, I wink at him. Fuck, I hope it doesn't come across as sleazy or creepy, but I can hardly take it back. "If these waffles are really great, then you're going to have a hard time keeping me away."

Who knew a guy pressing his lips together

and pulling them between his teeth could be sexy, but hell if I can keep my stare away from his mouth.

"Okay then." I think the squeak of his response surprises us both. I chuckle as he escapes, making quick work of disappearing behind the swinging door. And me? I'm left alone, trying to recite my list of rules.

DEAN WASN'T LYING. THE WAFFLES ARE OUTSTANDING. I'll need to run an extra mile though to work off the sugary and greasy goodness of my breakfast. But totally worth it, especially as Dean agreed for us to meet to work on our assignment.

My place is completely out of the question. There's the library, but since we haven't planned ahead and booked out one of the small meeting rooms so we won't get shushed when talking, it only leaves his house.

I'm curious to find out more about Dean.

While I know this isn't the neighborhood he grew up in, since he and his brother only moved a few months ago, I'll still get a peek into his life. All I know about the man is he's snarky, intelligent, witty as fuck, and he loves basketball. More than that, he knows the rules, appreciates the game, the plays. He also has a sweet side.

And don't even get me started on his cock. You all know how much I loved that experience.

Despite all of that, I'm keen to know more. I'm not even going to make excuses or justify my reasons, as I know you'll call bullshit. In that case, it's best we leave why I'm so invested unsaid.

Pulling up outside the compact brick home, I double-check the address he texted me. It's definitely the place. There's not much of a yard, but what I see looks cared for. It's positioned on the outskirts of the built-up suburb. Well, built-up for such a small town. It's nothing like my experience of a small town back home in Vermont, which is far from a bad thing. Just different.

I rap my knuckles on the door, my bag in hand, relieved I have something to hold on to to stop me from rubbing my palms on my jeans. Being nervous sucks. It's also super rare for me. What can I say? I'm blessed with my mom's confidence gene, but where Dean's concerned, none of that seems to matter.

The door opens, and his smile holds a hint of "holy shit, you actually showed up." Not that I can blame him for that reaction. Not after our rocky start.

"Hey." He backs up a step and invites me in. "You find the place okay?"

"My GPS hasn't let me down yet." I step into the house, my focus staying on him rather than scoping out the place.

He's quiet for a beat, and while his expression is still unreadable, it's obvious he's mulling something over. "Let's head into the kitchen. There's a table in there that we can work at."

With a nod, I follow him through the sitting area. It's cozy and homey. There are a few photo frames dotting the mantel, and an exercise bike wedged in the corner. Dean must see where my gaze is trained, as he explains, "That's my mom's. It's become a feature with the cobwebs gathering there."

"I heard that."

I falter at the sound of a woman's voice before quickly straightening.

Fuck, I'm meeting his mom? This is going to be awkward as hell.

When I realize Dean's attention is on me and his brows are high, an amused, if not confused smirk on his lips, I relax my shoulders and roll my eyes. I'm just not sure if the eye rolling is for me or directed at him.

When he sees my reaction, he turns back and steps into the kitchen. "I'm just making an observation and commending you for the part you're playing in the conservation of arachnids." His tone is so deadpan, my chuckle escapes, loosening my muscles even more.

Parents love me. Even at high school, I was the "responsible" one, keeping my friends in check. Well, as much as possible with hormonal horndogs, but still, the truth remains that parents, grannies, family members in general tend to think I'm a good influence.

I totally have this.

Dean's mom is in the middle of cleaning up the kitchen. Something delicious is obviously baking in the oven, and she's dressed for work. A nurse, from the looks of it.

I fill up the doorway pretty well, considering my height, and she notices immediately. Her eyes widen, and she takes me in, a tilt to her head that's a little similar to the way Dean does it. She's petite like Dean and has the same pretty brown eyes.

"Kieran, right?" Her smile is warm and assessing.

"Yes, ma'am."

Her smile twitches, and she steps from behind the counter, drying her hands before reaching out to shake my hand. I do so immediately, not wanting to crush her palm, but ensuring my grip is politely firm and friendly.

"Nice to meet you," she says. "But less of the

'ma'am.' Way to make me old before my time. Call me Tina."

I don't comment that she's so much younger than I expected her to be. Instead, I chuckle.

"I'd like to say I was expecting you, but since Dean sprung your visit on me thirty minutes ago, I'd be totally bullshitting."

My chuckle becomes louder. I like this woman already. She's maybe in her thirties, and with her greeting, it's clear she and Dean have more in common than their physique.

"And you wonder why I don't tell you anything." Dean snags the towel out of her hand and shoos her away. There's no spite in his tone, and when I search his expression, the soft smile I see makes my heart jolt.

She turns to him and swoops him into a hug, placing a smacking kiss on his cheek. "Right, kiddo. I have to head out to work. Lasagna should take an hour, so keep an eye on it." I don't miss her bouncing brows at that. "Zeke's curfew is at ten tonight, as he promised to work on that assignment first thing. Please text me when he's back, okay?"

"Will do."

His mom returns her focus to me. "It's good to meet you, put a face to the name."

I quirk my brow at that, trying not to let it show

how much my heart picks up speed. Has Dean been talking about me? After a smile at his mom and a quick "You too," I can't help but return my attention to Dean.

Once we're alone, my grin is quick to form and fills with too much heat and cockiness, considering I'm playing with fire. "Have you been talking about me to your mom?"

Dean looks at me for a long beat, his gaze roaming my face, before he narrows his gaze a little, then quirks his brow high. "You wish." A smug grin tilts his lips. "That'll be your new number-one fan, Zeke."

The fucker laughs when my face falls. So much for me playing it cool and keeping my reactions to him locked down. I attempt to recover, shrugging off my embarrassment. "Your brother has good taste."

Dean stops messing with the kettle, and his focus burns me. He's zeroed in on me so acutely that I'm pretty sure he's aware of every breath I take and the fluttering of the pulse in my neck.

"What's going on here, Kieran?" While his tone is completely matter-of-fact, the emotion flicking in his gaze fluctuates between wariness and interest. I can only imagine what he sees in mine.

Probably lust battling with me being on the cusp

of freaking the shit out of myself. Which feels something similar to panic.

"What do you mean?" I absolutely know what he means, but with my brain screaming "Danger" at me, weirdly in a robotic voice rather than my own, I need to deflect. I then hold up my bag and I wince. "Assignment." The wince isn't intentional, but that panic I mentioned? Yeah, it's gone from crawling across my skin to seeping into my bones and threatening to steal my breath.

He's not buying it, because of course he's not.

Heat rushes across my chest, up my neck, and my cheeks are on fire. My brain's also checked out, so it makes sense that I spew, "My rules. I have rules. I just can't… and fuck, I really want to see your cock again, but I have a plan, rules to stick to…" I shake my head, unable to stop the words from tumbling free. "Work. We just need to do the assignment." And then I'm nodding like some sort of manic puppet on acid, and holy J Christ, I manage to stop talking and shut my mouth.

During the whole stream of words, Dean's brows shot higher and higher, and the way he's looking at me now, I can't tell whether he's worried for himself or me.

"That's a lot of sharing in a short amount of time." He purses his lips, and while they twitch, concern shines in his gaze as he takes me in. "Perhaps you should start with sitting your ass down before you pass out or something." He nods toward one of the kitchen chairs, and I take his advice. When my butt hits the cushioned pad, all I want to do is rewind the last minutes and crawl into a hole and pretend like none of this ever happened.

What the hell is happening to me?

Dean Whittaker is turning me inside out, so much so, if I looked at myself in the mirror, I'm not sure I'd recognize the person peering back at me.

What the fuck is up with that?

He turns his back to me, and I silently thank him for the reprieve. I crack my neck and force myself to keep my hands steady and pull my schoolwork out of my bag. The pumping of my heart is loud and distracting, but if I focus on entering my password, then I'll be fine.

There's no other alternative.

"Here."

I startle at his voice and at the mug he places in front of me. The scent of lemon and honeysuckle reaches me, and my shoulders sag. "You got me tea?" I dare to make eye contact with him and hold his gaze.

"Just drink the tea." Settling opposite me, he places his coffee down. "Rules? Explain."

I straighten up before easing back into my seat and kicking out a leg. "Push much?"

"Avoiding much?"

I roll my eyes at him.

"I'm serious. What rules are you talking about? That's twice I've heard that now, and clearly it's affecting you." He looks at me pointedly. "And I'm assuming it has something to do with me too, so what am I dealing with here?"

There's a part of me that wants to completely blow him off—not to be confused with blow him, though that too—but since I'm a certifiable mess around the guy, fuck it. My plan, my rules are solid and have kept me focused and out of strife.

They've made sure I'm on target for going pro, and I'm not ashamed of that. I also don't owe him anything, but it doesn't mean I'm not willing to share. Maybe in doing so, it'll make all this easier.

CHAPTER 7
RULE 15: NO UNNECESSARY RISKS

DEAN

WHILE I ANTICIPATED WHAT KIERAN WOULD SHARE, THE extremity of his words, his "rules," and his logic boggles my brain.

Don't get me wrong, that he feels like he has to stay publicly in the closet is sad and hurts my rainbow heart. I also understand his thought process on some level, aware the professional sports world can be toxic. But hell, to live by such rules is admirable while being depressing as fuck.

One thing's for sure, he's committed.

So why did he suck me off?

I open and close my mouth three times before settling on "That sounds exhausting, living that way."

"Well…" He clears his throat and plays with the handle of his mug. "It just… is. It's been working and hasn't let me down yet."

I can't help but quirk a brow high at his words, silently calling him out.

He has the good grace to look shifty, and his cheeks turn a sweet shade of pink. "That was a blip."

Hurt unfurls in my chest. I'm a blip? For fucking real.

Perhaps some of my emotion escapes in my expression, and his brows spring high. "I'm… that's not what… Shit." He huffs out a breath, and mortification crosses his features. "I'm sorry."

I can't help but feel a bit sorry for the guy. It doesn't make the lick of hurt dissipate, but in his fastidious world he's created for himself, I understand what he means.

It seems I'm full of free passes lately, as I throw him one. "How about we just focus on the assignment and work hard at acing this project?" I tamper down my surprise at my ability to adult when I'm feeling a little butthurt. Wonders legit never cease.

But I've also been played and hurt by an athlete before. Holy jiggly balls, is this me growing and showing I've learned my lesson?

A rush of breath escapes him at my offer, and a

smile that makes my heart trip over itself is directed at me. "Yeah, great. Thanks."

Why the hell is Kieran so gorgeous? This smile of his should come with a warning label, and the more I'm discovering about the guy, it's clear he's not quite the prick I expected.

Attempting to shrug off my curiosity and the tingle of awareness between us that I'm fighting, I center myself and focus on the whole reason he's here. "So, I looked over your notes." He quirks a brow. Challenge settles in his gaze, yet there's a hint of uncertainty there too. I'm sure he's trying to hide it.

"Your responses are highly insightful."

A smirk lifts his gorgeous lips, and it's impossible not to fixate on the movement and want it directed at me.

"The analysis on syntax and etymology was on point." I expected to struggle to praise him, and honestly, had done a double take, a little slack-jawed at his analysis so far.

From what he's just told me, though, I finally understand that this guy, this basketball player who has some serious skills, is also smart as fuck.

You're thinking about that tick box of mine, right?

Ugh. The asshole is doing a ridiculously good job of appearing more and more perfect.

With the obvious exception of him not being out.

For me, that's nonnegotiable for a relationship. The relationship—heck, if you can even call it that—I had with a guy in the closet was enough to hurt and humiliate me for a lifetime. And that sucks, and to be so fazed when I was seventeen left its mark.

A fuck, though? It'd be rude not to.

I realize I've been silently staring at him while going over his potential dateability. Such a rookie error. "So yeah, I uhm...." I cringe. Being lost for words is so not me. Kieran Kendall is too distracting for his own good. "So yeah. I followed the same principals you did but on the second text."

"I saw."

Of course he has.

"What you did was... insightful." He quirks a brow, cutting through my hard-on fog, which is exactly what's going on right now.

Laughing, he picks up his tea and takes a sip, a smile of appreciation forming on his lips. The sound and gesture is enough for me to offer him a friendly smile. My shoulders relax, and I ease into a discussion of the text.

WE MIGRATED TO THE SITTING ROOM ABOUT TWO HOURS ago, not long after devouring my mom's lasagna. I have both legs on the couch, my laptop on my thighs, and have just dodged a throw cushion aimed at my head.

"No, asshole." Humor traces each word. Shaking his head at me, Kieran picks up his phone to check the alert that's come through.

"Hey." I chuckle and hold my hands up in defense. "You're seriously telling me you wouldn't jump Ryan Broadwater's bones given the chance?"

"I'm not saying he's not hot." His gaze is on his cell, and his fingers are flying across the screen.

"So why not?" Ryan Broadwater is a gorgeous and talented player in the League. It's his Australian accent that gives me a boner, though. That he's straight doesn't come into it. In this weird discussion that we started about twenty minutes ago—majorly drifting off topic—every hot basketball player is fair game, regardless of sexuality.

"Other than the fact when I'm pro I'm playing it straight?"

That he's put a serious edge to this "who would you fuck" conversation takes me by surprise. My gut clenches, hating the reality of his situation. It was so easy to get caught up in the banter and start relaxing around Kieran that for a moment there, I allowed myself to forget he's made himself off limits.

Not liking the direction of this conversation, I ask, "Your *bros* need your attention?" I eye the phone he's focused on from his position on the floor.

"Bros?" His snicker is ridiculously sexy.

"Yup."

"Well, my *bros* are feeling abandoned with all this studying I'm doing."

Ignoring the disappointment flaring to life in my chest, I close my laptop. "Okay, you want to arrange another meet, or do you think we can just text?"

Question fills his gaze. "I'm not going just yet."

"You're not?"

"You bored of my company already?"

Is he… flirting?

Fuck me, but if he is, that's impossible to ignore.

"Well, bored is such a relative term."

His snort is loud, and my grin is immediate.

"If you've got plans, though, I can go."

I shake my head, the movement a little too fast for me to be playing it cool. "No plans." I need to take control of this, so add, "Other than acing this assignment."

The grin he shoots at me is sweet and has my pulse picking up speed.

"How about we head out for ice cream? There's a great place in town." I ignore how the offer sounds a little date-like. "A bit of sugar pick-me-up," I clarify.

In a blink, he's standing. "I know the place. What's your poison?"

"I could do with a rocky road right about now." I stand and head to the hallway, fighting back the happy smile trying to break free.

"You have a weakness for marshmallows?"

"Marshmallows are cool."

Marshmallows are cool? What the ever-loving fuck!

I keep on walking, swiping my phone and keys, and pointedly ignore his chuckle.

We decide to walk to the gelato place. It's only a short distance away, and the stretch and bite of the autumn late afternoon feels good.

"You have siblings?" I ask, curious about Kieran the more I get to know him.

"Nope. Only child. Begged my parents for years for a sibling. They weren't swayed by my arguments. Is it just you and your brother?"

"Yeah. Unlike you, I wasn't too pleased by a new baby." I chuckle at the memory. "Had a full-on meltdown when my mom brought him home. I once hid him in a drawer." I cast a glance Kieran's way. He's wide-eyed and staring at me in horror. "Don't worry,

I felt guilty after a minute and rescued him. After that, it always seemed like the two of us against the world."

Surprise that I'm sharing this with him has me catching my breath.

I don't know whether he can pick up the tension pulsing through me or not, but when he says, "Are you feeling more settled now, at college I mean?" I exhale.

We've already briefly chatted about my move. Not the reason why—beyond wanting to be close to Zeke. Seriously, who wants to get into how broke my family and I are? "It's getting easier." Which it is, and knowing that and believing it is one heck of a relief.

While not much has changed in the grand scheme of things, I've sort of settled into a routine. Classes are going well, and my job helps with gas and going out, as well as helping my mom a little with groceries.

"That's great."

We reach the gelato place, and I all but falter when Kieran swings the door open and indicates for me to go ahead. I do so, trying to ignore the flip of my heart. This guy is not making it easy for me to not crush on him.

And I have no idea what to do with that.

Keeping my attention ahead, I focus on the ice

cream selection. While I know exactly what I'm going to order, if I don't have anything to concentrate on, I'm worried my eyes are going to be glued to Kieran's ass or his lips that I know taste so damn sweet.

"Hey, Marco."

Marco greets me with a friendly smile. "Hey, Dean. I was beginning to worry about your sugar levels. It's been, what… five days since I last saw you?"

I snort. "I'm not that bad." I totally am. But for real, this ice cream is to die for. It's a popular place, even with the cooler days and evenings, so I'm not the only one who thinks so.

The presence at my side makes me start, my breath catching in my throat when heat presses against me. Wide-eyed, I peer up at Kieran, who's practically glued to my arm. My reaction must get his attention, as he gazes down at me with a look in his eyes that makes my heart once again bounce around in my rib cage.

"My treat. What would you like?"

Before I can answer, Marco says, "Rocky road with a double hit of chocolate sauce and extra marshmallows."

Just as I'm about to glance away and give Marco shit and wind him up by making a fake order, I pause. Kieran's jaw's clenched, his gaze narrowed, and he looks seriously pissed off by the interruption.

Well, this is new.

"Is that what you want?" he asks, angling a little, his face precariously close to mine. "Or is it time for something a little different?"

And holy shit, his voice is low, gravelly, and screams of the shared intimacy from the party.

"I'm going for the salted caramel with added whipped cream." When his gaze drifts to my mouth, it's impossible not to react. My tongue flicks out, wetting my bottom lip, and all I focus on is the mention of salt and cream. Is he thinking about the taste of my cum?

"Okay." My voice is a squeak, and I don't even give a shit, not when all of Kieran's attention is on me. But when the fucker's expression morphs into a satisfied smugness and he flicks his attention to Marco, I finally realize what he's doing.

He's attempting a dick measuring contest with Marco.

If I'm right, what the fuck? Right along with, why is that so hot?

Either way, a wave of satisfaction rushes through me, alongside with the desire to flip him off and cackle at how wrong he's read mine and Marco's exchange.

Coming back to my senses, I turn my attention to Marco. Amusement fills his features. Admittedly, Marco is cute. He's a few years older than me. This is also his family's store. Want to know what else I know about Marco? He's happily in love with Julian and is looking at proposing soon. That's something I learned after only living here for two weeks.

While the guy is a little flirty, it's only with the regulars, which I'm definitely one of. And I know he's devoted to his boyfriend.

I aim for a sultry smile at Marco, and I can read him well enough to see understanding register. There's a slight twitch of his lips before he winks and leans forward, forearms on the counter and hands clasped.

"That what you want to try, Dean?" He quirks his brow. "If I knew you wanted to explore, I could have arranged that for you."

The urge to snort hits me. "Ooh, like a private tasting or something? You guys do that?"

Kieran shifts at my side, but I don't give in and glance his way.

"A private tasting? For you?" He bounces his brows. "You know I would absolutely make that happen."

"How about we just get our two caramels and

cream to go instead?" Kieran interrupts. His tone is absolutely unimpressed.

"Sure." He takes Kieran in and I'm sure is stockpiling questions to throw at me the next time I'm alone. "I'll get right to that." Marco winks again, and I stay put, smirk, and allow Kieran to pay. Something that would usually make me grouchy, as I have real issues with making sure I pay my way. But Kieran is being far too much fun for me to deny him.

Perhaps I should be putting the guy in his place.

You're wondering why I'm not, huh?

Okay, so you're totally not, because Kieran is beyond sexy, especially like this. And honestly, at this point, I'm entertained and curious about his reaction and intentions.

The sensible part of my brain, one that really wants to protect my foolish, interested heart, knows I should run a mile.

But do I?

Please tell me you're laughing with me and not at me for being a fool. We all know I have no intention of running. Screw that.

The guy can give head like he's been training for the Olympics. You know… if there was a sport for giving head.

Plus he's hot, as in, I'd even consider bending over for him. That's something I've done once, hated, and never planned to do again. But heck if he couldn't make me consider giving it up.

In my defense, all of this is making my brain malfunction. The excuse is real and I'm sticking with it, so hush.

It's the reason I shoot Marco a smile before we step out of the store, while he gives me an exaggerated wink. I chuckle, saying, "Don't forget the offer's still there if you need help shopping. Not sure you should be trusted by yourself."

"You just enjoy my company, Dean. No need to make excuses."

Kieran bristles beside me, making this so easy.

"Uh-huh. You keep telling yourself that. I just know your taste in clothes doesn't fill me with confidence when it comes to engagement ring shopping." I side-eye Kieran. He's absolutely paying attention.

"Hey, I'm not that bad."

Marco really is that bad.

"Uh-huh. Not sure Julian would agree with that assessment." I snicker and wave at him before finally stepping outside. I lick at the cream, going in for a second suck to get some of the caramel in. When it's just Kieran and me, I glance up, and we lock gazes. He's staring at me, and I wipe my chin. Of course my expression is super smug, and I like to think the pink in Kieran's cheeks and his slightly scrunched-up face means he knows I'm totally onto him.

But it's best to be clear, right?

"You know those rules you have?"

We stop walking, and with the slight tensing of his muscles, I'm sure he's paying complete attention.

"Yes?"

Somehow I hold back my loud chuckle at that uneasy question.

"I'm not quite sure you're as committed as you're claiming to be."

Wide eyes peer back at me. With a slack jaw, it's obvious he's fumbling at being called out.

"Bending the rules can be fun, Kieran, and since you're well on the way to having to rewrite them anyway, it's only right I offer my services."

Bravado. That's exactly what this is. If he could hear the loud pounding of my heart and knew just how clammy my hands are, there's no way he'd buy what I'm selling.

Hell, perhaps I'm a better actor than I thought.

I focus on the pavement and heading home, putting one foot in front of the other, and aiming for casual rather than it looking like I'm speed walking. It's difficult to eat my ice cream, despite how delicious it is. The house should be empty for a while longer, and the thickening of my dick makes it clear he has plans.

Screw being sensible. Plus… I did give myself permission for a no-strings fuck.

And from how quickly Kieran catches up with me, I have a feeling he's on board with my offer to see how far we can push those rules of his.

CHAPTER 8
RULE 3 SECTION B: NO CRUSHING ON BRIXHAM U GUYS

KIERAN

THAT THIS IS A BAD IDEA IS AN UNDERSTATEMENT. BUT I neither have the inclination or the willpower to stop it. With the tension thrumming between us, each breath a spark of promise, one thing is clear: Dean Whittaker is in complete control, and I'm powerless to stop him.

That I easily have forty pounds on him means nothing. Stepping away and leaving is not an option. Is it the challenge that he's thrown my way that's the draw card? I'd be lying if I said my competitive spirit isn't intrigued, but surely that would mean I should be proving him wrong and making clear that my rules are firm and inflexible, right?

Obviously I'm full of something, when all I really want to be is full of him.

Just the thought has my already fast-paced heart-beat picking up speed. Not only that, but my asshole is legit clenching, and my dick is chubbing up in a way that's completely inappropriate considering we still have a few more minutes until we arrive at his house.

The air is thick between us, and the need to speak and cut through some of it is on the tip of my tongue. The problem is, I can't get words out. Not only that, what the hell do I even say?

That I've never been in this situation before both terrifies and electrifies me. Both emotions are nothing to do with me bending or breaking any of my rules either. Hell no. What's got me sporting a boner and making me so tongue-tied I'm worried about my ability to control myself is the realization that Dean is likely to be the one guy who's not eager to be fucked by a basketball player. Nope. Instead, I'm sure he's absolutely willing to take control and give me everything I've been missing out on.

Just the thought has a grunt escaping. While it's quiet, it's enough to capture Dean's attention. He angles to look at me, his gaze searching, his cheeks flushed, and that pink tongue of his that darted out earlier when we were in the gelato place peeks out again.

Imagining what he could do to me with that tongue has my eyes widening, earning me a nostril flare and Dean looking like he's going to start trying out for competitive speed walking.

His reaction is enough to have me smirking, and some of the tension in my shoulders eases. He wants this as badly as I do.

Should I be playing hard to get?

Yeah, I just snorted too. I've reached the point of "fuck it." I might have only known Dean for a short while, but I'm sure he's not the kind of guy who'd out me. He'll be discreet, I'm sure of it.

Plus, he's feisty and bossy as fuck, and I like that a whole lot.

"Thank fuck."

I snort at his words as he pulls his keys out of his pocket and wrangles the door open. His hands shake, and I suspect it's nothing to do with nerves. Does Dean even get nervous? I can't see it.

Once the door is open, he steps inside and doesn't look back. I follow him in, and then he's on me before the door has time to click shut. My back being pushed against the door, though, gives us the privacy we need for me to welcome his tongue and grip his ass.

When his tongue swipes mine, I groan. He's straining to reach me, though that doesn't negate how he's controlling the kiss. I gasp for breath, and he eases away, pupils blown and cheeks flushed.

"That was the longest walk ever." He comes back at me, lips pressing against mine, not giving me time to respond. Amused and turned the fuck on, I kiss him back, seeking his tongue, seeking the heat.

And then the tease is pulling away again.

I sigh and angle back, pressing my head against the door. His chuckle grabs my attention, and I narrow my gaze at him. The smile he sends my way has my heart picking up speed.

"I have a double bed." A quirked brow joins his words.

I should be shutting this down. I'm not sure if there's uncertainty or indecision in my expression, but he leans into me, neck angled to scan my face.

"Hooking up is fun, and this..." He reaches for my cock and squeezes. A shudder ripples through me. "...this I can do something about."

"No strings?" I grunt out the words, feeling a bit of a dick for putting them out there, but I'm already ignoring my steadfast rules, and this is my attempt at keeping some control.

"Abso-fucking-lutely."

My grin is instant, and his is seductive, and then

we're racing up the stairs, me almost tripping, too focused on his ass. In his room, I spot the bed, and that's all the investigation needed.

There's no second-guessing or struggle when he backs me up so I can ease down on my back. Dean straddles me, his ass finding purchase against my jeans-clad cock.

"Fuck, I'm hard." I thrust to show him.

"Yes, you are." He grinds against me, and I grunt, tugging him down and ravaging his mouth. Our kisses are hard, almost feral in the messy heat, but I don't want to stop, don't want to calm the peaking desire swirling through me.

Dean's hand on my junk, though, that'll do it. I grunt into his mouth, and he grins.

"You want me to suck you off?"

"Is Eddie Phelps the highest-ranking forward in history?"

Dean laughs, the sound easing into my chest. Christ, it's good to smile and laugh with a guy, have some sort of connection and not a faceless hookup in a bathroom stall.

"I'm about to blow you, and you're thinking of basketball?" As he speaks, he's making quick work of my jeans. I lift up as he tugs them down.

"It's the only thing to keep me from coming as soon as your tongue touches my cock." I'm only half joking, but it doesn't hurt to lay on a little flattery, right?

Quirking his brow at me, Dean peruses my dick, which twitches in response. My junk has no issues with being admired. "You know, I think I need you naked."

Much to Dean's amusement, I sit bolt upright, kiss him hard, and then pick him up and set him down beside me. Less than fifteen seconds later, I'm naked, stretched out, and grinning at a highly amused Dean.

"Should I worry about the speed?" he sasses, shifting back to me, still fully dressed with the exception of his shoes. I perhaps should care that he's still covered, but it's all levels of hot.

"Keep looking at me like that, and I know I have more than one in me." I smirk, totally telling the truth. It's been far too long since I received head, and this is the first time ever with someone I know.

"*That* I can work with."

Dean trails soft wet kisses over my chest and along my abs. A sound of approval tears from me when he licks my six-pack. "You're so fucking hot." He nips at my skin and soothes it with licks before trailing down further.

It's impossible to not hold my breath. He's so damn close, and I'm already on the edge. Just as I'm starting to go lightheaded from lack of air, a whoosh of breath escapes me as he simultaneously takes a firm grip of the base of my dick and sucks my helmet before journeying down.

I sigh in relief. His mouth is perfect, the suction incredible, and pace enough for my eyes to cross. The grunts and groans escaping me are loud, and I'm on the cusp of whimpering. "Holy…" It's all I can manage, completely ensnared by his skilled mouth.

"Yo, Dean." The sound of a door closing punctuates the voice.

Dean freezes, my cock in his mouth. Both our eyes are wide, and I'm sure as shit mine are filled with panic.

"Fuck." I make a move to scramble for my clothes as Dean pulls away just in time for me to not lose my cock. I grasp my clothes and tug them on as Dean stands and wipes his mouth.

"Shit. Zeke's early." He hesitates before taking a breath. "It's fine. I'll go and speak to him. Just…" Dean's steady gaze trails over my face, the move and look in his eyes reassuring and surprisingly calming. "…stay here, get dressed. We're only studying."

If I hadn't been holding my breath while looking at him, I would have missed the tightness around his eyes. But it disappears instantly. A small, reassuring smile follows.

"Give me a minute."

When he leaves, I finish getting dressed. My hands shake, and for the first time in maybe ever, I feel sick. Sick at my reaction. Sick at my fear. Sick that I made the decision to live this way.

Right alongside that nausea is a heavy hit of guilt.

I'm privileged as fuck. My team knows I'm gay. Hell, all my immediate family does too, and I've received nothing but unconditional love and support. Yet here I am cowering and racing to get dressed so the rest of the world doesn't find out. And for what? Asshole fans and players and the goddamn media potentially being homophobic pricks and throwing some hate my way in a future that may never eventuate.

Self-loathing is a bastard of a thing. As is shame.

I have to get out of here.

Once dressed, I head downstairs, hearing voices in the kitchen. Where my bag is. I fix on a smile, scan the room, and aim it at Zeke. "Hey, Zeke."

He casts me a wide smile, and from that look alone it's obvious he's none the wiser. "Kieran, hey. Great game."

I ignore his embarrassed wince, since he already said that to me yesterday. "Thanks. Let's hope we can keep up this winning streak." Immediately my mind goes to Dean and wondering if he'll be coming to the next home game. No chance I'm asking. Zeroing in on Dean, I nod. While my lips are curved up, I'm not feeling it, and from the concern in his eyes, Dean's not buying it either.

"You leaving?"

I bob my head. "Yeah. The guys keep texting me about going out tonight. Someone's gotta keep them in line."

His lips pinch together.

"Thanks for today. I'll email you to make sure we're on track."

"Okay." It's impossible not to notice the shift. His tone is guarded, his expression shuttered. All it does is remind me that I'm a prick on so many levels, and as hot as this was, it was a big fucking mistake.

"I'll see you guys soon." I send Zeke one more chin lift and gather my things and hightail it.

Dean doesn't follow.

CHAPTER 9

RULE 9: LEAD BY EXAMPLE

DEAN

Who knew incredible chemistry and awkward meetings could result in earning an A? Though I'm sure we could have achieved that grade if post-BJ meetings were scored. Either way, I'm pleased with the grade and that it's keeping my GPA nice and steady. I just wished the three meetings we organized to finish up had gone differently.

But it's over. There's no group work in sight, and with the holidays fast approaching, and new courses in the new year, I don't expect our paths to cross again. Well, with the exception of me watching the games. So far, I've watched every single one. I'm a sucker, I know. But when Kieran's played at home,

I've made sure to remain as inconspicuous as possible.

I'm a glutton for punishment, but at least I'm owning it, right? He's got a spectacular dick, and I barely even got a taste. And that's totally all it is.

If you're rolling your eyes and calling bullshit, I'm going to plead the fifth.

I think about Kieran daily and how we connected. What a decent guy he appears to be is neither here nor there. Not since he ran and has been all but hidden beyond our civil group meetings.

I sigh, wondering if I should have just stayed in tonight. Campus is half empty, with most students already heading off for Thanksgiving.

Since I'm local, my Thanksgiving plans involve working as many hours as possible at the diner and hanging out with Zeke.

"I didn't think you were going to show."

"As if I'm going to stand you up, Simone." I lean in and kiss her cheek and relax a little when I inhale her honeysuckle perfume.

Hooking her arm through mine, something I found odd at first as I've never had this sort of friendship with anyone before, she takes a step in the direction of O'Connell Street. There's a Thanksgiving blowout party going on tonight. It's at Phi Alpha Delta. Is it bad that I roll my eyes just thinking that?

Me, at a frat party.

But hey, I haven't had a drink for weeks, so caught up in studying, working, and thinking about a basketball player who's been avoiding me. It means I'm ready to relax, have a few drinks, and while I'd like to add "hook up" to that list, I'm not holding my breath. I'm best off venturing into the city to find some action if I'm that desperate. Though, honestly, I'm not feeling it.

We pause at the curb before crossing the street. "What time are you leaving in the morning?" I ask.

"My flight's at one fifteen, so I have every intention of waking up hungover. You sure you don't want to come?"

Simone's asked me at least five times to head to California with her. Her parents have a beach house. The place sounds amazing, but I don't want to ditch Zeke for Thanksgiving. Plus, I barely have enough cash to contribute to groceries.

"Maybe next time."

"I'm going to hold you to that. Remember my twenty-first is this summer. The 'rents have promised me and a select group of friends"—she squeezes my arm—"a trip to Mexico. You can't bail on that."

Before I can provide another argument, she hip checks me. "I mean it, Dean. The 'rents are covering the flights and everything." When she's all peppy like this, it takes me by surprise. She's the same age as I am—I turned twenty-one early September—but sometimes I feel those extra two months have made me a little pessimistic to the world.

I scrunch my nose at her offer. Mexico at any time of the year sounds amazing, but taking a handout feels gross. "We'll see." It's a few months away, so I have time to pick up a few more work shifts and save if I really want to go.

She angles to look at me, and I know she's shooting lasers at me. I laugh and shake my head. "'We'll see' isn't an outright no." It's all I can offer. I really should get over myself and snatch the gift with both hands and give my absolute gratitude.

"Fine." Simone drags the word out, and we round the corner to O'Connell Street. There are students milling around and music playing, but not so loud it'll earn a visit from the cops. "Come on. You can be my wingman. I need to get wasted and maybe even laid."

"Maybe just one of those," I say, not liking the thought of her going off with someone while being off her face.

"You see, best wingman ever."

I groan but will absolutely watch her back if she's planning on getting wasted.

It doesn't take long for us to pay and enter the

party, knock back three shots that make me grimace, and find a spot in one of the rooms shooting off from the main space. The party isn't super crazy. While there are still countless bodies filling the house and making it loud enough that we have to raise our voices to be heard, it's fairly mellow.

There a bunch of people dancing on a makeshift dance floor in the main room, and with the moving bodies, it's warm enough for me to tug off my coat. The beer I've just finished and the sip of my second I've just taken is probably helping to keep me warm too.

"Off your ass and let's dance."

Simone drags me to the group of people dancing. I'm not exactly kicking and screaming, as I love to dance, and screw being self-conscious. I know I can move.

I let go in the crowd of bodies, loving they have strobe lighting in here. And despite the open space, the bass doesn't get lost. It thrums through the small crowd and the floor, traveling up my spine. The only thing missing is a fog machine, but it's worth it to have fresher air surround me.

I have no idea how long we've been dancing. I've lost count of the songs, but I know I'm feeling more sober. I'm also thirsty.

"Drink?" I signal to Simone. She gives me thumbs

up but makes no sign to move. Since she's had her sights set on a cute guy for at least the last fifteen minutes, I kinda figured she wouldn't want to leave. "No disappearing without telling me."

She plants a kiss on my cheek, saying, "Promise," before making a beeline to the dark-haired guy who's caught her attention. I take a moment to watch them, looking over the guy to try and get a read on him. He's sort of familiar, tall, and the way he's focusing on Simone, he's definitely interested.

Fairly sure she's at least safe while I go in search of a drink, I create a path through the dancing bodies and head to the kitchen. It doesn't take long to have a shot poured for me, but before I grab a second, I need to take a leak.

There are more people in the house than I expected, making it a bit of a mission to find the bathroom. I get there, though, and don't even have to wait.

After washing up, a glance at the time tells me it's close to midnight. Since I don't have a shift until tomorrow afternoon, I'm free to have a late night. I still have to Uber home, but I'm in no rush.

I unlock the door and stumble back when it opens before I get the chance to pull it. Heart pounding at the intrusion, I stare wide-eyed at the man filling the doorway. It's only a beat before he's stepping quickly inside and closing the door behind him before securing the lock.

Kieran.

There's an intensity in his gaze that I've seen before, but not since we ate ice cream. Is it possible he looks hotter?

"Kieran." I frown and work hard at not dropping to my knees to finish what I started a few weeks back. Instead, I pull forth my indifference, pretty much what he's offered me since Zeke interrupted us. "I've just finished up." It's best I go for the obvious and plead ignorance.

I don't feel like I have a right to be pissed off, especially as we agreed on no strings. Okay, I kinda do, but I'm trying to not let it… him bother me. But since he's been so aloof, it's hard not to be hurt. I didn't expect us to try again necessarily, nor did I expect to hang out and have a few beers together.

He still hasn't spoken, yet I feel his attention on me completely. It's enough for my hairs to stand on end under his perusal. That gaze of his is seductive and dangerous, which means I need to get away fr—

The abruptness of his mouth on mine destroys all thought. Kieran's kissing me like he's possessed, taking my breath and my sense with it.

Deep and passionate, the kiss is everything I've been craving. His tongue brushes against mine, tangling, before he's sucking, exploring. Heat licks up my spine, and I cling to him, not wanting to stop, but wanting to let go, wanting his mouth on mine, on my body, anywhere I can get it.

Kieran Kendall is addictive. Hell, I always thought coffee was my elixir. How ridiculously wrong I was.

Effortlessly, he eases me against the wall, pressing his hard body against mine. He's scooting low, and knowing it's so I don't have to stand on my tiptoes makes it difficult to not want everything with this man.

"You drive me crazy." His words are all growly, the gruffness sending shivers down my spine.

I clutch his hair and ease away. Once our eyes connect, I hold firm, and he winces at the pull. "You're a fucking idiot." Our mouths connect once again, this time slower but no less hot. It's a flicker of tongue, a caress, a gentle glide—

Someone knocks on the door. No, they fucking hammer.

"Seriously?!" Kieran is breathless when he speaks, as am I, as we abruptly part. But not completely, much to my surprise. When he rests his forehead against mine, that surprise morphs into a flutter of excitement in my gut.

"Kieran, you in there, man?"

Kieran winces, though his hold remains. "Shit, I'm so sorry," he whispers. "Leon," he hollers, thankfully not in my face. "The fuck, man, a bit of privacy."

A chuckle travels through the door. Leon's I assume. "Sorry, bro. Just looking at heading out. Gonna go for pizza. You coming?"

Kieran's gaze connects to mine, and he smirks. "Apparently not. Again."

I hold back my snort, not quite sure which alternate universe I've landed in. Kieran Kendall is being all cool and unfazed. He's not freaking out. I expected him to be out the window by now.

"You guys go ahead. I'm gonna head back."

"You sure?"

"Yeah, not quite feeling it." The asshole I'm clinging to thrusts his hips against mine for good measure. I narrow my gaze. He seriously wants to play this game with me?

They carry on a whole conversation as I make quick work of his jeans. Kieran's breath hitches when I grasp his cock. He's hard and all but throbbing in my hand. It's when I start jacking him off, a little awkwardly as his pants aren't fully open, that he grunts and grabs my hand to stop me.

The warning in his stare is hot as fuck. "I'll see you in the morning," he shouts, his gaze fierce as he holds my wrists. Yeah, plural. I've tried twice to get back to work, but the man is too strong for his own good.

Finally it's mercifully quiet.

"Your friends don't know when to leave a guy to take a shit in peace."

Kieran snorts loudly. "Tell me about it. You think that's bad, try living with them." Still holding my wrists, he places them around my back. "You were doing one hell of a job at distracting me there."

"I was?" I aim for nonchalance, not willing to let go of this playful exchange we have going on. It's unexpected, and I'm far too horny to do anything sensible like leave him.

"Where are you staying tonight?" His voice pitches low. "There enough room for me?"

I wince, wishing that were the case. "I'm heading home." No chance am I screwing around with my mom and Zeke at home. "Let's go to yours."

Frown lines appear on his forehead. "That's not a good idea."

"What, you can't keep quiet?"

A delicious pink crawls up his neck, and this close, it's easy to see his pupils dilate.

"You don't want me to swallow your cum?" I push, totally getting off on just how pink he's turning. His breathing picks up. "I promise I can be stealthy. Sneak on out of there without anyone knowing."

God, I'm an asshole. Stealth is not my middle name. But for the chance of a night with Kieran, I'll pull out all the stops. Shit, I'll even crawl out his bathroom window if necessary.

"You know," I continue, sure there's a special place in hell for me, considering just how hard I'm trying to convince him to finally let go, "I've got the perfect cure for making you really thankful this Thanksgiving." I stand on my tiptoes and press the lightest of kisses on his lips before trailing soft kisses toward his ear. "It involves my dick and your prostate."

I know I'm taking a real chance here since none of our conversations have ventured at all into this territory. But screw it. There's something about Kieran that screams he's a man who needs to be topped. I just hope he knows it.

And holy shit, his breath catches, his eyes blaze with heat, and he slams his mouth to mine. The kiss is brutal and far too short, since he drags his mouth away. I try to chase the movement, but he shakes his head.

"Meet me at the corner of O'Connell and Western in two minutes."

And then I'm alone, breathing raggedly and wondering how I'm going to survive having just one night with Kieran Kendall.

CHAPTER 10
RULE 3 SECTION C: NO HOOKING UP ON CAMPUS

KIERAN

THE ONLY HEAD THAT'S THINKING OR MATTERS IS THE one straining to be free. I'm also pretty sure if I look down, I'll have a wet patch from my dick weeping with joy.

It's that need that gets me out of the party and to Dean, then the short couple of blocks to my house, which, thank Christ, is dark and empty. It's what helps me lead Dean to my room and lock my door. It's the driving force that gets us stripped naked and on the bed, lube and condoms beside us, and Dean sprawled on top of me.

Frantic hands turn soft as they explore, and by the time Dean's swallowing me down and I'm riding his fingers, I can barely remember my name.

All that matters is this… his touch, his caresses, the way he penetrates me, the way my moan is loud and needy and demanding "More!"

"You sure?"

His question draws my attention away from the sensation, so lost in the moment. "Fuck yes."

Dean adds more lube and a third finger. It burns but in the best of ways. Should I tell him he's the first? Tell him that fingers and a pretty impressive dildo are the closest I've got to the real thing. But fuck, I can't wait until he's buried inside me.

What if telling him makes him freak?

Fuck that.

"You good?"

There's a sweetness to his question. It relaxes me further. He must feel it, as when he glances at me, there's a satisfied smirk on his lips.

"Yeah," I offer anyway. "Anytime now, though." It doesn't matter that I've never had sex this way before. It's not like I'm holding out for a special guy. It's all about finally having the opportunity, but as I take him in as he gets to his knees, I admit maybe a little is about trust too.

Dean loses his smirk as he covers up and smothers himself with lube.

I can't take my eyes off him or what he's doing. The movement, the prep, shouldn't be sexy, but it so is. Especially as I know why he's lubing up and exactly what he plans to do.

When he refocuses on me, his smile is slow, but there's nothing sweet about the expression on his face. Hell, he looks like he wants to devour me. In that case, slather me with chocolate and lick away.

"You're gorgeous." The words he shares are quiet and raspy. Goose bumps spring to life, dancing across my arms. "I can't wait to be inside you."

I lift my thighs, exposed and raw and so ready. The movement gets him angling toward me and positioning at my entrance. I exhale, wanting this. Needing this.

But fuck, I feel vulnerable. Nothing about this feels like no strings attached. It doesn't matter that I've known Dean for a couple of months, or that I've been dodging him since going to his house. This feels like… something.

When he pushes against me, my breath catches, the burn painful.

"Breathe and push against me, Kieran."

My eyes snap open. I didn't even realize I closed them. They connect with his and I nod, watching him focusing on me, following his breathing, and trying my hardest to exhale and push and accept the intrusion.

When he eases past the tight ring, I almost cry out

in relief. While my dildo is awesome, it's nothing compared to the real thing.

Real D is fucking phenomenal. Hands down. And the more he pushes in, the more I relax, and when he starts moving and finally hits the sweet spot he promised, I'm flying high.

Desperation claws at me. I scramble for purchase, my palms landing on his forearms. The move earns me a smile and renewed efforts. Dean's grumbling and groaning and cussing up a storm, and I join in, becoming more vocal the more he stretches me, pounds into me, and hits my sweet spot over and over, deeper than I've ever experienced.

"Fuck," I garble. I need more… something—

I gasp in relief when Dean palms my cock. "I've got you." He jacks me off, his grip firm and strong and giving me exactly what I need. "You're so fucking tight."

I grunt, feeling every inch of him, marveling at the sensation and the delectable sting.

"Nearly…," I say with a grunt.

He nods, a drip of sweat rolling down his temple with the action. He doubles down with his efforts, both on my dick and my ass. And then I'm stumbling, free falling. My vision blurs, my back arches, and Dean cries out. I finally spill my release, my orgasm rocking through me, seemingly lasting a lifetime and surely leaving behind a gallon of cum, rather than the cooling pool dripping down Dean's hand and landing on my stomach.

We're both breathing heavily, and I think at this point I should be saying or doing something, but I have no idea what. Instead, I focus on calming my breaths, but I still haven't looked at Dean.

His quiet voice makes me jump. "You okay?"

I nod and finally peer up at him. He's still inside me, and even when he's not, I expect I'll be feeling him for days. "Yeah." My smile is slow to appear, shy but genuine. "You?"

After a brief search of my face, he grins back, a different sort of smile than any I've received from him before. "More than okay." He sounds sleepy, the tone enough to make my own eyes droop a little. "Is it safe to go to the bathroom?"

I freeze, the reality of where we are crashing into me. "I'll go, just in case."

Disappointment floods his features, but he remains quiet and simply nods.

Once he's pulled out, I search for a pair of shorts and leave my room. The house is still dark, thank fuck. There's no way I would have heard anyone come in, not with the grunting and slapping of flesh all I could hear.

I waste no time rushing to the bathroom and

wash my junk and my ass before grabbing a towel and wetting one section of it. Pausing in front of the mirror, I risk a glance at myself. My eyes are wide and wild, skin heated, and my mouth's curved high.

Dean's in my room waiting for me. We're in my house, and I know if my friends find him here, they'll give me shit, but only because I can't keep my dick in my pants, and not for any other reason.

While Dean said he can be discreet and I believe him, after tonight, would it be so bad to keep this up? We could keep it on the down-low, perhaps just tell my housemates so Dean and I can hook up safely. He's not going to be that much of a distraction.

Hell, since meeting Dean and knowing he's watching games, I've been playing faster, harder. That was even the case at my last home game. It took me all of thirty seconds to spot him toward the back of the stadium—don't even ask how that's possible with the crowd we have—and when I did, my heart had beat triple time, liking too much that he'd come to watch, despite me ghosting him.

With renewed purpose, I dash to my room. If Dean stays, we could have BJs for breakfast. How fucking awesome would that be. Breakfast of champions. Am I right?!

I enter my room grinning, only to falter. Dressed in his jeans, he's tugging on his T-shirt. Dean glances my way, heat touching his cheeks when his gaze rakes over my body.

"You're leaving?"

Pausing, he peers up at me, confusion swirling in his eyes. "Yes?" He purses his lips, and a smile appears that is absolutely not real. "Stealth, remember?"

"But… morning ," I blurt. "Uhm," I croak, "I mean, you can stay, rather than go home tonight. My bed's big enough."

Questions are bouncing around in his head. I just know it. I only hope he doesn't throw any my way. I can't be trusted.

"But won't your housemates be back soon?"

Since he's stopped dressing, I take that as a positive sign and step into his space. Feeling bold, I remove the tee he's holding and throw it on the floor. "They'll get over it. Plus, you know how many times I've heard them going at it?" I quirk my brow. "It'll do them good. They'll probably think I'm watching porn."

Amusement colors Dean's face, and his brows shoot high. His lips twitch, and I'm happier than I probably should be when he drapes his arms over my shoulders. "So these morning BJs, we're aiming for porn-level action, huh?"

I chuckle. "We can always try, though you just

breathing on my dick makes me hard enough that coming is inevitable."

From the way he smiles at me, all soft and sweet, it seems like he likes what I'm saying. My ability to flirt and seduce are admittedly lacking, but maybe I'm not half as bad as I thought.

"I think we should test that theory right now." He punctuates his words with a slow kiss, and I just know breakfast is going to be my new favorite meal of the day.

CHAPTER 11
RULE 7: SHUT DOWN GOSSIP

DEAN

You're confused, right, by the hot and cold practically vibrating off Kieran? I swear, if the man didn't legit tick so many boxes, I would have been out of here last night after arguably the most intense sex of my life.

Hush yourselves. I know I'm just twenty-one so have a lot of living to do, but holy perfect ass! Everything about last night, or early this morning if we're being pedantic, was spectacular and mind-blowing. Everything we shared is the stuff of my hottest dreams imaginable. Times a trillion.

That. Fucking. Amazing.

What that means is I'm finding it hard to say no

while also preparing for him to freak out as soon as he wakes up.

After our explosive sexathon, Kieran was in an orgasm-fog. I'm sure of it. It's the only reason he encouraged me to stay. When his pouty bottom lip popped out, which should have looked ridiculous on the athletic, gorgeous man, I melted into a puddle of want.

Don't get me wrong, the joint BJ afterward using my favorite number, sixty-nine, was worth it. Plus the lazy handjobs at about four this morning made my toes curl. But I've been awake for an hour, and I can hear movement around the house. I can't help but wonder if Kieran's going to backtrack and get me to sneak out through his window, which, considering he doesn't live on the ground floor, means I'll likely break my neck.

But hell if I don't want him to mean it. To be okay with me being here and his housemates, his friends, knowing I spent the night.

"Hey." The rasp of Kieran's voice is sexy, and even though I'm on edge and exhausted, my cock valiantly stirs.

Feeling brave, I turn on my side to look at him. "Morning."

He offers me a lazy smile before rubbing a hand over his face and his messy hair. "Have you been awake long?"

"Not really." I don't think me telling him I've been cataloguing his features and the soft sounds he makes when he's sleeping is wise.

His eyes are wider this time when he looks at me, sleepiness disappearing. "You slept though, right?" There's a hint of concern in his tone that makes something stir in my stomach.

"I did." I can't hold back the curve of my lips.

"That's good."

The sound of something banging downstairs has him pausing and me holding my breath. I almost blurt out that if he's changed his mind, that's okay. But I keep my mouth shut. I don't want to take it easy on him. Not after last night. If he asks me to go, I will. In a heartbeat, even though it will sting. That doesn't mean I'm going to gift him the easy out.

When he returns his focus to me, he scans my face. I have no idea what he's thinking. His soft gaze makes me relax a fraction, and his "You want breakfast?" has my pulse picking up.

"I could eat."

He turns on his side and leans into me, brushing his mouth against mine. There's no chance of deepening the kiss, as he pulls away. "I just need to check what kind of breakfast we're talking about here."

My dick twitches, and I thrust against him, my

cock cheering that we're still naked so there's no material between us. I grin. It's wide and overeager, but I can't keep the excitement from my face.

The fact is, despite the hot and cold from Kieran since meeting him, I really like the guy. He's fun, and smart, and cute, and witty, and he can play a mean game of basketball…. It's hard reining my developing emotion in.

"You're not satisfied from the last two *breakfasts*?" he sasses.

"In my defense, last *breakfast* I didn't get a taste."

His eyes widen. "I seem to recall you licking my hand clean."

My semi turns into a full-blown stiffy at the memory. "It seemed such a waste."

"Waste is never a good thing."

My breath hitches when he angles over me and I'm happily forced on my back.

"I think I'm hungrier than you," he says, kissing along my collarbone.

"While I'd usually think that's not very gentlemanly of you…" I groan when he nips and sucks at my nipple. "I think I'll let it slide."

He chuckles, continuing laving my nipple.

While he's doing an impressive job at making me writhe and beg for his mouth, I touch him everywhere I can reach. I'm half tempted to ask him to spin around so we can perfect my favorite number again, but his mouth is finally dipping past my belly button. I suck in my stomach—

"Kieran! Ass out of bed."

I push my head against the pillow and cover my face with my forearm. "Your friends have the worst timing ever."

With his mouth no longer on me, he shifts and moves to his knees. Amusement dances in his features. From a glance at his cock, it's clear his dick isn't half as amused. It's flushed and hard, and the vein I familiarized myself with last night is pulsing.

"Between your brother and this lot, I think they're taking cock-blocking to a whole new level."

A flicker of relief appears in my chest. He's not bolting for his clothes, for the door. He's not ushering me out, getting me to hide. That's a good thing, right?

"Come on. Looks like we're having the conventional type of breakfast this morning." He follows up by planting his mouth on mine and dipping to kiss my cock.

"You can't do things like that and expect me to think straight."

"That's the point, right? To not think *straight*?"

I roll my eyes and snort at his ridiculousness. He taps my thigh as he stands and starts getting dressed, shouting, "I'm awake, asshole," to whichever of his friends hollered out to us.

Dressing quickly, I use it as a distraction to center myself. The only one of his friends I've met was a dickhead. Both times. It's a good thing I'm made of tougher stuff than athletes with egos the size of Texas.

Not bothering to ask what Kieran plans to say, I follow him out of the room. What I really need is to shower, but it'll have to wait. For now, I'm rallying. There's also no way I'll ever allow myself to feel intimidated by athletes. Never again.

We step into the surprisingly tidy kitchen. There's a guy loading the dishwasher, another at the stove, and a third sitting at the oversized table. They paint a picture of domesticity, which doesn't compute.

"What needs doing?" Kieran says by way of greeting.

"About fucking time you—" The guy at the stove cuts off when he turns around. His brows are so high they're almost touching his hairline. A bubble of amusement rushes to my chest. He looks like a damn cartoon character in his surprise. You know, if there were any six-foot whatever, gorgeous-as-hell basketball players in any cartoons I'd heard about.

His words cutting off attracts the attention of the other two. Double takes and surprise spring to life, and I suppose one thing's for sure, Kieran wasn't lying about never bringing a guy home before. Not with reactions like this.

"Holy shit. Kendall got laid. Why the fuck have we never bet on this happening?"

"Sammy, man, seriously?" Kieran shoves him as he passes by, heading into the main kitchen area.

Feeling like I'm on show hanging back in the doorway with three sets of eyes on me, I offer a friendly smile and take a seat at the table. Kieran said we were having breakfast, so it's best I make my intentions clear.

"Dean." My attention immediately moves to Kieran, who's standing next to the coffee pot. He indicates toward it.

"Yeah, please."

He smiles and sets about pouring me a cup, saying, "The loudmouth at the table is Sammy."

I nod and say hi, realizing this is the guy who gave me a shot the first time Kieran and I hooked up. Now I'm fully paying attention, I recognize everyone in this room as a player for the Bears. I let Kieran carry on with the introductions, though.

"Leon." He indicates toward the guy who's cooking bacon and eggs, from the smell of it. "Bentley."

Bentley smiles at me from next to the dishwasher.

He's a big guy, definitely the tallest in the room, and with the flush coating his cheeks I think he's adorable. "Hey," he says gruffly, the depth surprising me. Sure, he's huge, but the sweet smile conflicts with the rough voice. "Dean, right?"

"Yeah. Hey."

"And you know Tyron." I don't miss the hard look he sends the man walking into the room. He's behind me. I only just registered his footsteps before Kieran spoke.

I angle to look around as Tyron steps more fully into the room. He's not smiling, nor is he looking at me. Instead, he wears a resigned expression, one that makes it clear he wants to have a few words with Kieran. Hopefully that's once I've gone.

Don't get me wrong, if the ogre says anything to me or in front of me, I will absolutely put him in his place. My dick's more than big enough to weigh in and shut him down.

Not pushing my sugary sweetness too hard, I still offer a smile, albeit more reserved. "Hey, Tyron. Give me a heads-up if you're close by and I'm holding my coffee, yeah?"

Kieran snorts, and Tyron flicks his attention to me. His scowl slips, his gaze turning assessing. "Thank fuck you drink coffee, not like this precious asshole over here."

And holy twat waffle, I think I've won him over. It can't be that easy, right?

The guys crack up, and I smirk, the tension in my shoulders fading.

"Bro, you'll find this precious asshole is responsible for this afternoon's training session." Kieran quirks his brow at Tyron.

It's interesting seeing him like this, out of the limelight and in the company of his friends and teammates. And as the guys continue to rib each other, I settle in for the show. Not only are they hot, they're slightly ridiculous with their teasing. Each of them constantly pulls me into the conversation, all taking it in turns to one-up each other.

"So what are you doing for Thanksgiving?" Sammy asks. We've finished breakfast, and I'm on my second coffee.

"Not a lot. I live in the next town over, so I've just picked up some extra shifts at work. Try and get ahead with the reading I need for when school's back in session. How about you?" I'm actually curious about one man in particular, but Sammy is being super welcoming, so I'm happy to chat about his plans.

"We only get decent time off over the main holidays," he explains. "We have six games before then, and training as well."

"So you're all staying here?" I glance around to a series of nods.

"Yeah. We do a Friendsgiving tomorrow, then we have a game the day after."

"A busy few weeks." I turn my attention to Kieran at my side. He's angled slightly toward me, his legs stretched out, and one foot pressing against my calf. I like it a little too much that he's seeking contact. "What about you?" I ask him. "Are your parents okay with you not going home?"

"Yeah, they understand. They're going to fly in and watch the game after Thanksgiving, though."

I make a mental note to be as inconspicuous as possible during that game. "Are they able to get out to see many games?"

"Not much. But they watch them regularly on TV. And they try to be around in spring, for as many games in March Mayhem."

"Your team is on fire in the conference. March Mayhem is yours."

What looks like a shy smile morphs onto Kieran's lips, and I want to kiss him so badly.

"You follow the game?"

"I'm a hardcore basketball fan, yeah," I say to Tyron. He's studying me again, which makes me believe that I haven't been given the sign of approval after all. Not that I give a shit what he thinks. "I've only just become a Bears supporter, though." My cheeks heat at the memory, and I force myself to not look away from Tyron's probing gaze. "I'm a hard-core Eagles fan in the League."

I wonder if Tyron is remembering when he caught me and Kieran hooking up after a game.

"Why not before?"

Ignoring how he fires off the question and how the tone rivals that of an interrogation, I keep my tone light. "I only moved in July and transferred here in September."

"Where were you before?"

"LA."

He nods. "And were you hooking up with a player out the—"

"The fuck, Tyron. Jesus." Kieran shakes his head at my side. "Back off."

"What?" Tyron shrugs, his attention drifting from me to Kieran and back again.

I wait, wondering what else he's going to say. The other guys at the table look like a mixture of confused and embarrassed. Me? He can come at me all he wants. The fucker won't know what's hit him.

"I'm just saying that twice you've had a run-in with this guy, and now all of a sudden you stumble into him again last night. Makes you bring him home, screwing up your plan and putting what you're working so hard for at risk. You know hoop hos aren't just women, right?"

I press my lips together, on the verge of laughing. Sure, I'm indignant and want to rip him a new one, but seriously? Christ on a cracker, I've met far too many arrogant pricks like him. Does he seriously think he can intimidate me? I can't help but snort, even as Kieran jumps out of his seat. While his movement startles me, it doesn't stop my snort turning into a full-on laugh.

It's controlled, genuinely amused. It's also a sign that this fuckhead needs to protect his balls.

Kieran is midtirade before he realizes I'm not laying into Tyron and am instead finding this whole exchange ridiculous. I glance at Sammy, Leon, and Bentley. Their expressions are priceless. They have no fucking idea what's going on. They're also looking at me like I'm unhinged. But that's okay.

Kieran stops short of what ever he's shouting and peers down at me, concern in his gaze. At his expression, I try to quell my laughter, a few additional bubbles spilling over.

"Dean, are you okay? Sorry ab—"

I wave him off and stand. His eyes widen when I angle up, but he accepts my kiss. I keep it short and sweet, and I pull away, smoothing my fingers over his brow. Am I savoring the moment? I sure am. "I had a great night."

Back on the soles of my feet, a pang hits me when he frowns. I figure he knows I'm preparing to leave. Ignoring the flip of my heart, as Kieran is seriously a beautiful man, I swallow the emotion away and turn to the four pairs of eyes all directed my way.

I really do find Tyron spouting off shit both hilarious and ridiculous. I also know he's looking out for his friend. That's not to say underneath my genuine amusement I'm okay with being spoken to like I'm a piece of crap.

Never again.

I smile at the three of Kieran's friends who've been nothing but friendly. I make eye contact with each man, saying. "Thanks for breakfast. It was nice meeting you all." I turn my attention to Tyron. While he seems like he's sitting there without a care in the world, I can see the signs. He's uncomfortable and preparing for a confrontation.

I don't plan to give him that. Or at least, I don't plan for him to have the chance to say a single word.

"You might be looking out for your friend, but in the nicest possible way, fuck you. You don't know me. You don't get to ask questions or throw shit my way. You have issues, you talk to your friend when I'm not around like a decent fucking human being." As I turn back to Kieran, I check my keys and phone are still in my pockets and am relieved I have my shoes on.

The pang returns, and I genuinely feel sorry for Kieran. Maybe we could have had something good. I don't say that to him. What's the point? "Good luck with the conference. I hope you make it to the finals." And I'm out of here, my feet moving as steadily as possible. I manage to reach the door before the sound of Kieran's footsteps race my way and he's at my side as I pull it open.

"Wait, Dean. You don't h—"

I close my eyes and take a deep breath before looking at him, fixing a tight smile in place. "I really did have a great night. But it's best if I just go."

"Ignore Tyron. He's an asshole. He doesn't know what he's talking about."

I nod in complete agreement, but it doesn't matter. Not in the grand scheme of things. "This, last night, it could never go any further. Not really." His face falls, but I see the truth in his eyes. "Your rules, remember?" I don't bother to add that I have rules of my own too.

"Fuck." He rubs his hand over his hair. "But I still have another year…"

I shake my head. "I know that would be an even bigger mistake." Surely I don't have to explain why.

Just the thought of us being together, having what we had last night for a whole year, for him to then push me aside to go pro, no way. There's a tightness in my chest already. After a year, my heart would be decimated if that happened.

I step outside and make the mistake of looking back. With no idea what to say that won't make me sound like a dick or desperate, I offer a sad smile and turn away.

He doesn't follow, and while I'm grateful, I really wish he would.

CHAPTER 12
RULE 1 SECTION D: BE PREPARED FOR GAMES

KIERAN

I'M OFF MY GAME. STILL PISSED AT TYRON, PISSED AT Dean for not answering my calls, and so fucking pissed that each game over the past two weeks has been a total bust. Coach is worried and more frustrated than I am. One more loss or draw, and we're not going to be ranking for March Mayhem.

Not only that, I made the mistake of following Tim Delaware on Twitter. The amount of hate and bullshit directed his way is gutting, made even worse when he shared his boyfriend with the sporting world. Shit, you'd think he's been demanding the fans watch him sucking his boyfriend's cock while pitching, considering the amount of disgust thrown his way.

I don't remember it being this bad for Max Barton, the baseball player who came out two years ago. But then again, he's never admitted to having a boyfriend. At least not publicly.

It's like the public play the game by offering support for being inclusive, as long as the reality of what that means isn't seen. The rainbow letters are easier to swallow as long as they don't actually see the dicks involved.

"Shakespeare, my office. You too, Channing."

I groan at Coach's order. We've just had a grueling practice, and I still stink. Making Coach wait, though, is not an option. A shower will have to wait.

A few of the guys eye me as I leave, Tyron ahead of me. Only my three other housemates who were there the morning with Dean know what's going on between me and Tyron, and while I'm grateful they haven't blabbed, the rest of the team is curious and confused at the animosity between us.

It's not lost on me, or anyone, there's been a disconnect. The problem is, I don't know how to get past it.

"Sit your asses down," Coach Maple instructs. His face and voice are currently void of inflection or emotion, but I know he can flip at the drop of a hat.

Sitting bolt upright, I keep my palms on my knees

and center myself for what's coming. The whole time Coach is perched on his desk, head and shoulders above us, arms folded and just waiting.

Awkward doesn't even cut it. I bite my tongue and keep a lid on any reactions and tells.

Tyron breaks. "Coach, listen—"

He cuts off abruptly at Coach's sharp stare. After a few beats of deathly silence, Coach says to Tyron, "You're not really trying to give me orders, right, Channing?"

"No, sir," he's quick to answer.

Coach grunts, his focus returning to me. "What about you, Kendall? Got any directives for me?"

He's clearly pissed, since I'm being last named. "No, sir." I clench my jaw and feel like I need to start counting down to my demise or some shit. I've been failing my team. Failing myself.

Fuck.

Shame hits me, almost floors me with its staggering weight. Something must show, as Coach eyes me hard and nods. "There it is," he says, and I make eye contact with him. "Feels like shit, right?"

I nod and stay mute, not daring to speak. He knows, and I don't even need to confirm he sees my shame and the realization of it. I think it's worse than if he truly tore us apart and benched us.

"Did I make a mistake?"

I go to answer but realize he's waiting for Tyron to respond.

"Coach?"

Coach's gaze hardens. "Making Kendall here captain. Was it a mistake?"

Shit, the words gut me.

"No, Coach," Tyron answers immediately, his voice firm, holding weight.

"Kendall, you agree with Channing here?"

"Yes, Coach. It wasn't a mistake."

"I thought fucking not, since I don't make mistakes on my team." I hold back my wince and wait in silence. A few more beats pass by, the silence more intense than any punishment he could throw at me. "Do I need to remind you both how you carry this team, lead this team, and your bullshit… whatever the hell is going on… could break this team on Thursday?"

We shake our heads. "No, Coach."

"You sort this shit out today. You do not leave my fucking office until you're holding hands and singing 'Kumbaya,' you hear me?"

As we both agree, Coach stands and leaves the room, the door closing with a soft snick.

"Fuck." Tyron groans into his hands. "I thought for sure he was going to make us eat dirt, then get us to jack each other off."

Unbidden, loud laughter erupts from me. "The fuck, man. Jack each other off?"

He grins at me. "I'd totally do it for the good of the team."

I shake my head, my laughter dying down. "You really pissed me off, Ty. And the way you spoke to Dean, man, you were so out of order."

He has the good grace to flinch at the mention of Dean. "You really like the dude?"

I hesitate. I can totally bullshit here, but what's the point? Before Dean came along, I told Tyron everything. Maybe that's where I went wrong: holding back. "I do."

The nod he gives is slow, the look on his face calculating. "I'm sorry for how I acted, what I said."

"It's not me you owe an apology to."

"I know, and I'll fix it, but Key, since the day I met you, you've been so clear and determined, focused. Then this guy shows up out of nowhere and every- thing changes?" He shakes his head. "I'm sure he's a nice guy; I just don't get why you'd risk everything."

"It wasn't out of nowhere," I admit. "We'd been chatting and meeting for a couple of months." I don't tell him about my freak-outs within that time.

"You have?" Surprise flickers to life in his gaze. I feel shit that I see hurt there too.

"My Lit 129 course, he's in it. We ended up in the

same work group." I give a "and the rest is history" shrug.

"Oh shit, okay, wow. So not what I expected."

We both go quiet, and I think about Dean and how shit he must have felt listening to Tyron. But fuck, he was magnificent when he spoke up before leaving. In that moment he'd rendered me speechless, leaving me completely in awe of the man he is.

"So he's genuinely a basketball fan and not just trying to hook or snare you or some shit?"

This time I find it in myself to chuckle. What Tyron did was fucked-up, but I've no doubt he was trying to be a good friend. "He loves the game. He's been at every home game since that night when, you know…"

"When I walked in on you giving him a happy ending?" His smirk is contagious.

"Yeah, asshole. That night."

"What about the games since Thanksgiving?"

My gut sinks. Every time my mind wasn't on the game, I'd searched the crowd. Always coming up empty. "No."

"Holy shit." Tyron jumps up from the seat, his brows lifting and his voice strangely high-pitched. "You've been kicking ass since *that* game." I make to speak and to tell him he's talking shit, but he shuts me down. "Nuh-uh, no way, man. You ask all the guys. You've been bringing your A game. Fuck, he's only your lucky fucking charm." He collapses back in the seat as if exhausted, the color draining from his face. "What have I done?"

The way he looks at me has me clamping down on my lips to stop from laughing. He's deadly serious, which is as terrifying as it is hilarious.

"We need to make this right. He needs to be at the games." He's now talking to himself. There's a change in tone, one that's absolutely his plotting tone. In fact, this *tone* scares me half to death as Tyron's been known to do some crazy shit. "Maybe we need to make him an official mascot. That means we can actually get him on the bus to come with us to away games. And definitely for March Mayhem." He stands once again and paces the room. "You think he'll be okay in a bear costume?"

Words are difficult. Honestly, I have no idea how to respond. Do I want to work things out with Dean? Yes. I don't even have to think about it. While I have no idea what that means for the future, I'm simply following my gut. My dick has some say too. The thing is, so does my heart.

I take deep breaths, trying to work out how to calm Tyron down while figuring out if there's a way to have Dean speak to me again. "He works at the diner over in Grounder." And I have to tackle the next thing carefully. "I know we don't have a mascot because of the drama a few years back, but being a team mascot is real hard work. Not sure he'd have time for that even if he agreed."

That gets Tyron's attention. The maniacal grin worries me a little, but if it means he's going to help me with Dean and it also means he's back to being the guy I can rely on, then I'll take it.

"Perfect."

I do a double take. What's "perfect" about Dean not having time to be a mascot? Or the dean preventing the Bears from even having a mascot for the past five years?

"You know if we make this happen, school can help with scholarships and shit."

"He already has a scholarship."

"A full one?"

I shake my head. "No, I don't think so."

His grin is back. "We can *so* make that happen."

I have no idea how Tyron can be so cocky or confident. It's impressive, if not kind of worrying. But if he… *we* could make that happen, wouldn't that be a great thing for Dean? It would be, right?

"Let's grab a shower and the rest of the guys. I'll get Sammy to start looking into costumes. And I need to speak to Coach and Dean Chadwick."

Reaching out a hand for me, Tyron tugs me up and hauls me into a hug. "I really am sorry, man."

I nod, hugging him back. "I know."

He spins me around, arm around my shoulder, and we step back into the locker room to a chorus of cheers. Shit, the probability of Dean kicking my ass is high with these guys as my friends.

DEAN IS NOT A PUSHOVER. I KNOW THIS, YET I STILL allow Tyron to talk me into visiting. I have no idea if Dean's actually working, but this is Tyron's plan, and I'm just going with it. It doesn't take a genius to work out why either.

I can't stop thinking about Dean. And while I gave him a piece of me I've never given before—access to my ass, just to be clear—that's not even the real reason. Sure, sex was phenomenal. But I miss his sweet snark, his bite, his ability to own his space.

And I totally sound like a sap here, but when Dean smiles at me, I swear my heart flips, making it impossible not to want to kiss him and bask in the looks he sends my way.

What the fuck, right?

Kieran "Rule Book" Kendall, confirmed bachelor since who the hell knows when, is pining for a guy and willing to rewrite the rules. The jury's still out, though, about just how many rewrites are needed. It's not something I can think about just yet.

"I feel like a dick."

Sammy chuckles at my side and claps me on the shoulder. "When it all goes wrong, blame Ty."

"When?" I shoot a look at him, my brows dipping. "You think this is stupid as fuck too and we're going to get kicked out?"

Sammy, the swell guy he is, just laughs harder. "When have you ever known any of Tyron's schemes to pan out?"

"Ah fuck." I rub a hand over my face. The diner is just ahead, and each step I take feels like lead. "He's gonna call the cops on us, have a restraining order put against me. Coach is going to go apeshit."

While I appreciate the show of solidarity with another shoulder squeeze, that Sammy doesn't contradict anything I say doesn't make me especially optimistic.

Before I can back out, we're filing into the diner. It's no surprise five tall guys grab almost everyone's attention. That, and maybe our faces are just a little recognizable. We're the closest college to Grounder for miles.

A waitress smiles, running her gaze over us and then looking around the room. I expect she's figuring out how she's going to fit us all around a table. "There's one big booth to the right over there. Why don't you all go grab a seat? We'll be with you in a minute." She passes us menus, and we give our thanks.

I focus on my feet and keeping my head down. It's been too many days since I last saw Dean, and while I'm desperate to get my fill, I honestly don't know how he's going to react to being ambushed.

I recall him kissing me goodbye. He wasn't angry at me, which is something, but the resolve on his face was clear. Really, I should let the guy go. I know this, and that makes me an asshole.

A selfish asshole at that.

I'm owning it. And if that means Dean will give me a chance, I'm willing to let my friends embarrass the fuck out of me.

"Incoming," Leon whispers after we've been sitting for about a minute. I've been pretending to look at the menu but have really been listening out for any sign of Dean.

"Ooh… he looks pissed," Sammy adds helpfully.

"You should have brought flowers," Bentley offers. I lift my brows at him, wondering how me bringing flowers keeps my sexuality on the down-low. "Works every time my dad screws up."

It's no use. I have to look.

Okay, so Dean does look a little pissed off. One brow is slightly curved higher than the other, there's no smile in sight, and he's targeted completely on me. I think I get a glimpse of curiosity, though.

With the combination of fire and confidence in his gaze, there's no doubt that Dean simply does it for me. He's hot, in a cute "you don't wanna get on the wrong side of me" way. Seeing him like this, I swallow hard, lust and resolve thrumming in my veins.

A mistake or not, I smile.

How can I not when he looks so fucking fiery?

At my smile, there's the slightest twitch of his lips. Thank fuck. Maybe I've got a shot after all. Christ, I hope so.

Tyron speaks before anyone else has the chance to say anything. "Dean, bro. Good to see you." He bobs his head like he's having a friendly conversation with a long-lost friend. "You're looking good, relaxed." I pinch my lips together as he continues, just waiting for Dean to react. "So, funny thing, a couple of weeks back over breakfast, it seems like I hit my head, and in doing so, put my foot in my mouth and said a few things that were not my place."

Surprised, I jolt back. So not what I expected him to say. Sure, he's attempting to be funny, but when you cut through his bullshit, it almost sounds like a genuine apology.

"So we're here for a late lunch and to leave you with a generous tip and to also say I'm sorry I was a dick."

I hold my breath as Dean scans him from head to toe before he turns his attention to me. I don't keep it for long. "This your attempt to buy me off, some sort of hush money?"

"Fuck no. That's not what he meant," I rush to say, horror crashing into me. "Ty, fucking fix this, man." My gaze locks on Dean's. "That's not what he meant. He really is sorry."

"I remember a similar conversation we had about why your friend here was a dick. I have to wonder why you'd think I'd be interested in any conversation or apology when your friend isn't a dickhead just once, but twice. And that last time he pushed the boundaries of what a half-assed apology could fix."

"Dean, bro—" Tyron stops dead from the daggers Dean shoots his way. I should have perhaps mentioned the whole "bro" thing and what Dean thinks about it. "Uhm, Dean, I was out of line, trying to protect Key, and pushed it too far. I'm sorry. Please accept my apology."

Damn, Tyron's good. How could anyone deny

those puppy-dog eyes? Plus this time, he legit sounds sorry.

When there's a wavering of the resolve on Dean's face, my stomach tumbles. I hold my breath.

"If I accept your apology, will you order and leave me alone?"

More than aware that's not Ty's plan at all, I wince. It's time to intervene.

"Dean."

His eyes travel to mine, almost reluctantly.

"Is there somewhere I can steal you away, for just two minutes?" Uncertainty clouds his features, so I offer, "Just two. I promise."

Despite his hard gaze, there's definitely the curiosity I thought I saw earlier. He looks away, scanning the other customers. With a huff of breath, he focuses on me. "Two minutes." He turns and walks away while I scramble out of my seat.

"Don't blow this," Tyron whispers.

I roll my eyes at him, more than sure he's done a good enough job of that as it is.

Dean leads me to a side door. He has a quiet word with a waitress, who eyes me speculatively. I offer a polite smile and am relieved when Dean carries on, me hot on his heels.

We reach a small corridor, pass a couple of rooms, and he finally leads us to a space that's clearly a locker room of sorts. It's cramped but private.

Once there, he turns toward me. The curiosity is gone, and his body language screams "hurry the hell up."

I step toward him, closer than friends would, but I can't help myself. Being so close to him and having not seen him makes me desperate for his touch. Heck, I'll even take a hit of his scent at this point.

His eyes widen as he has to angle to look at me.

"I've missed you."

Dean's brows shoot high, and he shakes his head. "You don't even know me."

"That's not true."

"It is." A humorless laugh escapes. "Hooking up doesn't mean we know each other."

Swallowing hard, I focus on controlling my thoughts. I really don't want to come off as desperate, despite what being so close to him is doing to me, but being here with him feels right. I don't want to lose that… this… whatever it is I'm feeling.

"I know that you don't take shit from anyone and you've been through some things, yet you don't let that stop you from being positive. I know that you love your brother and want him to be successful and are determined to keep him grounded and focused on school."

With the pounding of my pulse in my ears, I can barely hear myself, but a flush spreads up Dean's neck and caresses his cheeks, so I keep going.

"I know how you like your coffee and how you're super smart and determined. You're going to make an excellent teacher. Just seeing you with your brother tells me as much. And you're passionate." I take a small step so there's just a few inches between us. "Not only about literature and basketball but when you kiss me and touch me… and with all that, I can't stop thinking about you. I trust you and want to get to know you even better." I shake my head, lift my hand, and trace his cheek with my fingers.

"I should have fought harder and got you to stay. I'm sorry I didn't."

Indecision stares back at me, but beyond kissing him, I have no idea what else to say or do. Since I won't force myself on Dean, I wait. Each millisecond feels like an eternity as I watch his gaze dart around my face and emotion flitter across his features.

"So you're saying," he starts, his tone quiet and breathy, "that you miss me?" The smile is slow to spread, but it's there, and he's teasing and fucking perfect.

"I do." He leans into my touch, and I angle to press my mouth to his. Sighing into the kiss, I wrap my arms around him, drawing Dean close. Our lips slide against each other's, and I luxuriate in the heat and taste of him. It's only the sound of someone in the corridor that has us pulling apart.

I'm breathless and grinning like a fool. Since Dean's staring up at me with a similar expression, I don't feel so goofy.

"What time do you get off?"

"Four."

"I have training soon, but can I come by after?"

He tilts his head. "Maybe since your housemates know about me, it's best if I come to your place?"

The twinge in my heart takes me by surprise. "Thanks," I offer, the word nowhere near good enough for him agreeing to keep us on the down-low. "I'll text you when I get back."

He bobs his head and looks at the time. "Shit, Bessie is going to kill me."

I kinda figured we've been longer than two minutes, but considering that kiss, I don't feel too guilty about it. "Let's head out." After one more brush of our lips, we pull apart and we leave the way we came. Dean darts past me to go and pick up orders he knows will be waiting while I go back to the table.

Four expectant sets of eyes are burning holes into me.

"Well?" Tyron leans on his elbows.

Me? I simply grin, and the jerks that they are all cheer and offer a round of high fives. I snort, knowing they're getting ahead of themselves. There's no way Dean's going to get caught up in Tyron's hairbrained scheme.

CHAPTER 13

RULE 5: EAT FIVE FRUIT AND VEG A DAY

DEAN

"No."

For an hour, Tyron had been filling my drink, pleading with me, and plying me with cookies, which I witnessed him bake. I know… mind blown that the protective doofus asshole baked me delicious goodness.

His permanent scowl is gone too. It's kinda freaking me out.

I started off horrified at his request. That morphed into amusement, and I'm currently leaning toward exhaustion. While I've known plenty of asshats in my life, Tyron is the first who comes off as slightly endearing. I'll never admit that, though.

But he's determined. I'll give him that.

I also think he has some magical powers of persuasion, as he's wearing me down. The ass can sense it too. It's in the way he bats his ridiculously long eyelashes at me, which is weirdly sweet considering I don't think I like him very much.

"But Dean…" My name has become a whine. "Think of all the good you'll do. Did you see that we didn't win a single game recently?"

A grimace escapes. I do know that. While I managed to stay away from the home games, like a glutton for punishment, I watched the highlights and saw the scores.

"The whole team agrees you're our good luck charm. You put a fire or something in my man here."

Kieran snorts softly at my side and leans in, pressing his lips against my head. We've been snuggled on the couch, which is ludicrously surreal, since I arrived. It should feel odd, alien even, especially as all his housemates are here. But it's not. Rather than question it, I'm lapping up the contact, having missed Kieran more than is healthy. Something I'm not ready to examine more closely.

Breaking free from the haze Kieran's sweet kiss put me in, Tyron's words register. "The *whole* team?" My muscles lock up, not sure how to feel about that. I turn to the man I'm all but draped over and stare at him with wide-eyed horror. "You've told the team about me, about us?" I hate the squeak at the end of my question and clear my throat. "What does that mean exactly?"

But seriously, what does it mean? We haven't discussed anything, not really. We haven't mentioned the *B* word or even the *E* word. Fuck, I'm confused, but that doesn't conceal the thrum of excitement in my stomach.

"Only the guys here know about you, as in you and me," Kieran says.

I hold back my snort, confident he has no idea how to describe what we have either. It makes me feel slightly better.

"But things have been... tense in the team—"

Sammy barks out a laugh. When everyone looks his way, he puts up his palms and presses his lips together.

"What lover boy is trying to say is, he's been mopey and all woe is me and shit, and freezing me out since you left." Tyron holds up his palms much like Sammy just did. "Which I totally deserved for interfering and misunderstanding—"

"And for being an asshole," I supply. I'm good like that.

Tyron smirks, appearing slightly chagrined. "And being an asshole," he agrees. "We only sorted things out today, and that's when I figured he wasn't just playing a shit game because of our argument or you leaving."

"He wasn't?" It's foolish of me to engage, but I still don't quite understand what this good luck charm stuff's about.

"No. Ever since you met, that first game you attended, Kieran's games have improved… exponentially. Like, even compared to the preseason games the difference is obvious."

"Hey," Kieran calls out. "Last year I was awesome."

"Yeah, I'm not denying that, but since meeting Deano here, your stats have been record-breaking."

"It's true." Leon bobs his head. "The whole team's noticed a shift, and with your playing, your focus, it's… I don't know, buoyed us or something."

"Exactly." Tyron looks thoroughly pleased with the confirmation. "It's made these past few games and how shit-tastic they've been an even bigger kick in the gut. But you"—he focuses back on me and points for good measure—"you're the common denominator. And while I don't want to presume to know what's going on in Kieran's head… or other parts of his body—"

"Gee, thanks, asshole," Kieran grumbles. I side-eye him and see his pink cheeks. This reaction feels kinda nice.

"—I expect he's playing better for you, or because of you… I just know that you're the reason." He waves off whatever Kieran's about to say, adding, "Yeah, yeah, I know it's your skill, but I dare you to deny it."

"I still say he has a magic cock."

All five of us whip our attention to Bentley. He's been sitting quietly, impassively even, so this outburst is one heck of a declaration that gets our attention.

"Jesus H." Kieran tilts his head back, his exasperation clear. I'm battling between the urges to double over in laughter and run out of the room.

Tyron fills in the awkward silence. "Uh, well… I wasn't going to say that, but back to you being a better player because of Dean."

Curious, I return my attention to Kieran. His cheeks are flushed, and he's sending Tyron some sort of look I can't read. Next he makes eye contact with me, his gaze piercing, searching.

Just as I'm about to give up and look away, a little bit of disappointment unfurling in my chest, he shrugs, saying, "I'm not denying it."

Everything is too intense, too much. It's too damn personal to be dealing with all these feels while we have an audience. Since arriving here, it's felt like I've entered some alternate universe. While I've known my fair share of jocks in my formative years, these guys are a unique set of too much and intense. In layman's terms, they're nosey assholes with impulsive streaks that are a little endearing.

"Oh shit," I say, the words breaking through my silence and free from my thoughts. "This whole group is freakily reliant on each other and *involved…*" I shake my head. "If Kieran and I, uhm… hook up regularly, does that mean I may as well be 'hanging out' with the whole team, because you know—"

"I don't share, so that's a hard no."

Surprise and arousal flare to life inside me at the assertive and immediate reply from Kieran. A hint of a smirk I give him swiftly changes into a "your answer will do just fine" smile, or at least that's what I'm aiming for.

"Thank Christ, because I need privacy and space, and I don't know how I feel about being surrounded by so many giants all the time."

"So, does this mean we can size you up for the bear costume?" Tyron is literally at the edge of his seat, the plate of cookies in his hand. The eagerness on his face is a little unnerving, but those damn eyes of his… Shit, I know I'm going to regret this.

"Are you sure I can't just tag along as myself?" As soon as my words are out there, I know that'll raise a whole heap of questions, ones that Kieran doesn't want. I sigh. "You guys will owe me so fucking big if I do this and you win March Mayhem."

I'm mauled, honest to god mauled by five hot basketball players who find it hilarious to shove me in the middle of their group hug. While it's not the worst place to be in the world—hello abs—they're a rowdy bunch, and I feel like I'm with a gaggle of middle schoolers rather than the college students they are.

Kieran finally pulls me away, much to the grumbles of his friends. It's sweet but still weird.

"You wanna go to my room?"

"God yes. Anywhere away from this rabble." I'm only half joking.

Kieran's chuckle is quiet, but still ripples across my skin. He has a great laugh.

To the jeers of his friends, we head to Kieran's room. As soon as the door is locked, I collapse on the bed face first. "Your friends are exhausting."

"They can be a bit much." The bed dips when he settles next to me. I angle to take my fill and soak him in. The man is easily the hottest guy I've ever been with, times ten, truth be told, and that's because he's pretty much the whole package.

Those tick boxes are filled with smiley faces. Don't get me wrong, I'm ignoring the elephant in this… relationship, or whatever it is, about the exception I can't help but be hung up on. But I'm willing to take the risk and see what happens. Believe it or not, I can be discreet, and I can also keep my hands to myself in public.

Now is a different story.

After texting Mom to let her know I won't be back, I return to bed. Naked and still sweaty, Kieran shoots me a sweet, content smile.

"I think we need to do that at least once a day."

I snuggle up to him and sigh when he drapes his arm around me. "You think? That might be a problem if we end up staying away for a game—not sure how your coach would react to us sharing a room—and you know, Christmas is fast approaching. Then before you know it, it'll be the summer."

Maybe I shouldn't be talking about this stuff now, not after everything, but I'm putting myself out on a limb here and need to prepare.

"Summer is still months away. And the holidays are only a handful of days for me with games. Let's not worry about it now." He dots a kiss on my head, the move becoming familiar.

"Live in the moment, huh?"

"And this room. My bed, ideally."

I nip at his chest.

"Ouch."

I roll my eyes. "That didn't hurt."

"So no licking it better?"

"Isn't that meant to be kissing it better?"

"That'll work too." He chuckles, and I lean up on my elbow to peer down at him. "What's going on in that head of yours?"

I twist my mouth as I try to gather the right words. "It just seems all a bit surreal, you know. And a bit fast. And don't get me started on your housemates."

"They're full-on." His voice is a little guarded. "But I promise they mean well."

I'm nodding before he's finished talking. "I get that, but whatever this is, you and me, I can't have a third, fourth, fifth or hell, sixth wheel."

"I get that, and they won't be. It's just Tyron can be intense."

"You think?" I snort. "He's also slightly insane."

Kieran's smile is soft. "I think me flipping the way I have, going off MO has really thrown him for a loop. I know we're a buncha jocks, but believe it or not, the guys rely on me."

"I understand that." Not only have I witnessed that in games, but based on the dynamics I saw downstairs, it was super obvious. "I feel like we need to talk about your 'rules,' as I'm not quite sure where I stand here."

Talking about this stuff is mortifying. I wish I could shut up, just spend all our time fucking him into the mattress, but that's not me. "I've never been in a relationship before," I admit, cheeks burning. "And I don't need a label, or shit, maybe I do, I don't know, but I'm confused about what you expect here, what you see happening between us."

The words are out there, and while I'm a jittery mess inside, as offering my truth is a hell of a thing, I'm impressed my voice doesn't shake once.

Making myself vulnerable is hard. I've been shit on so many times, I can't help but be wary.

"I've obviously never dated before," he starts. The pink in his cheeks makes me feel better. God, I feel like a goofball. I keep that observation to myself and pay attention. "I can't imagine coming out to the League, should I get drafted." He winces. "I just wanna play and be recognized, and fuck, what if I ended up in Florida or some shit. Can you imagine?"

My shudder is real. When just the word "gay" is

deemed practically a felony, I can't imagine the struggle it would be living there and forever looking over your shoulder. I need to be around bigots as much as I need a hot needle in my dick.

Sorry, not sorry… I winced too.

Remaining quiet, I nod, hoping he'll continue.

"I know I like you and enjoy spending time with you. I also know it's asking a lot to keep our hooking up…" He raises his brows and waits a beat, searching for a reaction. When my lips curl high, he exhales. "…on the down-low. It means no holding hands or PDA. But it doesn't mean we can't hang out outside of here. Once the season's over, I won't be as busy. Is that going to be okay?"

Ignoring the voice in my head telling me that it so is not okay, I listen to my heart and the fizz in my stomach instead. "I can make that work." His smile lights up his eyes. "And our hooking up is exclusive, right?" Since we're having this talk, I may as well go all in.

"Yeah. I wasn't lying downstairs when I said I don't share. Obviously I've never been in a position to share, but you know, I don't want to share you."

That Kieran gets a little tongue-tied and wordy when he's caught up relaxes my shoulders and forces away the tendrils of worry trying to take root. "I don't want to share you either." I punctuate my sentence with a kiss before pulling away. "I do want to share a pizza, though. I'm starving."

He chuckles and sits up, the sheet pooling at his waist. This man is a living, breathing fantasy come to life. A happy sigh whooshes from me, and I lean in as he opens the app for the pizza place.

A night of pizza and sex sounds pretty spectacular, and I wouldn't want to be anywhere else.

CHAPTER 14
RULE 6: DON'T LIVE ON TAKEOUT

KIERAN

"Do you think I eat too much pizza?"

The question's enough for Dean to stop chewing his cereal. "What?"

"Pizza. Do I eat it too much?"

This look he's giving me isn't unusual, not when Tyron is speaking. All I can do is shrug at Dean, letting him know I have no idea why Tyron is talking about pizza.

When it's clear I'm not going to respond, Dean shoots me the stink eye before saying, "I suppose 'too much' is relative, right? As long as you're eating healthily the majority of the time and your calorie intake is right for your training—" He cuts off and looks at me, his brows furrowing. "That's a thing, right, food and training?"

"Sure is."

He seems happy with the confirmation and turns back to Tyron. "So I suppose you need to ask yourself if you're eating right and if pizza is a treat rather than a staple." He waits expectantly now he's been drawn into Tyron's randomness. Meanwhile, I don't get involved. It's only been a couple of weeks of Dean hanging out frequently, so he's not yet used to this side of Tyron. He'll soon learn, though.

Tyron seems to think about that as he's eating his egg-white omelet. Without answering, he shrugs and shovels another forkful in his mouth.

And that's it.

Seeing Dean about to say something to Tyron, I nudge him and shake my head when I have his attention. "It's better not asking. He does random shit like this all the time."

"It's weird."

"Yeah. That's Ty."

It's obvious Tyron can hear us, but his head is all but stuck in his phone, and he's tapping away on the keyboard. I expect that's the only reason he's not flipping me off.

"What time's training?" Somehow I keep a straight face. I value my balls too much to laugh.

"Urgh. At two."

"It's going okay though, right?" While the thought of him in the bear costume tickles me, I still can't believe he said yes and is going through with it. Nor that Tyron made it happen. Knowing Dean's going to be around at every game, though, makes me happy in a way that surprises me.

"Yeah. I'm having some begrudging fun. I would not want to be dressed up in the thing in summer, though." The look of distaste on his face is comical. "Even my eyelashes sweat. It's not pretty."

I chuckle. "Not wearing your eye shit must suck." My mouth twitches at his reaction, which is exactly as I predicted. I should feel bad for getting a rise out of him, but since we've been spending time with each other, and the both of us are usually going about life dazed and happily fucked, he's been super mellow.

I love that we're getting on so well. But the fire he gets in his eyes whenever he's indignant makes me hard.

"Did you just call my forty-five-dollar mascara eye shit?"

"Forty-five dollars?"

Narrow eyes shooting lasers are especially sexy. I just hope he never realizes just how much I think that.

"You saying these eyes aren't worth good-quality mascara?"

"I wouldn't dream of it. You know I think you look especially hot when you're wearing it."

His narrow gaze softens a little.

"Is this really the sort of shit you guys spend time talking about?" Tyron puts his phone down and stares at me as though he has no idea who I am.

Rather than answer, I smirk at him. "There are other less suitable topics of conversation we could be having over breakfast if you prefer?"

He stands and pockets his phone. "That'll be a hard no. Come on, get your ass in gear." Tyron dumps his bowl and mug in the dishwasher and leaves the room.

"You about ready?"

Dean nods. "Yeah. You still okay to meet for lunch?"

"Definitely, especially if you're still planning on heading home tonight and abandoning me."

He rolls his eyes, but I don't miss the hint of a smile he's trying to hide. "Zeke has a game tonight, and I don't want to miss it. Plus, my mom is pummeling me with questions about where I've been hiding."

"I know." I trail my fingers over his forearm. "But

in less than a week it's the holidays, so I'm heading home."

Dean knows this, but it doesn't hurt to remind him. While I'm only at home for seven days due to games, it still feels like a long time without Dean. This on-again, off-again thing we've had going for almost three months finally seems to have settled. I don't want to rock the boat, and in all honesty, I'm enjoying spending time with the man. Like… a lot.

"You'll be fine."

I grunt, not so sure.

He stands up and chivvies me along. We both have a nine o'clock class. I've then got a meeting with Coach, followed by another class. I need to get in some study time too. But lunch with Dean is going to be the highlight of my day. Especially as we have a late practice, which is why I can't go and watch his brother's game.

I indulge in a lingering kiss before we leave. It would be easy to get frustrated by the number of times I have to stop myself reaching out to him when we're in public, but since he's being so incredible at doing as I've asked, I don't feel like I have a right to complain. At least not to him.

Just putting it out there. I fucking hate it, and if this thing between us grows, I know I've got some hard decisions to look forward to in my future.

We head out to college, Tyron and Sammy joining us. As we get closer to campus, more and more people say hello, several shooting curious looks Dean's way. Nothing about Dean blends in, not when he's with the three of us. Dean, though, doesn't even blink. He's taking everything in stride, usually rocking a fun tee or hoodie and appearing completely unaffected.

When we reach the south campus, I let them know this is my stop. The guys nod and tell me they'll catch up with me later while I stand a respectable distance away from Dean.

"You know, eye fucking me in public is going to get old fast."

Dean's words are so unexpected a loud, harsh laugh bursts out of me. "Is that right?" I manage, aware my laughter has caused heads to turn in our direction.

"It sure is, especially when it makes me hard and want to climb you like a tree."

Wide-eyed, the visual slams into me, and from Dean's snicker, he knows it.

"Catch you later," he says before I'm able to respond, and like the pitiful man I am, I watch him go.

That man of mine knows how to drive me to

distraction. And before you make a comment, please don't. Let's just skip over my word choices and pretend it never happened.

With a sigh, I head to class, focusing hard on gross things like drinking coffee to will my half-hard dick to behave. It works, thankfully, and I'm able to survive my morning, with only a few risqué thoughts about Dean Whittaker.

COACH MUST HAVE A DATE TONIGHT. IT'S THE ONLY explanation for cutting practice short. It's that rare that the whole team stands still for at least thirty seconds, waiting for him to call bullshit and make us do a hundred burpees.

It's not until he yells at us to get out of there before he changes his mind that we make a run for it.

Leaving early is how my housemates and I manage to head out to watch Zeke's game. I'm not even surprised that my friends are tagging along. At the moment, Dean is pretty much a god, according to them all.

"It looks busy," Bentley comments, looking around the parking lot we struggled to find a space in. "What if they've filled the seats?"

Tyron glances over at him. "I think they'll let us in even if that's the case."

He's not saying that to be a jerk, and there's no arrogance in his tone. The thing is, he's absolutely right, especially with all of the local college feeder towns. They'll recognize us, so there won't be an issue.

I haven't texted Dean to let him know we're coming. It feels fun to show up unexpectedly. There's a bubble of anticipation in my gut knowing he's going to be surprised. Even knowing I can't greet him with a kiss doesn't bring me down. If I earn one of his smiles that I know he reserves just for me, it'll be worth it.

There's no issues getting in. Plenty of double takes, but no one stops us. The game's not due to start for another ten minutes. It means the cheer-leaders are on the court, the players with their coaches, some running drills, and most spectators already have their asses in their seats.

Not that it's difficult to peer over heads when you're my height, but it makes searching Dean out easier.

"He's over there."

I whip my head in Leon's direction and follow where he's pointing. Dean's close to the court, sitting next to his mom, and while I can only see his side profile, it's obvious he loves the thrill of the game. And that's even before the game's started.

"What do you want to do? Find a seat here or go to him?" Leon asks.

It's like my friends don't know me at all. Okay, admittedly, they've never seen this needy-as-fuck side to me, but still, isn't the answer obvious?

Apparently my expression is answer enough as Leon chuckles, saying, "Lead the way, Captain. I'm sure people will be clambering to give up their seats for us." While he rolls his eyes, I really hope he's not wrong. I'm not that much of an asshole that I'd ask someone to move, but if someone offered, damn straight I'll take their seats if it means I get to press my thigh against Dean's.

Jesus H Christ, do I know how to live danger-ously or what?

"They have nachos," Tyron says as I start down the steps. "Save me a seat." No one has a chance to respond before he's gone.

As we head toward the court, closer to Dean, there's a noticeable change in the atmosphere. People are pointing and staring. There's nudges and hushed whispers. Dean is so invested in a conversation he's having with Tina though, he's completely unaware.

It's not until I'm at the end of the row and I see movement on the court that I pull my attention away from Dean. It's Zeke, and from the giant grin he's shooting my way, the kid's pleased to see me. He heads on over, and rather than leave him hanging, I go down the final few steps to greet him.

"Hey, Zeke." I reach out and shake his hand.

Wide-eyed, he blinks after releasing my grip. "You're here."

"Yeah, thought I should come and see these mad skills your brother's been telling me about."

When his grin stretches even wider and a light blush colors his cheeks, he looks to his left… toward Dean.

Finally.

I follow his gaze and capture Dean's. His eyes are even wider than his brother's, but it's the smile I'm more focused on. It's warm and gentle and so fucking happy, and there's no doubt causing a stir is worth it for that reaction alone.

Turning back to Zeke, I say, "What are these guys like?" I indicate toward the opposing team.

He shrugs. "Good, but we can hold our own."

I nod. "You be sure to do that. Play hard."

"I will." He turns away to the call of his coach. "I gotta go."

I wave him off before refocusing on Dean. He's standing and making his way out of the aisle, saying something to Leon, who's laughing. A second later,

Bentley is signing a few caps, and a group of kids who were in the aisle grin and vacate the row for us.

And then I'm beside Dean. Peering up at me, his gaze bright, he smiles. "This is a surprise."

"I thought it was about time I watched Zeke work his magic."

His gaze is on my mouth, and his hand twitches. This is so hard. Easing out a breath, I indicate toward his mom. Her head's cocked, and I'm pretty sure any questions she's had about Dean being MIA have been answered with the way she's studying us.

"Game's about to start," I say.

"Shit, okay, let's sit down."

I follow him in, Leon at my side, and we all settle in our seats. When Tyron arrives with his hands full of nachos and who knows what else, I grin, as I have no choice but to scoot closer to Dean.

When our thighs touch, we both release a breath, and I chuckle low. From the corner of my eye, I catch his smirk but don't dare fully look at him.

My attention turns to the game, though I'm absolutely aware of Dean's every breath and every movement. It's when he claps, cheers, and hollers that I'm completely fixated on him. It's not until Leon knocks me and I tear my gaze away, receiving a pointed stare, that I focus on the court again, trying to ignore my heated cheeks.

With renewed focus, I pay attention to Zeke.

The kid has some talent. The game is faster than I remembered it being when I was in high school. That sounds crazy since high school was only three years ago, but it's a fun game to watch. There're probably four players who have a spark to them, ones I'm sure college recruiters are already keeping an eye on.

At halftime, we're approached by multiple fans. The guys and I happily sign some autographs while Dean looks on, bemused. I know this is a side of me playing ball that he struggles with.

When I finally sit down again a couple of minutes before the second half begins, Tina leans forward. "Good of you to come and watch Zeke."

I smile. "Coach was in a good mood and cut practice short, so what better way to spend our Friday night?"

She quirks her brow at that, and I can only imagine what she's thinking. A bunch of college guys hanging out at a high school game on a Friday night admittedly isn't the norm, but she doesn't call bullshit.

"What are you guys doing after?"

Instinctively, I look at Dean, looking for some kind of answer. When his gaze snaps to mine, his brows are high, and I figure my reaction is so fucking obvious, at least to his mom.

"Uhm…"

I have no idea what to say, how to answer. It's not like I can come out and say, "Well, I was hoping to kidnap your son for a sexy-time sleepover."

Tina's lips twitch. "Well, we're going to grab pizza if you want to—"

"Did someone say pizza?"

I wince and snort when Tyron enters the conversation. The guy has a built-in radar that's on pizza setting.

If Tina is taken aback, she hides it well. With a grin, she focuses on Tyron, who is standing and leaning toward us. "Pizza at my place. You're all free to join us."

"Hell yes. Thank you, ma'am."

Tina's eye twitches a little, and Dean smirks, saying to his mom, "These guys polish off a pizza each. Be warned."

She looks us over, amusement in her gaze. "Just look at the size of the guys. I'm not surprised."

Dean gapes at his mom and her teasing, while I snort, Leon doing the same at my side, and then it's time for the second half, but that doesn't stop Leon leaning in and whispering, "Is it me or is Dean's mom hot?"

"Dude," I rush to say and give him a shove.

"What?" He laughs. "Just saying."

I shake. "I dare you to 'just say' in front of Dean."

I barely hold back my raucous laughter at the look of horror that spreads across his face. Yeah, my friends have a healthy respect for Dean and his ferocious self. The thought makes me beam.

CHAPTER 15
RULE 1 SECTION E: PLAY LIKE IT'S THE PLAY-OFFS

DEAN

THE FIRST GAME AFTER CHRISTMAS IS AT HOME, AND while a legit Bears mascot costume has been organized and sized, I'm able to watch the game from great seats, sitting next to my brother, since my training isn't complete. Though apparently, this is the last game I can be sitting out. Come the New Year, I'm officially the Bears mascot.

I swear, I don't know how I get conned into this sort of shit.

Oh, that's right. It's my dick's fault, and maybe a little bit my heart's too.

But this mascot stuff is a big deal. There's a whole bunch of cloak-and-dagger stuff about the role, which is pretty cool. But also, because of some legal stuff a few years back, our college dropped having a mascot altogether. That means a contract, a scholarship negotiation, which I can hardly believe, and mascot training to make sure I do a great job being Bryson Bear.

The game is fast, and the Bears seem to do no wrong. Every pass is caught, and they're 94 percent on target. Not only that, but their defense is on fire. As I watch, I also think about what I've learned so far about my new role and how I'll play the part, what I'll do at halftime, how I'll encourage the crowd and diss our rivals.

At the end of the game, while I can't go out and celebrate since Zeke's with me, nor can I congratulate Kieran the way I want to, his gaze is glued to mine. The next night we celebrate with handjobs and epic shower sex, so I have zero complaints.

The second game is away, and I'm here shitting bricks. I'm also struggling between being overheated and feeling ice-cold from the nerves slicing through my system. It doesn't matter that I've survived the intro to the game, the first half, or even the halftime when I did a full-on dance-off with the opposing team's meerkat.

So why am I shitting bricks?

The game is close. Kieran's been fouled three times, and his right ankle is a little unsteady.

I can't help the gasp that tears free from me when number fucking twenty-nine fouls Kieran again. I throw my hands in the air, cussing up a storm in my head, and manage to pull my gaze away from him only when he's upright and steady on his feet.

I turn my large furry thumbs down and rile up the crowd, getting them to boo along with me. It doesn't take much before our not-so-small crowd of away fans are so vocal that I find myself grinning. Triumphant that the fans are as pissed off as I am, or at least almost, I refocus on the game.

Kieran is there, hands on the ball, gaze on me for one, two beats, a smirk on his face. Then the whistle blows and he passes the ball straight to Sammy. I can barely keep up with how fast he moves to get in position, and then the man only goes and scores.

I whoop. Forgetting for a second to keep my mouth clamped shut. Bryson is meant to be silent. Oops, but seriously, that shot was epic. I'm doing a victory dance, complete with twerking, ass directed at the home team, when I feel a slap on my padded butt. I spin, and holy shit, it's a good job I'm completely in disguise.

Kieran's grinning and spares me a quick glance and a wink before he's once again all over the ball. This right here is more than I ever imagined.

Being a mascot rocks.

And if my… Kieran keeps playing like this, he's going to have one hell of a reward when we get back to his place.

The game carries on, and while Kieran definitely needs his ankle strapped and iced, he's playing like he knows exactly how I'm going to reward him.

When the crew chief calls time, I bounce up and down, the away crowd jumping with me. I'm then grabbed from behind. Unbelievably it's Tyron.

"Bro, killer twerks." He hugs me hard before moving off. Stunned, I can't respond, nor am I given time to, not before Sammy hugs me.

"Good game."

Bentley's next. He's grinning wide as he pats my arm. "Good work."

The whole team are in my space, one after another, hugging me, congratulating me, and a bubble of emotion makes its way into my throat.

These guys are too much, too everything. I swear they've already latched on to me, making me feel all the freakin' feels for them and their adorable bro-ship.

And then there's Kieran. He's before me, gaze bright and wide. I only have a moment to drink him in before he's clinging on to me, hugging me so hard it penetrates through the padded suit.

"You okay?" I ask, battling with the emotion

that's come with the sense of belonging. "Your ankle?" To hell with not speaking. How can I not?

"I'll be fine." He hugs me harder. "You were amazing." He pulls away, his smile so broad it hits me hard in the chest. "I'm so proud of you."

Surprise has me catching my breath. It seems crazy, receiving this praise, reacting this way all because of a costume, but to the team, to Kieran, it means something. It also means something to me.

I smile even though he can't see it, and I ignore the way my eyes fill. "I'm proud of you too."

He squeezes my arm before easing away. Coach is calling. "See you in fifteen."

I nod, following his retreat, while wondering how I'm going to manage to keep my hands to myself on the three-hour bus journey home.

In case you're wondering, I don't manage. But I'm discreet, and I don't do anything too delinquent. Honest.

Traveling on the bus, though, is kinda surreal, and between sweet, sneaky kisses, and laughing at the guys as they celebrate by talking shit, I spend the time going over my debut.

I think I did okay. The team seems happy.

This new role is worth the shift changes at work and the reduced hours, especially since the scholarship I've scored is practically a free ride, and I can't help but wonder how this is my life. You already know drama is not my thing, but dancing, heck yes. Plus I can be flamboyant as fuck when I want to be.

It's a buzz, and even away with not as many Bears fans, the supporters lapped up my debut. They're also just as vocal and supportive in the consequent games I'm involved in.

A big draw card for me about the games, home and away, is when the Bears kick ass and win, I'm able to hug Kieran in public. The wonder of being incognito in costume.

I'm talking full-on fluffy bear suit, complete with Bears cap and jersey and shorts. It's unbelievably warm and I sweat like I've run a marathon, but you know what, it's fun. I can dance around and be an idiot, knowing no one knows it's me. And of course there are those hugs.

The second game in February is a close call, and it's a nail-biting final three minutes that cinches the win for our team—because over the past two months the team has become "ours." I'm absolutely invested. That has a lot to do with the guy I'm sorta dating—but not officially. Some of it is because of my hard-core-fan status of all things basketball, now specifi-cally all things Bears.

The players are great. While our PDA is on the down-low with the team at large, the occasional sneaky holding of hands or sweet exchange of kisses we share when we catch a break receive no comments or double takes.

It's empowering and sexy, and it makes the "not out in public" thing bearable.

Between school and games and work and making sure I carve time aside for Zeke as well as Kieran, I'm exhausted. But with their last game—I know, I blinked too and the month practically whizzed on by —the team cemented their entry into March Mayhem.

But it gets better.

They've kicked ass, like my chest-is-hurting-with-how-proud-I-am kicked ass. The Sweet 16 was a close call, and I was sure I was going to pass out with excitement and terror, but that was nothing on the apoplexy that threatened during the Final Four game.

Final fucking Four!

This month has been undeniably the best of my life, and I haven't even been playing. Tonight's the championship game though, and I honestly don't know how I'm going to cope doing my job on national TV while the whole time I'm thinking about Kieran and pouring every ounce of energy and positive thought I have into him and the team winning this.

"You sure you don't want us to wait for you?" My mom's stacking the dishwasher as I'm frantically searching for my keys.

"I'm good, thanks. I'll get the bus with the team, and win or lose, there'll be a party." I'm fidgeting, nervous energy thrilling through me. Mom eyes me warily, but she doesn't comment on it.

"And you've got somewhere to stay?"

I smile and fight the blush trying to creep up my neck, kind of appreciating the distraction of thinking about spending the night with Kieran rather than tonight's game. "Yeah, a few guys on the team have said it's okay for me to stay on their couch." Lying sucks. Not that I'd overshare anything about my sex life with Mom, but it doesn't mean it doesn't sting.

"That's good. And you'll be safe, right?"

She absolutely knows about Kieran and me, but like the great mom she is, she's letting me open up when I'm ready. That's not something I want to spend too long thinking about, though, as I expect it'll be in heartbreak and over a gallon of ice cream.

Even though she doesn't always believe it, my mom's doing a pretty incredible job at managing life and doing this mom gig. She was only seventeen when she had me, and I know sometimes she thinks she's screwing up in some way. But that couldn't be further from the truth.

She loves us unconditionally and works her ass off to provide us with the best life possible. And she put herself through college, with a kid, and without help from her parents or my sperm donor. Honestly, I think that makes her the most incredible woman ever.

"Always." I spot my keys under a bunch of papers and snag them. "You've got your tickets?"

She pats down her pockets. "I absolutely do. You'll have to thank Kieran again for the great seats."

With a simple nod, I offer an innocent smile. She doesn't need to know I already thanked him profusely for the gift with an intense BJ that had us both seeing stars. It was the fact that I never asked for them and he simply thought my family might like to watch the final game in the conference that made my stomach fizzle with some sort of emotion.

"Go Bears!" She fist-pumps as I'm leaving. "I can't wait to see you kitted out." I snort and wave at her, appreciating her enthusiasm. Before I can step out the door, though, she calls my name.

I glance back at her and take in her soft smile.

"I'm so proud of you."

Emotion leaps into my throat, catching me unaware. Mom's relieved the new and improved scholarship means I won't be taking on so much debt.

"Thanks."

"We'll be the ones cheering the loudest for you. And I've set the DVR."

I roll my eyes to shake away the emotion. "Secrecy, remember. It'll ruin the whole illusion if anyone finds out it's me."

She zips her lips. "I'm the queen of discretion."

"Sure you are."

She chuckles. "I so am. And that goes for anything else you may or may not wish to tell me about any tall, gorgeous member of the team."

And there it is. My eyes widen before I can school my reaction. "Uhm… yeah, nope. I'm outta here."

The snort escaping her at my expression is loud, and her grin is wide. "Have fun."

I wave again and hightail it out of there.

I go straight to college and gather my costume, still not believing we're heading to the last game of the conference. Honestly, the team have it in the bag. Other than the blip around Thanksgiving, their stats are incredible. But those stats no longer matter. Not in the final.

We're heading to Atlanta for the game. We're so lucky that the championship game is so close, only a couple of hours away, rather than a flight out. The game isn't for another eight hours and we're due to leave soon.

I haven't seen Kieran for a couple of days, so when I spot him outside the bus, the hitch in my breath is more pronounced than usual. "Hey," I greet, and when his eyes light up and he rakes his gaze over me, it takes everything in me not to step into his space and kiss his face off.

"Hey." He takes my costume from me and hands it off to someone who's loading the bus with equipment before indicating for me to step on. When he follows, I realize he was waiting outside for me. Damn, the man knows how to turn me inside out. "We're at the back," he says quietly, leaning into my space as I'm climbing the steps.

While I hold back the pleasant shudder from him being so deliciously close, there's nothing I can do about the goose bumps.

"Captain's prerogative, huh?" I tease, trying to force my brain to safer ground.

"Yo, Deano!" a couple of the guys holler, and what seem to be genuine smiles and a few high fives are sent my way as I walk by. I grin, feeling ridiculously like a celebrity, saying hi along the way. This mascot gig rocks.

When I reach the back of the bus, Kieran's housemates are there, and it seems like they're forming a protective circle almost, a barricade between where Kieran and I sit in the corner and the rest of the team.

I've never thought about it before, but it's how they've sat on the previous trips as well. "Do you always sit here, in these seats?" I ask, wondering if I'm reading into this more than necessary.

"Huh?" Confusion furrows Kieran's brows.

"You and your housemates, do you have assigned seats or something?"

"No, we sit where we want."

"And you always sit here like this?"

Searching my gaze, Kieran tilts his head. "No. This way I get some quiet time with you before the game."

Seriously, did your heart leap too, maybe do the merengue? I have no idea what the merengue is other than it's a dance, but you get what I mean. Because, seriously, Kieran Kendall keeps giving me the feels.

Rather than respond with the ineloquence of mushy words I'm sure would come, I ask, "Did you have a good training session this morning?"

For a beat, he doesn't speak, as he's paying close attention to my expression. Other than a small smile, I don't offer anything else. It's not that I'm deliberately trying to be an asshole, but whatever we have has an expiration date. The summer probably being it.

I have no misconceptions that our hooking up is anything but that.

"Yeah. We didn't push it too hard. Mainly watched some film, talked strategy." He angles a little in his seat, back to the window. "Honestly, I think it's still sinking in that we're so close to winning the tournament. Last year we got close…" He shakes his head.

"It's incredible. Your team's dynamics… I don't know, you just gel, you know?"

"They're good guys and players."

"They are." I kinda feel privileged to be able to agree so honestly. It's amazing how a few weeks can change my perspective so dramatically. "Before I got to know some of the team," I admit, "I knew you were all amazing on the court, but now, seeing you from this side, off the court and how you work together…" Struggling to find the words, I trail off.

"Not what you were expecting?"

I chuckle. "Seeing even a glimpse of the inner workings of a team has been interesting, an eye-opener even. But you guys, you're like a well-oiled machine, but… not." I snort at my inability to explain myself. "That makes it sound like you're robotic and formulaic or something, which isn't right at all. It's just now I'm understanding some of your personalities better, I see how that complements you on the court." My gaze drifts to his four housemates, who are chatting across to each other while doing their whole protective shield thing. Since I'm sure it's intentional, I realize it shows how much they care for Kieran and how they understand what he needs.

"You're a great captain," I settle on.

The pink, which I find ridiculously endearing, spreads across his cheeks. "Thank you."

I grin and sidle over to him a little, never more certain that this is actually a safe space since his housemates have his back. I like that he doesn't deflect, nor does he puff out his chest with arrogance. I allow myself to indulge in the briefest of kisses before angling away and putting a couple inches between us. It's enough space for me to comfortably rest my hand on his thigh. When he holds my hand, I gently bite the insides of my cheeks to stop from beaming.

As the time passes by, we quietly chat about our last couple of days, upcoming assignments, and random things his friends have gotten into. What I've noticed about these trips is the quiet. The team stick to hushed conversations on the way to a game. The quiet has tension thrumming through me. I have no idea what it's like for the players, but it just makes me more nervous and eager for it all to be over.

The guys are all different. Some are snoozing with headphones on, some focused on their phones, while a few like me and Kieran chat quietly. Though not once have I ever heard any conversation about the game they're heading to.

I've never asked the why of it all, and I don't plan to do so now. Superstition, I expect. Or maybe not. But just in case, I don't want to be the jinx by asking. Heck, I'm still reeling about being a mascot of all things, all because of my ability to give Kieran a happy ending.

While none of the guys have put it that way—beyond my magical cock—it's what I believe, and I expect most of the guys do too. Since I get a very happy ending each and every time, there's zero complaints from me. And after the walls I've built over the years since I was royally screwed over in my last year in high school, I'm finally figuring out I need to take the happy wherever I can find it.

By the time we're pulling up at the huge stadium, there's electricity in the air. It's eerily quiet as the bus parks, but I know that will change once the players are in the locker room and getting ready.

As the team start to stand and file off, I squeeze Kieran's hand and chance a glance at him. "You good?"

He bobs his head, his lips in a thin line and his body all but vibrating.

"What's hotter?" I whisper, startling him from wherever the glazed look had taken him.

"What?"

"You riding me or you fucking me?" The latter is not something we've done. Yet.

His pale cheeks regain some of their natural color and his eyes darken. "You want me to fuck you?"

"I'm not usually into it, but I'll definitely consider making an exception for you."

His eyes spring wide at that. "I—" He clears his throat. "Me riding you," he answers. I smile in response, but he's not finished. "Bareback."

Now that gets my attention. "Yeah?"

"Fuck yeah."

Before I answer, a quick glance around shows me not everyone is off the bus yet, but we definitely have privacy. Something I suppose I should have checked before I attempted to distract him. "How about we make that happen next week?" A whoosh of heat zips through me at the thought. I can't even believe I'm suggesting it.

"You'd do that?"

"If we're both negative, heck yes." There's a bigger conversation to have about PrEP, but considering this discussion has taken me by surprise, it can wait.

"And now I'm hard."

"And now I'm horny," I fire back.

"Key, come on, man." Tyron's voice hauls us back

to reality, and after a discreet adjustment, we get our asses into gear and head off the bus.

THERE'S SOMETHING FREEING ABOUT THE ANONYMITY OF being the new Bryson Bear. What I hadn't fully realized but completely respect was the whole persona I have to adopt, the secrecy involved, nor just what strings Coach pulled to ensure I fast-tracked training.

I have no idea what Tyron said to him or whoever, but I owe him one. Or maybe this makes up for him being such a dickhead.

Pregame, I focus on our fans and building the atmosphere. Bryson Bear used to have a signature running dance move back in the day, which I've been asked to adopt. Considering it's been a few years since the last mascot, it was suggested I add a few updated moves too.

Twerking is a hit, especially when my ass is directed at the Bluehawks team as they enter the court.

Brixham Bears aren't far behind. I allow myself an indulgent moment to track Kieran. Does he glance my way and shoot me a wink? Damn straight he does. And when the team passes me by, I raise my hand, and every single player gives me a high five.

We're making new traditions, new aspects to Bryson, and I'm quickly remembering—from years of watching the sport—why the mascot is so important at a game and to its team.

With renewed energy and soaking up the insane atmosphere, I set about keeping up with my Bryson persona. That means being a bear with attitude, while being upbeat and energetic, all without talking.

It's exhausting, and I'm melting—I'm also going to need a gallon of water soon—but with the spectators responding so enthusiastically, it's a high I never anticipated.

What's more is I'll find out tomorrow if I'm going to be offered a contract for next year too. It's something I never realized I wanted.

When the game starts, I'm able to take ten to cool down, refresh, and make a super speedy change so I can return to the game as myself. I don't know whether to watch the ball or focus on Kieran alone. Both are moving so fast.

There are no pauses, no time for any of the players to catch their breath, and it's abundantly clear why Bluehawks are a championship team.

They're phenomenal.

They're also ahead.

I wish I could say something to Kieran as he walks off the court at halftime, but since I'm already back in character, that's not possible. I just hope he knows I'm rooting for him and our team.

Come my halftime performance, I don't do anything too extravagant. Maybe next year after a whole season doing this, it'll be different. But I do the appropriate jeering with the Bluehawks mascot and work on buoying the crowd.

We're still down, frustration is high, but the game has been spectacular to watch.

Once the game is back in full swing, I can leave again. I race to change so I can watch, but the whole time dread sits heavily in my gut. There's no contest that basketball is epic, but being so invested brings an intensity I never prepared for.

There's also the nagging voice in my head that wonders if they lose, does that mean I'm no longer a good luck charm and my "skills" are no longer required. I shake my head at myself. If that happens, fuck them and everyone. My worth is not attached to me being a good luck charm and giving the team's captain spectacular orgasms.

Whatever happens, I'll deal. But fuck, I want them to win.

Ten minutes before the end of the game, I have to redress and return to the sidelines. I make it back with three minutes to spare and try to focus on building the cheers while watching the clock and our team. I'm also seriously hoping we don't go into overtime. My nerves can't take it.

It's only when the timer sounds and the scores are fixed in bright lights that I can breathe.

Holy hell. We won.

Victory slams into me as does jubilation. The roar in the stadium is deafening, and streamers pour from the ceiling.

This moment right here is phenomenal. The championship game is ours. Brixham Bears are the motherfucking champions.

My breath is knocked from me when arms grab me from behind and pick me up. It doesn't matter that I can't see who's got hold of me. I know who it is.

And hell if we're not going to have our very own celebration tonight after the real party.

CHAPTER 16
RULE 13: USE YOUR NONDOMINANT HAND TO JACK OFF

KIERAN

The trip back to campus was a whirlwind. I feel like I'm dreaming. Everything I've been working so hard for, that the team have been pushing for, has happened.

A development like this is potentially career making. While I have one more year of college basketball, just the taste of victory, at playing professionally, is starting to look more and more real.

The party is crazy, and for once, I'm all in. Not to get me wrong, I don't want to get wasted. I'm too horny for that; but I'm not ready to leave just yet.

"I'm gonna sleep for a week." Bentley spent the last hour dancing and has just crawled back to the lounge area we've commandeered. He unceremoniously collapsed on one of the couches, his head on Sammy's lap.

Tyron shoves Bentley's feet off his thighs for the third time. "You'll be sleeping for a lot longer than that if you don't get your canoes off me."

"They need to be so big to help support the size of my dick. No getting butthurt that you take a size six."

Bentley's words earn him a jab to the side from Tyron. "Fuck you, asshole. You want a dick-measuring contest, I can whip it out right now to shut you up. There's a reason why I have to use both hands to jack off."

"Are they always like this?" Dean's at my side, his thigh touching mine—all we can manage considering the wall of students at this party.

"This is them being well-behaved." I'm not even joking. We really are all exhausted, though. The adrenaline crash has hit us all hard, and Dean doesn't look much better. "Some interesting twerks earlier."

He barks out a laugh. "You saw that, huh?"

I lean in so no one else can hear. "It was kinda hot."

"I think the word you're looking for is 'ridiculous.'"

"Maybe on anyone else, but knowing it was you in the suit made it not the case." There's no denying having Dean invested and involved feels good. Before Dean, I thought I'd been giving my all. Our wins were high, my screwups minimal. Since meeting him and having him at every game and actively supporting us, I feel like I'm playing even harder while having a shitload of fun doing so.

The man makes me feel like I'm free-falling. We still have a lot to discover about each other, but with him by my side, it feels like I might have a parachute.

It's different.

Unexpected.

"You want another drink? I'm going to grab one," Dean asks, standing.

"Yeah, that'd be great. Thanks."

He smiles down at me before he steps away. With my gaze glued to his ass, it takes me a beat for me to realize Tyron is talking about me. Glancing at him, I raise my brows.

"Good of you to remember we're here." There's no bite to his words.

"Whatever, man." While it's just me and my housemates around us, there are a few other players close by, and so many other students there's no chance of privacy.

"First tournament win. Feels good, bro." He raises his Solo cup, and I follow suit, the other guys joining in.

"We keep fighting hard next season and go out with a bang." I wink and finish off my drink.

"It was Tyrel, Linc, and Maxwell's last game. Let's hope Coach gets some talent in to replace the guys," Leon says.

It's always a shitshow starting off a new season, especially making sure the team connects. Egos are always a pain in the ass to deal with too, but with the rest of the guys at my back, we'll get it sorted, and it's nothing I need to worry about just yet.

I trust Coach and know he'll already have contracts signed and filed. "It'll be fine. Coach knows where the holes will be," I reassure. "Just focus on not failing your ass the rest of the semester."

Leon launches his empty Solo cup at me. "As if I'll fail. You're talking to the wrong guy." Immediately he turns to Sammy, who flips him off.

"Fuck you, dick for brains." Sammy returns to stroking Bentley's hair, which should be weird, but it really isn't. What can I say? We're a bunch of touchy-feely guys, and I thank my lucky stars every day that not once have they displayed any form of toxic masculinity.

That doesn't mean they don't talk smack or about whipping out their dicks all the damn time. But bro-hugs and stroking of hair... meh. None of that shit matters to these guys.

The cushion shifts next to me, and I snap my head around, knowing immediately it's not Dean. Relieved it's a face I know, I smile. "Hey, Lex."

"Hey, Key. Good game. Congratulations." She presses her shoulder against mine before pulling away.

"Seriously, what about me?" Tyron sounds mortally offended by his sister.

"What about you?" She rolls her eyes for good measure, which I know pisses Tyron off. Lex really does love giving her twin shit.

"Where's my congratulations?"

"What, were you there? Playing? I was following the ball and therefore the hands that made a difference."

Tyron's gasps, the sound so incredulous we all bust a nut laughing. "No, you didn't. You take that back."

Lex makes him stew for a little while before standing and launching herself on her brother to give him a hug, ruffling his head for good measure. He splutters and complains, but we all know he adores his sister, despite her being a pain the ass at times and not able to handle her liquor.

"Okay, praise time is over. You can leave now. You're destroying my cred and chasing away the ladies."

Lex stands, a look of disgust on her face. "One, what cred? You're a lame-ass. And two—" She searches the space. "—ladies, where exactly? They're hardly lined up. You're too damn butt ugly for that."

I'm still chuckling as I stand. These guys will be at it a while, and I'm more interested in finding Dean, who's yet to return. Throwing Sammy a smirk and an up nod, I leave them to it. They'll know where I'm going.

I look for ten minutes. Not because there's that many rooms to search, but because people keep stopping to congratulate me. It's difficult not to be an asshole when all I want to do is be left alone, but I smile and say thanks.

It's when I'm being held hostage by a gaggle of girls that I hear his laughter. How that's even possible with the music coming from the next room, I have no idea, but it grabs and holds my attention. On alert, I peer around, taking advantage of my height. He's standing on the opposite side of the room next to Danny fucking Lloyd.

Honestly, I'm going to come across as an arrogant prick here, but beyond my team, I don't socialize or even know many other people. Life's busy during the season especially. It doesn't leave me room for much in terms of working on friendships.

But Danny Lloyd, I know.

Why, do I hear you ask?

I'm glad you did, because if I simply say "prize prick," you'll understand my feelings toward him. The last thing I want to do is engage in any sort of dialogue with the track star, but the fucker goes and puts his dirty hands on Dean, which has my feet moving.

Before I have the chance to speak, Dean glances over, a smile on his face.

"Hey, I got drinks."

My smile is tight, and from the furrowing of his brows, Dean sees it. "Thanks." I want to haul him away, but how do I manage that without it raising all sorts of questions? Christ, I hate this.

As if understanding my dilemma, Dean gives me a small nod before turning back to dickwad Danny. "Good to see you again, Danny. I best get these drinks back."

I can feel Danny's gaze and try my hardest to not look, but of course he doesn't make it that easy.

"And here's the basketball star of the moment. Heard you played a decent game today, *Shakespeare*."

God, I hate that name. It's lame, which is why none of my teammates use it. But him saying it makes me detest it even more. With an internal sigh, I give him my attention. "The team held their own."

The dick side-eyes Dean and tilts his head before his focus slides back to me. "Interesting."

I refuse to bite, but not Dean.

"You guys know each other?"

The laugh spilling from Danny is false as fuck. God, how I detest this man. "You could say we've run into each other every once and a while. We run in a similar sort of crowd."

"No, we don't," I deadpan.

"How about you guys?" Danny asks.

"Class," Dean says simply, his tone more reserved than a moment ago. "Anyhow, I'll see you around."

"Definitely. Actually, how about I give you my number?"

I grit my teeth, hating that this guy is playing me, playing Dean.

"No, I'm good thanks." Dean moves and stands by my side with a distance between us that I don't like.

"You sure? Us gays need to stick together and keep ourselves entertained."

"He said no." Venom drips from the fast words.

Delight lights up Danny's features, and I want nothing more than to punch the look off his face. "Never mind. A gay's gotta try, especially when they have a shot at an ass as good as yours, Dean."

The hand on my wrist pulls me up short. I don't

even realize I've made to move. Focusing on the man at my side, I discover he's not paying attention to me, but where he's gripping leaves the sexiest of burns.

"Danny, the asshole in you is strong. I didn't realize. And here I was thinking you were a stand-up guy. I suggest you take yourself and whatever else you're trying to sell here far, far away. And if you see me, pretend you don't." A squeeze of my wrist follows before he lets go and indicates for me to go ahead.

A grin splits my cheeks, and there's no holding it back. A feisty Dean Whittaker never gets old. And hell, was he defending my honor or something? If that's what that was, I'm so down for it.

When we're in the next room, I pause until he's next to me. "You just wanna get out of here?"

"Do you not need to celebrate with your team?"

"I'd prefer to be celebrating with you."

"In that case, let's go."

We turn in the direction of the exit, and I pull out my phone, shooting Tyron a text to tell him where I'm at. I snort at the eggplant and water emoji he flicks back and tuck my cell away.

As we head away from the party, the music and laughter die down. It's late, and so far, we haven't passed anyone on the way back to my place.

"So, Danny?"

"Urgh. Fuck, he's a dickhead."

"Apparently," Dean says. "I never realized until tonight."

"You know him well?" Stiffening, I wait for his answer, desperately hoping they haven't hooked up.

"Relax, big guy." He pats my chest, and I exhale. "We're in a class together. I've only spoken to him a handful of times, but never like that. How about you? It sounded like you have history?" Caution is clear in his tone.

"Yeah. I just happened to go to a club in the city last year, and he was there." The memory of it has me sneering. "He seemed to think it meant an open invitation to hook up. When I said I wasn't interested, he didn't take it too well. Since then, he's been an asshole."

"He's not said anything, outed you?"

I shake my head. "No. I thought he was going to, but it seems that a miniscule amount of decency in him exists. Maybe the recognition that there's no coming back from being a prick by outing someone."

"Well, that's something."

I snort. "Still doesn't make him less of an asshole, and then him hitting on you like that…"

"You didn't like that, huh?"

I side-eye him and see his smirk. "You caught that?" I dip my gaze to fully look at him.

"Just a smidge."

"Did it get you as hard as I am when you shut him down?"

Dean flicks his gaze and zeroes in on my dick. It's dark, so he can't see anything. My cock doesn't know that, though, and twitches happily under his scrutiny. "I think so. You can feel for yourself as soon as you're naked and riding me."

Heat surges in my stomach and tightens. "You meant what you said earlier about getting tested?"

He nods. "Yeah. I'm already on PrEP."

"I can do that."

"You don't have—"

"No." I shake my head. "I've thought about it. And we want to be safe, right?"

His "Yes" is breathy, and I wonder what it is about my answer that he likes.

"But we still said exclusive, right, no dicking around?" The thought of sharing causes a spike in my pulse. I can pretend all I want that being exclusive will help keep my sexuality to the confines of my inner circle, but it's so much more than that.

"Is that what you want?"

"Yeah." I rub my hand over the back of my neck and feel like I need to say this now before we're inside and in the light. "I like you and don't want you being with someone who's not me."

There's just a few more steps under the cover of darkness before we reach my door. When he stops, I do the same and turn to peer down at him.

"You like me as a good luck charm or…?"

There's no point playing games. I'm too tired for bullshit. Every ounce of energy I have left, I want to dedicate to having sex with Dean.

"Everything I know about you, I like. We're having fun, and I enjoy hanging out… spending time with you." Hearing those words aloud forces me to keep going, and I just hope he doesn't hate me for it. "But nothing's changed. I still plan to enter the draft, and as it stands, I do not want to be out to do so."

Silence echoes between us, but I can't backtrack or make false promises. Playing pro is my dream. I'm not going to change that for a guy I've known for a few months, no matter how much I like him.

"I know you're already eligible, but since you didn't enter the draft last year, I'm assuming you're finishing school, right?"

I nod. "One more year. The draft is usually in May." I don't ask why he wants to know or what he's thinking. All I know is when he finally nods and stands on his tiptoes, I lean down to reach him. The kiss is short and sweet.

When he pulls away, he stays close, saying, "How about we keep focused on the present and let's not think about the future? We can hang out, have fun, and if it stops being fun, we can step away with no dramas or issues."

I sigh in relief and shove away the sharp nudge in my chest that doesn't like the last few words. But this is what I want. Dean, fun, and incredible sex.

"I like how you think, Dean Whittaker."

Without any fanfare, I haul him up over my shoulder, receiving a screech and a thwack on my ass, and race the last couple of steps to the house, then charge up the staircase, unceremoniously planting him on the bed before backtracking and locking the door.

"Let's seal this plan with your dick in my ass." I wriggle my brows.

Dean's laugh is immediate, and he wastes no time stripping down and showing me just how incredible riding a dick can be.

CHAPTER 17

RULE 11: CLEAR YOUR SEARCH HISTORY

DEAN

With the semester almost over, it's time to start looking for more work. While I live in the next town over, we're still pretty much a college town, or so I've heard, and Maylene, my boss, doesn't have extra hours for me.

It would be nice to kick back and relax over the summer, but I'm trying my hardest to cut back on loans, and I want to help Zeke and my mom as much as possible. Plus, I gave in to Simone.

I gratefully accepted the paid-for flight, after her convincing me her rich parents were paying for everyone's, which that means I have an incredible vacation coming up.

"No luck?" Kieran's sitting on the floor by the

side of the bed, throwing a mini basketball into the hoop fixed to his door. Meanwhile, I'm lounging on his bed, trawling through job adverts.

I grunt and push my laptop away. "Nothing. At this rate I think I'm going to have to look farther afield and just deal with a long commute."

"There's still some time. Something might show up."

"While it's sweet when you're all smiley and optimistic," I say, planting a kiss on his cheek, "school ends in a week, so the chances of that happening are slim to 'no way is that gonna happen.'"

He snorts and angles around, settling on his knees. "You like me smiley and optimistic, huh?"

"No, it's annoying." I smack a pillow on his head, needing the distraction. If Kieran sees my face, I don't doubt he'll spot the love-heart eyes that have been sneaking into my gaze recently. No way am I telling the man I like everything about him.

Well, maybe except his feet. They're kinda gross, with his big toe being freakishly long. A few weeks back I made the mistake of sharing that with him. The big-toed freak found it hilarious to chase me around the house trying to get me up close and personal with the oversized digit.

Needless to say, I distracted him by fucking him into the mattress. I swear it's the only way to shut him up. Though saying that, when he goes down on me, that works too. Nothing like a filled mouth to get some peace and quiet.

"We still going to go watch that movie?"

Don't get too excited… it's not a date. We don't do dates. Not officially anyway. Kieran's housemates are coming with us, which we've sort of made a habit of if we want to go out. While we've never talked about it, there's safety in numbers, and it's easier to hide.

I push away my frustration. I knew what I was getting into. There's also the fact that in a week, he'll be heading home.

"Yeah," I finally answer, tucking my emotions back in the steel box surrounding my heart. "You're totally buying me my own popcorn, though."

"I share." He sounds indignant.

"Uhm, no, you're a seagull and eat almost every piece before I can get a second handful."

He narrows his eyes at me, but he knows I'm right. Off-season, while he and the guys still practice and head to the gym to get all sweaty and stinky, their eating habits take a dive. I know there's still Tyron's pizza obsession, but he's convinced that's part of his staple healthy diet. But at the cinema, it's like the guys have never seen candy before. Literally every single one of them had their arms overflowing with sugary and salty goodness last time.

I've learned it's best to get my own treats and keep them to myself.

Offering me a smirk filled with delicious promise, Kieran angles up to the bed, knees hitting the mattress. Apparently, discussion time is over.

The bang on the door has me falling back with a groan. "I swear they can smell the pheromones or something." I've lost count of how many times his housemates have cock-blocked us.

Kieran falls next to me with a grunt. "How the fuck do they know to come at the worst possible time?"

I snicker, knowing that this is so not the worst time, considering some situations we've been in when the door has been knocked on.

"What?"

If I was on the other side of the door, I'd probably not answer. Not with Kieran's pissed-off growl with that one question.

"We're going to grab pizza before the movie." I can't hold back my snort at that. I imagine Tyron was responsible for the choice. "Get your assholes covered and hurry up."

I close my eyes, half wishing they'd leave us

alone while the other half of me is laughing my completely covered ass off.

"Do you think it's too late to find new roommates for senior year? The way this is going, my balls are going to get so blue they're going to think we're part Smurf. Another year of this and we're goin—" Wide-eyed he cuts himself off, and I have no doubt I know exactly the reason why.

One year and planning ahead?

My heart's in my throat before it drops and punches against my rib cage. These are the occasions I remind myself I haven't spilled the words desperate to break free. And don't even pretend you don't know the ones I'm talking about.

"Uhm… let's get those blue balls of yours up. I could murder a pepperoni." I'm giving him the out, eager to change the subject and for this moment to not be awkward. Nor for me to crumble and beg for him to pick me. No way am I coming between him and his dream.

"Yeah." He scoots off the bed, not quite like his ass is on fire, but it's too fast for him to not be wanting to take back the last minute or so.

I'm up and we're presentable and we leave his bedroom. There's a weird tension between us. While I understand why that is, I don't know how to cut through it, change it, or go back.

The only thing I can do it sweep it under the proverbial rug and pretend the brain fart that just happened won't happen again.

I'm not the only one who exhales in relief when, as a group, we step outside into the late spring evening. Being out with his friends gives us the distance we need. Shit, should I just go home?

"You know what, I think I'm just going to head home, check in on Zeke. It's been a couple of days." Not sure I'm pulling off the natural tone, I only manage brief eye contact with Kieran, and instead focus on his housemates.

"Bro, but it's Jason Statham. The only man it's okay for me to get a hard-on for."

Pressing my lips together, I hold back my snort at Tyron. The thing is, I'm not even surprised by this statement, or anything that comes out of his mouth. I stopped being shocked or confused about three months back when he cornered me for an hour explaining the pros and cons of circumcision. I shit you not.

All I'll say is the guy has a lot of opinions, and some really screwed-up "facts."

"Okay," I draw out. "Well, it's still okay to get a stiffy if I'm not there."

"But it's weird if you're not there."

I open and close my mouth, having no idea how

to respond to that. I look to Kieran for help. But when our gazes connect, it's clear he's not paying attention to his best friend. Nope. The man is studying me, and by his furrowed brow, I kinda think he's upset… maybe.

"For the love of god, please come to the movies, Dean. If not, Tyron's not going to shut the fuck up, and he's going to be weirder than normal." Sammy's almost at the point of pleading, and even Bentley and Leon pipe up, with Leon saying he'll spring for M&Ms for me if I get Tyron to stop acting like a freak and go with them.

I sigh and simply bob my head. "Fine, but I'm not sitting next to you in the movies, Ty."

He grumbles a little, but he seems placated.

We start walking down the street, Kieran not at my side and his voice noticeably absent in that whole exchange. *Way to go, Dean.* There's nothing like making an uncomfortable situation ten times more awkward.

By the time we reach the pizza place, I'm not feeling quite so out of sorts, courtesy of Leon, who's kept me occupied talking about his internship over the summer. It sounds like a decent gig, and I can totally see him going into marketing.

When Kieran sits next to me, I relax a little more.

While I didn't think he'd necessarily distance himself from me, I wouldn't have laid my life on it.

"You good?" he asks.

"Yeah. Hungry. You?" Am I being obtuse? Maybe a little. But there's no way he really wants to talk about any of this either.

"I could eat," he says quietly, offering me a tentative smile before being drawn into something Bentley is saying.

This pizza place is a college hangout. The dough's fresh, the place bright and clean, and it doesn't break the bank. Plus, you can order by the slice if you want to.

After a debate about pizza toppings, we settle on sharing four pizzas. This is always a risk, as these guys can pack it away.

"I'll go order." Kieran stands, and the guys, me included, throw cash on the table for him. As always, Kieran hesitates before picking up my money. I shouldn't find it so adorable, but we're not technically dating, so I'm extra aware of paying my own way. He heads to the counter where there's a small queue, ignoring the second and third glances of some of the other customers. But he does engage in conversation with a guy and his kid.

"Does that ever get weird?" I ask Leon.

"What's that?"

"Going out, being recognized? Strangers talking to you as if they know you?"

A quick glance from Leon toward the counter, and he nods in understanding. "Sometimes. It can get a bit much, but it's usually worse when we've had a loss. There are a lot of pricks out there who like to share their opinion."

I cringe at the thought. "I bet they do. How do you all handle it?"

He shrugs as though he's never really thought about it before. "Just accept it's part of the game. We get great scholarships, airtime, playing a game we love. We all knew what we were getting into. But Key, obviously he wants to go pro in the League, so once endorsements are added to the mix, that's when shit's gonna get real."

It is that. There's this crazy, amazing future laid out before Kieran. Why he's fighting so hard for it is understandable.

"You're not planning on entering the draft?"

"Nah. I love playing ball and can hold my own, but the four years are enough for me. Bentley feels the same. Sammy considered entering last year, but he was having too much fun with our kick-ass team."

"What's that?" Sammy asks, probably only hearing the mention of his name.

"You loving us so hard that you decided not to

enter the draft last year." Leon quirks his brow, and Sammy simply rolls his eyes.

"Yeah, *that's* the reason." He snorts.

When he doesn't elaborate, I don't pry. Returning my attention to the counter, I see Kieran finally making our order. The girl serving him is a college student, I expect, and the way she's leaning over the counter, her cleavage exposed, she knows exactly who Kieran Kendall is. Or at least she thinks she does.

My lips twitch at the over-the-top signals she's giving, and from Kieran's ramrod positioning, it's clear he's uncomfortable.

"And does that happen to you all everywhere you go?" Amusement colors my words.

Tyron angles around to see what I'm talking about. When he turns back to me, he's grinning. "Oh yeah. Pussy on a platter."

I quirk my brow at him and shake my head.

"Getting laid isn't hard work," he continues, seeming mighty proud of himself. "The thing is trying to avoid the stage-five clingers—"

"And the hoop hos?" I throw at him.

The guys snort, and Tyron has the good grace to offer me a shifty smile. "You can never be too careful."

"What are we being careful about?" Kieran settles

in the seat next to me, this time moving a smidge closer than when we first sat. There's still a respectable distance, but I can feel his body heat. He also shoots me a soft smile.

"Hoop hos," I clarify, and Tyron throws a napkin in my direction.

"You're always gonna remember that, huh?"

"Maybe. It depends on how silent you can be during the movie," I sass.

At my side, Kieran chuckles. "Yes, let's make that a thing. All the stupid shit you do that we need to forgive you for, you earn back by not talking when we're watching movies."

"Does that mean no more ten-minute ramblings of Ty trying to remember the name of an actor, then listing off the twenty other shows or movies he's seen an actor in before?" Sammy's eyes are bright with mischief.

"Hey, you do it too," Tyron tries to defend.

"Uhm, no we don't." Sammy shakes his head. "What we do is ignore you for as long as possible, then correct the actor trivia mistakes you're making."

"Is this pick on Ty day?" The pout Ty attempts is anything but adorable. He looks ridiculous, which is frustratingly endearing.

"We only do it because we love you," Bentley sings, pulling laughter from all of us.

We carry on teasing Ty while shooting the shit. By the time the pizza arrives, delivered by the girl with her unbuttoned top, much to my amusement and Kieran's hilarious embarrassment, I'm relaxed and pleased I came out.

And once in the cinema, with my very own popcorn, M&Ms, and 7UP, I relax for the movie, thankfully not next to Tyron and happily beside Kieran, who places his hand on my thigh when the lights are out and the movie's playing.

"We okay?"

The question's changed.

I turn my face in Kieran's direction and capture his gaze. My smile is quick to appear, as is the thump in my heart when he looks at me like this, but this time it's easy to say, "Yeah, we are."

Maybe that's only for a week, or hell, maybe it is for another year. Either way, I'm still having fun, still crushing hard on the man with the intense brown eyes, and I'm just going to take each day as it comes.

If Kieran and I can break so many of our rules for each other, then I feel in my gut that this is where I'm meant to be.

CHAPTER 18
RULE 14: KNOW THE NUMBERS

KIERAN

Home's quiet, my parents are cool and let me do my own thing, and I spend a few days with my grandparents helping them out with their decorating.

And things with Dean?

Well, my plan to cool things down over the summer is laughable. I'm calling or texting him more often than I'm not. And my family? Yeah, they know something is off.

Spring is almost turning into summer in Vermont. Though just to be clear, I'm talking Vermont heat here. The days are sunny, and I'm not having to layer up quite so much when I step outside. My dad says Georgia has made me soft.

What I do consider is how I can try to make my

way back to Georgia to spend some time with a man I should be moving on from. We weren't clear with how we left things.

All I know is I speak to him every day and I miss him like crazy.

I'm on the ladder in Grams and Pops's dining room, hating painting and especially cutting in. There's no chance I'll complain, though.

"Come on down. I've made some iced tea, and your pops got back from town a while ago with some subs."

My stomach is more than okay with the break. "Thanks, Grams."

After washing up, I take a seat at the kitchen table and glance around for Pops. Just as I'm about to ask where he's at, he heads on in, trailing mud and covered in oil. I startle at the sight.

"What have you been getting into, Pops?"

Grams tsks at my side and sets about turning the faucet on for him, placing a pan and brush on the side and giving Pops a pointed look.

"Trying to fix that damn engine."

"On the boat?"

"You know it. It hasn't got me beat yet."

Grams snorts as she sits back down. "The thing's older than Kieran here. Stop being a cheap ass and buy another one." She focuses on his boots. "And if there's even a speck of mud on my clean floor, you're going to find yourself sleeping outside."

My grandparents are awesome. They bicker and cuss and love each other with such brutal honesty that I can't help but want that for myself one day. I swallow hard thinking about the man my heart leaps at and who heats my blood at just the thought of him.

Is Dean the man I could imagine falling for and bickering about leaving dirty socks on the floor with? When my pulse picks up speed, I have my answer.

"What are you looking all flushed about?" Grams's power of observation is scary. Even though she's my paternal grandma, I think my mom learned it from Grams in her twenty-seven years of marriage with Dad.

"Leave the man alone, Jean." Pops sits down, his hands clean, his boots kicked off near the kitchen door, and he's pointedly ignoring the mess he's made. "He's pining and doesn't need you all up in his business."

My gaze snaps to his, my face heating to the point where there's no denying he's right. But I'll try anyway. "What? No way, Pops. You've got that all wrong." My snort hurts the roof of my mouth. It also sounds a little strangled.

Sub raised toward his mouth, Pops stops before

taking a bite. "You think I don't know what pining looks like, boy?"

"It's true," Grams says. "When your pops headed out to Vietnam in 1970, he missed me like crazy."

"You're pretty missable." Pops winks at Grams, and while they're teasing, there's always an edge of melancholy when Pops talks about Nam. And with him mentioning that time in his life, the last thing I feel able to do is continue lying to them.

Or even myself.

"Is your pops right, Kieran? Is there a boy you're missing?"

I huff out a breath and manage a light chuckle. "His name's Dean."

Shock registers on Gram's face. "Your pops is actually right?" We glance at Pops, who's not holding back his smug smile.

"I told you that grand plan you had wouldn't last the distance."

I sigh, because Pops totally did. I'm also wondering why I open up so damn easily to them. Though truthfully, it's the same with my parents. Not to get me wrong, I know how lucky I am, and how supported I am by all four of them.

When at high school, my friends thought the relationship I had with them all was weird. I think it boils down to me being an only child. Not only that, but they're incredible human beings.

"So tell us all about Dean," Grams prompts.

So I do. I tell them how smart he is, how he has spine of steel, how he's uniquely himself. I also tell them how we first met and what an asshat I was, and how that developed into us seeing each other.

Pops wrinkles his nose and shakes his head. "I just don't understand how dating works these days, and all the terms. If you like someone, you tell them and ask them on a date. If that goes well, you ask them to go steady. Done deal."

I don't get into how heteronormative that way of thinking is, partly because I don't want to share how a BJ in a bathroom stall is how I've survived the last few years. It's not only that, though. That timeline of dating, falling in love… I wish I didn't believe it and want it for myself. If I didn't, this connection I have with Dean and how my heart legit pines for him would be so much easier to ignore or move on from.

"It doesn't always work like that though, Martin." Grams pats his arm. "Sexual liberation is a wonderful thing."

Pops squints at her. It's not quite a scowl, but it's enough to get a reaction from Grams.

"Now don't you go looking at me like that, Martin Kendall. I was nineteen when I met you.

Would I have liked to have a roll in the hay guilt-free with a few of my suitors?" Her smile and shrug are so sassy I can't help but burst out in laughter.

Pops sensibly just rolls his eyes. "All that would have done was to help you realize what a stallion I was earlier."

I bite the insides of my cheeks, happily watching the show.

"Stallion. Pur-lease, Martin. Let's limit this fantasy world you have to a more realistic creature. How about an ass?"

My laughter spills out, loud and uncontrolled. It's enough to have my grandparents focusing on me and chuckling. "I've missed you guys," I finally say after pulling myself together.

"Missed us enough that you might want to invite this young man to my anniversary dinner?" The twinkle in Grams's eyes is impossible to miss. "No pressure or anything."

"Uh-huh. No pressure."

Grams smiles. "I just want you to know if he's a good friend of yours, whether he's more or not, he's more than welcome."

Seeing Dean would be incredible, and I'd love to have him visit. I also know he's working lots, and splurging on a plane ticket won't be something he's budgeted for. I have enough knowledge of the world to know I'm privileged, just as I know his mom's a nurse and doesn't get paid as much as she deserves.

I suppose I could at least ask him. That way he knows I'm not only thinking about him, but that I want to see him.

Grams's gaze is tender as she squeezes my arm. "I have no wish for you to hurry up and settle down. You know I've never been one to push for great-grandkids."

I blanch a little at that. "Since I'm just twenty-one, I'm hella relieved."

"What I will say is love is rare and precious."

"And it's okay for plans to change," Pops adds. "While I don't fully understand why you've set yourself on the plan you have, I respect it, Kieran. And I know you're young and have the rest of your life to settle down, so I suppose I just want you to think with your heart and your head."

"When did you guys get so wise?"

Before Pops can respond, Grams answers, "For your pops it was when he married me." She follows with a wink. "Now eat your sub so you can finish off my walls. I want it done and not stinking up the place for our anniversary dinner next week."

I lift my sub and take a big bite. As I chew, I mull over what they said. I just don't know where to go from here.

I SPEND THE REST OF THE AFTERNOON DECORATING FOR my grandparents.

I don't leave until a little before six, and figure now's a good as time as any to call Dean. Since Grams mentioned the invite, I haven't been able to get it out of my mind.

"Hey."

My smile is instant when I hear Dean's voice. "Hey back. How're things?"

"Just on a break. I've only got five minutes before someone comes looking for me." Dean follows up with a light chuckle. "Everything good with you?"

"Yeah," I say immediately. Aware he's short on time, I simply dive into the reason for calling. "So, my grandparents' wedding anniversary is coming up."

"It is. Is everything okay?" Tenderness fills his voice, making my heart squeeze. Not only does Dean know how much my grandparents mean to me, but he also knows how last summer Grams had a heart attack.

"Yeah, all good. Grams is more than okay."

Air rushes through the line. "That's good."

"So, I was wondering if you'd like to come for my grandparents' anniversary dinner. Stay for the weekend maybe." I pause, but he doesn't say anything. "Uhm, yeah, it's not a big party or anything, and I may have told my family about you."

There's another whoosh of air down the line. "You told your family about me?"

Heat flushes my cheeks. "Well, yeah, it helps that Grams is a mastermind at reading me, but if you can come, then it would be awesome."

"Oh, wow… thanks." The sound of a door opening hits my ears, along with muffled voices. "Let me have a think and see what I can do, okay?"

"Okay, no pressure, though. I know it's last minute." I want to tell him I've already looked at flights and one of the smaller airlines has a sale on at the moment too, but I don't expect he'll want even more pressure.

"Okay. I'll speak to you later or likely tomorrow as I have a late shift."

"That's fine. Talk soon."

"Yeah. Talk soon."

I'm left staring at my cell, my stomach a knot of emotion. I think he sounded a little, I don't know… overwhelmed maybe? Exhaling, I tuck my phone away and concentrate on starting the car. I asked him, and seriously hope he says yes.

By the time I get home just ten minutes later, Dad's cooking a pasta dish and Mom's finishing off in the garden—something she likes doing when she gets home from work and it's been a stressful day. I focus on scrubbing the specks of paint off me, then setting the table.

I know for a fact my parents don't always sit at the table to eat dinner, but they do whenever I'm home. I used to think it was lame, but I'm appreciating it more now I'm not home often.

Dad's in the middle of telling me about the design he's working on for a hospital expansion in the city when Mom comes in, not looking so dissimilar to Pops earlier. Rather than oil coating her hands, she's covered to her wrists in soil.

"Hey, baby boy." She dots a kiss on my cheek as she's passing, only able to reach because I'm bent over to lay the cutlery. I don't even roll my eyes at her endearment. I fully expect it will stay that way unless one day I decide to have a child and it happens to be a boy. "Did you make good progress at Dad's?"

"Hey, Mom. Yeah. All the cutting in is done, and one coat is up."

She bobs her head and indicates her hands, saying, "Give me ten," as she leaves the room.

"It's like she forgets I exist when her golden child returns home." Dad's whine is totally put-on.

"What can I say? I'm pretty damn remarkable." I receive a dishcloth in the face.

"Go collect the Chardonnay from the wine fridge, smart-ass."

I salute him, avoid another dishcloth, and collect the wine and wineglasses. While I'm not a huge fan of wine, I can enjoy a glass at dinner.

"So when will you be finished with the project?" I ask as Dad's pulling the parmesan out of the fridge.

"Another couple of months at least before the designs are finalized, so it's really early days yet."

"I imagine Mom's happy you've got a contract that's fairly local."

Dad grins. "I'm not so sure. Apparently I'm messing with her whole TV show schedule."

"Best not come between her and Netflix, Dad."

"I heard that." Mom appears at the doorway, complete in pj's and wet hair.

"Dressing up for dinner?"

I receive a middle finger from Mom for my snark.

"You know, I think I preferred it before I turned eighteen and I didn't hear either one of you cussing. Did you simply wake up the day I graduated and decide the guards were dropped and you guys were going to lay it on me?" I'm totally joking with them, even though I'm also telling the truth about when it happened.

The day after graduation, my mom dropped the F bomb when she burnt her finger and carried on like nothing had happened. It had taken me a good couple of minutes to drag my jaw from the floor. Yeah, yeah, I know I've been sheltered, but it's just the way I've been brought up.

"Yes, we have a checklist every time you come home… a daily quota to achieve," Dad deadpans.

"What needs doing?" Mom heads directly for the wine I've opened and pours herself a glass.

"Looks like you're already doing it." Dad shoots her a wink.

"And I do it so well." She sits down and takes a sip, her gaze turning to me. "I received a call from Mom earlier. Said we might be having an extra guest for dinner. A friend from college."

I know my grandparents wouldn't tell my mom or dad the specifics about Dean.

"That will be nice if one of your friends is able to come out. Give me notice if it's Tyron, though." She chuckles and I join in, knowing that the twice she's spent any time with Tyron has resulted in her drinking far too much wine.

Dad carries over the plates and I take a seat. The whole time Mom is focusing on me, waiting for me to respond.

I think about Dean and my feelings for him. I also

consider how much my parents would like him. It's that thought that has me telling them the super basics of me meeting a guy and liking him. And that he might be a little more than a friend. I keep the details brief.

"Dean must be nice if he's caught your attention." Her tone is gentle, her gaze assessing. Mom takes another sip of wine. "You've always been so committed, Kieran. It's admirable. That doesn't mean you can't have fun too."

That fun remark? Well, that's based on the clear worry that was in my tone when I spoke about Dean, and me downplaying my feelings for the man.

"I do have fun."

She quirks her brow at me. "I just don't want you to look back on your college years with any regrets. You have the rest of your life to be sensible."

"Everything is reliant on me entering the draft."

When Mom purses her lips together, it means she's debating how hard to push. She's proud of me, not only for school but my basketball ambitions. That doesn't mean she hasn't expressed her worry a time or ten. It's the reason I promised to see out college and get my degree.

"So how long have you been 'sort of seeing' Dean?"

I finish chewing, and my smile comes quicker

now that I have a mind full of Dean. "We met at the beginning of the school year, had a bit of a run-in, but not long after that we started—" I don't want to say hooking up to my mom. I clear my throat. "—realized we liked each other." I can barely contain my eye roll at the words I settled on. "Like" doesn't even come close to how I feel about Dean.

That truth is becoming easier to admit. To myself at least.

"And what are his plans this summer?"

"He has a part-time job at a local diner and is doing a bit of tutoring. When I spoke to him this morning, he told me he's just taken on another kid a couple of hours a week. It means he's unlikely to be able to come for the weekend."

Mom's brows lift, and a small smile paints her lips. "Do you talk to him every day?"

"Vanessa, give him a break."

I've never wanted to hug my dad as bad as I do now.

Mom darts a look his way, but I miss whatever he's silently telling her. "Sorry," she says when she focuses on me. "I just want to see you happy, and I'm curious about the young man who's put that smile on your face."

Have I been smiling while talking about Dean? It's more than probable. I have found myself dazing away wearing a goofy smile in the last week or so since being home. And I'm not even embarrassed about it. Not really. Okay, maybe a little when it's Mom calling me out.

I offer Mom a smile, saying, "I am happy, Mom." At those words, a tightness in my chest takes me by surprise. I'm lucky and I'm grateful and we won the championship…. So considering all that, why did saying "happy" taste a little like a lie?

CHAPTER 19
RULE 1 SECTION B: NEVER MISS PRACTICE

DEAN

Queasiness is not a good look on anyone, especially not on my pale skin. I could pretend it's excitement or that I'm airsick after my three-hour flight from Atlanta, but what's the point in bullshitting myself?

This was such a bad idea, and it's going to blow up spectacularly in my face. I just know it.

When I exit arrivals, my carry-on luggage in hand, I open up the Uber app after reminding myself of the address Jean sent me.

Who's Jean, do I hear you ask?

Jean Kendall. I know, I freaked out and did a double take when I received her message last week too. There I was, just finished a two-hour tutoring session with Isaac, a nine-year-old who wanted to be hanging out with his friends rather than being schooled in math, when my phone beeped.

And now here I am, wondering how Kieran's going to react and confident it's a ridiculously bad idea that I haven't told him I'm attending the small family dinner for Jean and Martin's wedding anniversary.

This was all after me saying no initially to Kieran. But Jean is a persuasive woman, and before I knew it, I agreed to come out after all. With the added flare of it being a surprise and the addition of her paying for my ticket. By the end of the call, she'd buoyed me enough to get me excited and agreeing with her about pretty much everything.

But yeah, since then—keeping it from Kieran, checking in, and the flight—nerves are my companion.

I study the signs to figure out the direction I need to take for pickups. Shelburne Airport is small, and I'm not even convinced they do Ubers out here. Once I spot the area for collections, I follow the directions, which leads me to a busy strip. Stepping to the side, I study the app, wondering if it's too late to change my mind. I could just turn around and book myself onto the next flight to Atlanta and Kieran would never k—

"Dean?"

My head snaps up so quickly, my brain wobbles in my head and my eyes are unfocused. They must be, because it doesn't quite compute that Kieran is standing next to a Buick, brows strained high, and confusion written all over his face.

It's as if my hand is disconnected from my mind as it gives a dorky wave. After swallowing hard, I offer a lame, "Hey." Knowing it's too late to run, I force myself to straighten and focus on projecting confidence I really don't feel.

And from the way he's still looking at me, I am the last person he was expecting to see here.

"I don't…" He shakes his head. "You're here."

I nod, trying to form a natural smile. It's going to slip any minute, though, if he freaks out.

"But…" He angles his head back, studying me. "…how? Why?"

Before I can answer, his cell rings. When he doesn't answer immediately, I indicate for him to go ahead, welcoming the reprieve.

What the hell am I thinking by coming here? And as a surprise? I swear Jean is a white witch or some-thing. It's the only explanation I have for doing something so reckless and relationship-like when Kieran and I have no plans to define what we are.

"—Yeah."

I've zoned out of most of the one-sided conversation he's having, but I pay attention when he laughs, his shoulders relaxing.

"You're unbelievable." Lips pressing together don't do a great job of hiding his smirk. "I will. Yeah. Love you too, Grams."

This feels so awkward, standing here, feeling like I don't belong. At least hearing him speaking to his grams—I'm assuming Jean—I'm able to chill out a little.

Sliding his phone into his pocket, Kieran takes the few steps needed to stand in front of me. How is it possible I forgot what a giant this man is? Not being the little spoon in bed these few weeks hasn't been a fun time, not when I'd just started getting used to it.

When his lips stretch into a wide smile, his gaze no longer holding the same confusion as they did before that call, I shift a little under his scrutiny.

"Grandma Jean sure is something, right?"

A whoosh of breath escapes me. "I think you're all part of a witches coven and she's the high witch."

His laugh is loud and boisterous. "Please tell her that. It'll make her day." Becoming increasingly aware of his proximity and the softer smile he aims my way, a new flutter of nerves spring to life inside me, especially when he says, "Thank you for coming."

Surprise has me jolting. "Really?"

That soft smile of his that melts me even more is fixed on me. "Definitely. I know she's taking advantage and getting her own way with literally everything." It's hard to not lean into his space and capture his lips when he's looking at me this way. "But I wouldn't have it any other way." He glances over my shoulder before indicating toward the car. "Come on. Airport security will tow my car away if we're here any longer."

I nod and follow him over to the Buick. Before I can open the door, he takes my bag and puts it on the back seat. I smile my thanks and get in, waiting for him to join me. When he does and he's started the engine, a thought hits me.

"Why are you here? Were you due to pick someone up?"

In answer, he chuckles. "My great-uncle Alfie. Who apparently isn't coming at all." He shakes his head. "Honestly, I was confused why he'd be coming since he hasn't been to any family celebrations since I was a kid."

"I feel like I should be saying 'surprise,' maybe with jazz hands or streamers or something."

My brows dip when he looks around the area where we're still parked, wondering what he's doing. But when he leans toward me, gaze darting to my lips, I can't help the hitch in my breath.

"You being here is a great surprise." A gentle touch of his mouth against mine follows. It's over before I can savor it, but my lips tingle. He straightens up, his cheeks pink, and I'm sure mine are a similar shade. "A fair warning," he says as he buckles up and pulls away from the pick-up zone. "My family are nosey and can be a bit much."

"Considering how your grams contacted me without you knowing, I kinda figured."

"When did she do that?"

"Just last week, a few days after you asked me. It started with a text, and then she called me. Your grams is a difficult woman to say no to."

Kieran snorts as he puts the blinker on and pulls onto a main road. "Difficult? More like impossible." There's a note of sweet amusement in his voice that tugs at my heart. From what I've learned about Kieran's family over the past few months, he's close to them, much like I am with Mom and Zeke.

It's one of the reasons that I came and why my heart keeps going crazy in my chest. At least his grams knows about me. I'm not sure how or what she knows, but that she knew enough to reach out to me makes me giddy if I think too hard about it.

"How is your grams? Is she okay?"

His grams had a heart attack early last year. It's something that still plays on Kieran's mind and is the reason why he calls his grandparents once a week without fail.

"Well, if you listened to her, she'll have you believing that her heart attack was nothing more than her heart getting carried away after watching *Magic Mike*."

Through my laughter, I manage the words "No shit?"

"A bit much, remember?"

There's no doubt in my mind he's not exaggerating. I'm even more curious to meet his family. While Kieran is confident, he's super easygoing. Yes, he knows how to have fun, but he's one of the most focused people I've ever met. There's a determination that runs through him that's admirable.

What he's not is batshit crazy. Not like Tyron, for example.

"I suppose I need to ask what your family knows about me."

Kieran side-eyes me, his lips quirking. "You're here because I told Grams and my pops all about you."

My head whips in his direction. "You did?"

"Uh-huh. And my parents." The pink is back in his cheeks.

As I stare back wide-eyed, I can barely hear the engine over the volume of my pulse as it pounds in my head. What the fuck has changed since the end of school? That's not what I ask, though. "So, are any of your friends coming?"

"Not that I'm aware of, but who knows with Grams."

I smile, as he's making a legit point. "And the rest of your family?" From what he's told me, he's out to his immediate family, but I have no idea who's going to be at this dinner.

"Grams only wanted immediate family. Including you, there should be eight of us."

I exhale in relief. I can absolutely play the good friend at a restaurant. I just hope it means I get to spend some one-on-one time with Kieran while I'm here.

"It's just at their house too. Mom talked her into getting caterers, which was a battle in itself. That means it's super casual and chilled, though."

"Sounds good." It also means I don't have to be overly careful with where I put my hands. Considering my palm is currently on his thigh and gravitated there almost by its own volition, that's probably a good thing.

"I'm going to head home first. My parents are at work but will be back just past five." A quick look in my direction and how he wets his bottom lip makes me think that he has plans for the two of us in his empty home.

"You're saying I get to see the legendary Kieran Kendall's childhood bedroom?" I bounce my brows, earning me an eye roll. "Please tell me you have posters on your walls and a bunch of trophies."

"What I have is a king-size bed and lube."

Alrighty then. That shuts me up pretty spectacularly, and we drive the rest of the way with tension so thick, it's only him telling me that we're close that makes me keep my hand from reaching into his pants. Any longer, and I'd be eagerly sucking him off while he's driving.

When we pull up, I'm distracted enough by his home that I can think clearly. While I expected his parents weren't struggling financially, this isn't quite what I was expecting.

There's nothing gaudy or even ostentatious about the brick home, but it's really freakin' big, especially as I know there's just the three of them. They live on a large, quiet estate of small acreage blocks, so next door is easily three hundred yards away.

When I step out of the car, I focus on the view. "Is that the Connecticut River?"

"Yeah. Dad has a small boat. We can perhaps go out later if you want."

Wide-eyed, I glance toward the shoreline. Yep,

there's a boat. Not sure his version of small is quite fitting, though. "And you grew up here?"

"We moved when I was ten. I was pretty pissed off that we were so far away from my friends and had to change schools. As you can imagine it's quiet here, but I found a good group, and for a small school, I had an excellent coach. Plus my grandparents just live over there." He points off in the distance.

I nod, not quite sure what else to say.

"Come on. Let's get inside. You hungry?"

Mentally shaking myself, I focus on Kieran and the sweet kiss he greeted me with. It doesn't take me but a second longer to remember my half-hard dick and just what I plan to do with it.

"Hungry for your ass." I quirk my brow and step into his space, angling up to see his face.

"Three weeks is a long time."

My cock twitches happily. When he left for summer, we didn't reaffirm our exclusive status, but that one sentence makes me giddy and horny as fuck. "Twenty-two days, to be precise. Not that I'm counting." The smile he casts my way, teamed with his lowering lashes, amps me up spectacularly. "I think you better show me this king-size bed of yours."

It's pointless even trying to get a proper glance of his home once we're inside. Kieran gives no room for any misunderstanding his intentions, but when we enter his room and he ignores the bed, dragging me into his bathroom, I search for an explanation.

The red on his cheeks makes me pause, and when he says, "I wasn't quite expecting you," my heart leaps. How can such a giant, gorgeous guy be so adorable? It should be a crime, or at least he should come with a warning label.

On my tiptoes, I angle up, press my mouth to his, and say, "I'll take care of you." There's barely a second that I can appreciate the desire swirling in his eyes before he's stripping off, turning on the shower in the large bathroom, and urging me to hurry up.

Not one to keep him waiting, I undress and step behind the glass wall into the shower. I've barely got any spray on me before he's fumbling around and placing a bottle in my hands and turning, palms on the tiled wall.

Loving his eagerness, I grin and press my front to his back. While it would be hard to fuck him like this without his bending his knees and scooting forward due to our height differences, I have no issues with washing him down or working him up. Dotting a kiss on his wet back, I whisper, "You missed me, huh?"

He groans when I trail my fingers down his side and toward his front, gripping his hard cock. The man is well hung, and my asshole twitches in interest. That's still not something we've done, but I'm keen to explore soon if he's up for it.

"I really have." His voice is breathy, needy. "It's been too fucking long."

"It really has." I angle away and focus on the bottle he handed me. "Soap free, huh? I like a man who's prepared."

He chuckles, but within five seconds his laughter cuts off with a sharp intake of breath as I dip fingers between his ass cheeks and circle his opening. Kieran being this way, eager and on the verge of desperation, is a high I never knew I needed, and when I penetrate him, I savor his heavy exhale and grunt.

Tightness surrounds my fingers, and by the time I'm using three, he's pushing against me, panting. My cock is throbbing, and I'm impatient to get inside. "Bed," I grunt. "You're so ready and sparkly clean that…" Hell yes, there's an idea.

I draw my fingers out of him.

"Wha—?"

As quick as his word attempts to escape, it disappears. I suppose that's a direct result of my tongue probing his ass.

"Holy fucking… nngh…"

A chuckle sits on my chest, but no way am I stopping. Kieran's whole body vibrates, and the noises coming out of him have my dick throbbing so hard that I may just come without being touched.

The grunts, groans, and desperate pleas escaping him are a garbled mess. I memorize every sound and every shudder that racks through his body. It takes me a moment to realize he's trying to pull away from my tight grip spreading his cheeks wide.

"Cock. Bed," he grunts as he spins around. I'm caught off guard, receiving a dick slap to my cheek.

Laughter spills out of me, fast and loud, Kieran's joining in.

"Fuck," he wheezes. "You okay?"

Somehow I keep my attention away from his bobbing cock that's within licking distance and nod, still laughing. "If I get a bruised cheek, it'll match the ones I've left behind on your ass."

Reaching down, he tugs me up, his expression full of humor. "Best make a cock-shaped bruise on my ass then to makes sure it matches."

"You're such a wiseass."

"I have an empty *ass*… and a thoroughly prepped *ass*," he deadpans.

Happiness sparks in my chest. The fucker's done a ridiculously good job at making me miss not only his ass but him too. "Best get your ass dry and on the bed so I can do something about that then."

He quirks his brow. "Are we seeing how many times we can use ass in a sentence?"

I snort and grab a handful of his... butt. "You're ridiculous. *Ass* on the bed now, and spread 'em."

The smile he shoots me is disarming and full of so much promise, I have no choice but to drag him out of the shower, snatch a towel, and haul him to his bedroom. He comes willingly, of course, else me trying to literally haul the man anywhere would give me a bad back and probably turn me into a pancake when he squished me.

I throw the towel on his sheet. "So much talking about ass means we've wasted time." Besides, him dripping wet with water rivulets trickling down him is sexy. "Lube?"

"Bedside drawer on the right," he answers, crawling onto the bed. I'm momentarily distracted by his muscular backside, and when he flips over, it doesn't help at all. Kieran Kendall is breathtaking.

An amused clearing of his throat, right alongside a quirked brow, gets me moving. I don't even have it in me to be embarrassed at being caught ogling the man. No chance of that when he's what wet dreams are made of. What makes it better is that he's currently all mine.

Lubed and before him, I work my coated fingers back in him. The time in the shower was well spent;

he's more than ready for me. On my knees and angling toward him, I line myself up, watching where I nudge my cock against his balls, then his taint, until I'm finally where I want to be.

Flicking my gaze to his, our eyes connect. With his bottom lip caught between his teeth, he paints a perfect picture of need and desire. Ensuring we don't lose contact, I breach him. The dark pink of his lip turns a lighter shade as he bites down harder, and his eyes widen before becoming half-lidded.

There's almost no resistance as I push farther, so much so, I'm in balls deep, my dick throbbing, and I'm holding my breath.

"I need you to fuck me."

I huff out my breath, my body shuddering at the sensation. Fuck, I've missed him. Missed this.

"You doing all right there?" The man's being dicked yet still manages to throw me a knowing smirk.

"My cock's missed your ass a little too much," I admit, hardly recognizing the sound of my own breathless voice.

The asshole shifts his hips, effectively pulling back before slamming against me.

We both groan.

"It's missed you too." Some of the cockiness is

gone, and he reaches out and puts his palms over my hands that are gripping his hips.

I need his mouth.

I angle down, and he leans forward a little to help me reach him. The kiss is messy and hot and fucking perfect. It's also enough to get my hips moving. After a couple of thrusts, I angle back for more leverage. Each push into his tight channel notches up my desire; each gasp and moan that escapes from him has me falling deeper and knowing it's too late to pretend like I'm not all in.

"You want my hand or my mouth?" Each word is breathy.

"Nngh… hand. Wanna come with you in me."

Holy shit, when he says such things, exposing himself this way, I want to give him everything that's mine to give.

Latching on to his cock, I focus hard on not missing a thrust, working my hips and hand in tandem. "Lift your thighs," I instruct, and he does so immediately, giving me a new angle. I drive hard and deep and welcome the fire coursing through me.

Finally Kieran gasps, "There," and I double down my efforts, pegging his prostate and needing to come so bad that I'm worried I'm going to pass out soon.

"Fuck." I grunt and moan. "Fucking come all over me."

His gaze snaps to mine, his mouth opens, and he's coming. Spurts of cum shoot out of him, covering my hand and his chest, and I'm seeing stars. I don't want to close my eyes, but it's impossible to not disappear into the orgasm, get lost in the welcoming heat and flames that embrace me. I shudder and gasp and am finally able to peer down at Kieran.

He drops his legs, but my attention is drawn to his content smile. Catching movement, I focus on his finger trailing down his chest, running through his cum. He then holds his finger out to me.

I smile, my cock twitching valiantly as I lean down and draw his finger into my mouth. Pulling away with a pop, I rake my gaze over every inch of skin I can see. "Let me lick you clean, and then I'll wash you down again in the shower."

His smile softens even more, and as I follow through and lap at his coated skin, I can't help but wonder how different things would be if the world he envisioned for himself included me.

CHAPTER 20
RULE 3 SECTION A: NO DATING

KIERAN

I owe Gran a shot of her favorite whiskey. She's unbelievably stealthy, and I've never been more grateful for her interference. Do I feel like an idiot for not even considering inviting him here myself or reaching out to organize a visit sooner? Maybe. Okay, the answer sways closer to yes, but he's here, my ass is deliciously sore, and I'm grinning so wide that Mom keeps throwing me knowing smirks.

Am I embarrassed?

No. It's as simple as that.

I like simple, and being here at home, away from college and hundreds of bodies and possible cameras, I can finally relax and marvel in the wonder of simplicity.

Yesterday we went for a walk before my parents got home, held hands, and skimmed rocks. And after a flying visit to my grandparents and then an introduction to Mom and Dad, we headed out on the boat and made out under the stars.

"So how's the tutoring going?" I turn on my side and trail my fingers down his arm. The mild summer sun caresses us as we bob in the lake. I've taken us to a sheltered spot that tends to be quiet, even with summer break in full swing.

"It's okay. I'm not loving it as much as I hoped I would. The kids hate it, which probably doesn't help."

"I bet. School work in summer sucks."

"That it does." He latches on to my palm when my fingers caress his hand, and I smile into the touch.

"How's Zeke?"

"He's good. He's working my diner shifts for me this week." A sultry smile follows his words. "I may have promised him some ball time with you one weekend."

I chuckle. "He can have more than one weekend since it means I get to keep you for the week."

The blush that colors his cheeks is impossible to ignore and deserves my attention. I lean over him and trail kisses up his neck to his cheeks, absorbing the heat that touches my lips. Dean's breath catches, and my heart constricts.

With emotion in my throat, I angle to peer down at him. At the movement, his lashes flutter open and he no longer has to squint as I'm offering him shade.

"What is it?" He tilts his head, his tone light, the volume barely more than a whisper.

I swallow hard, pushing aside the bubble of fear in my stomach as I think about Pops's words. "Go steady with me."

Do I feel like a fool? Well, yeah. But my embarrassment lasts for barely a second as the sweetest of smiles appears on his mouth. It then turns into a full grin, and I know with that reaction, I can expect some teasing.

"You want me to be your boyfriend, Kieran?" He quirks a brow, and though he's grinning wide and I hear the lightness in his words, that he's breathing faster can't be ignored.

"I don't know if 'boyfriend' is a strong enough word."

His brows shoot high, and he wraps his arms around me, grasping my naked back. "What are you saying here exactly?" Every murmur of teasing evaporates in that one question. With his gaze darting around my face and the widening of his eyes, he's never looked more beautiful. Handsome doesn't do this moment justice.

"I… I love you, Dean." Heat prickles my skin as I take him in, watch his reaction. But the words are out there now, between us, and there's no taking them back. While I've known I've felt this way for a while, it feels right to share them now. He's already changed so much for me, and I want to give him this. My truth.

His gaping mouth isn't the ideal reaction I'm looking for. The seconds feel long and awkward, and I'm beginning to flounder, beginning to—

"I love you." The words have barely hit my consciousness when he's both angling and tugging me close, his mouth connecting to mine. I groan into the kiss, relieved at the contact, and so fucking happy it's possible my heart is going to break free from my chest.

Despite the urgency running through my veins, the kiss is soft and slow. It's as though I'm kissing him for the first time. I explore his mouth while I luxuriate in the emotion of feeling so much.

When he wraps his legs around me, I sink into him, to this moment, to knowing that this is real and it's happening. My brain blanks, and I struggle for breath, tearing my mouth away.

He's gasping too, and as I stare down at the man

who absolutely has my heart, I know for sure there's no way I want to be without him this summer.

"Don't go back home."

"But Zeke—"

"Let's fly him out."

"What?"

"I'm serious. He can stay here for the summer. He'll love it by the lake. It means your mom doesn't have to worry about him and neither do you." I know his mom works as many shifts as humanly possible. Dean's also told me she hates that Zeke's left to his own devices so much.

The expression he's directing my way is hard to read. There's a sinking feeling in my gut that he'll say no. I open my mouth to speak, but he beats me to it.

"I have commitments, a job."

"I know." I bob my head and don't want to sound like a privileged prick, as I have no first-hand experience of all he's gone through. With that in mind, I choose my words carefully. "But your hours were reduced over the summer, right?"

When he nods, I keep going.

"And I'm sure if you need to find some work locally, as I know that's important to you, you'll find something. Hell, Mom will give—"

"I'm not asking your mom for a job."

"Okay," I say slowly. "Fair enough. But there are

plenty of kids around the lake who I'm sure you could tutor a few hours a week. There's also a whole bunch of diners in town."

Since he remains quiet, I hope it means he's taking my offer seriously. I'm more than aware I could head back with him, but the quietness of my home has given me a taste of what it's like to be out with Dean. I want to hold on to that for a while longer before I figure out what my next play is. And selfishly, I'm hoping I don't need to make a decision until the end of summer.

"But will your parents be okay with us staying?"

"Yes. They already love you."

His smile is soft. "After one night?"

I press a kiss to his nose before pulling away to him twitching it. "Yes, after one night, and maybe me talking about you constantly the last week." It's true. After I finally opened up to my parents, conversations about Dean all but poured out of me. Maybe just knowing I could talk about him made it difficult to hold back my words. I don't know, but I don't doubt for a second my parents will open their home to Dean and Zeke.

"You really want me here?"

I expel a breath, feeling him submitting. "You and Zeke."

And that does it. Dean melts into me. We're back

to kissing and he's tearing at my shorts, tugging them down and sucking me off. I happily go with the flow, a grin on my face, my cheeks flushed, and my eyeballs rolling back in my head.

By the time I'm going soft in his mouth and trying to get him to pull away so I can suck him off, he eases off me, a cat-that-ate-the-canary smile on his face. I glance down when he gets on his knees, seeing his spent cock poking out of his shorts.

"Ugh," I grumble. "I missed you jacking yourself off." There's a legit pout in my complaint. I fucking love seeing him wrap his palm around himself.

"I'll let you lick me clean." He waggles his brows, and he's clearly joking, but screw that. In his next breath, he's exhaling with a laugh as I tug him up my chest and inch him closer to my face. And when I do exactly as he suggested, his laughter abruptly dies, and I take delight in working him up all over again.

This time so he shoots his load in my mouth.

"This," I say as I come up for air, "is exactly how I want to spend our summer together."

TINA ORGANIZED FOR AN EXCITED ZEKE TO COME AND hang out for the summer. The multiple conversations included Dean sharing that we're officially dating but we're keeping our relationship quiet. Plus, Tina talking to my mom.

After two weeks of having a boyfriend and spending our evenings muffling our faces in a pillow to stop from being loud, it's absolutely the best summer ever. Each day we're laughing and goofing off, and when Dean isn't tutoring the couple of kids he's taken on for four hours a week, I hang out with Zeke, usually shooting hoops.

"Call Simone and add me to the list. I'll sort my own flight." Do I sound as whiney aloud as I do in my own head? But can you blame me?

While I knew that his Mexico trip was coming up, I never dared dream it was possible to go with him. But some things have changed. One of the most important things is me spending as much time with Dean as possible, and doing that on a beach in Mexico? Hell to the yes.

I don't really know Dean's college friends all that well, and that's one of my arguments. "I feel bad for stealing you away all the time. You know my friends so well." It's true, since he practically lived at my place last semester. "This gives me the chance to get to know them."

Dean doesn't appear to be so convinced. "And how are you spinning this?" He points between the two of us, and I immediately understand where his concern is stemming from.

"If they're your friends and you trust them, then we tell them the truth."

Surprise morphs on his features, springing his brows comically high. "Really? You're okay with that?"

Rather than answering immediately, I absorb his words. The thought of coming out in the League still makes a ball of dread form in my gut, especially from the latest news I really shouldn't be listening to. But it's impossible not to be curious about Tim Delaware. Sure our sports are different, but the reality I'm sure is the same.

Each article or Tweet I read that focuses on his sexuality and his boyfriend heightens every fear I have. Too many people lose sight of the sport and of the athlete, focusing instead on his sexuality.

And the amount of "does he top or bottom?" bullshit I've read compounds that even more.

Exhaling, I answer truthfully, "I love you." Immediately everything about Dean softens. "I'm happy for your close friends to know, but I'd appreciate it if they kept our relationship quiet." I don't miss the hurt in his gaze, but he follows up with a nod.

"I understand. And I do trust the friends who are going."

"So that's a yes?" Excitement flares to life in my gut. Fuck, I hope he has skimpy swimwear. That's something I can totally get on board with.

"That's a 'let me check with Simone.'"

I grin wide. That's totally a yes.

"I'll fly back with you to Atlanta with Zeke and then we can fly out to Mexico together." When his lips twitch but he remains silent, I prod him. "Admit it, you're excited about sun, sea, and all the sexy times we're going to have."

Dean rolls his eyes and passes me a bottle of water. "It does sound tempting." He follows up with a heated kiss, which is abruptly cut short by a splash of cool water.

We both startle and pull apart, becoming aware of Zeke's laughter. He's hanging on the side of the boat. "Do you guys ever stop?"

"Nope," I shoot back, standing and sticking out a hand to pull him up, then tying the canoe to the boat to stop it floating away. "Have you not seen how hot your brother is?"

Zeke proceeds to gag. It's over the top and hilarious. "Uhm, no he's not."

"Hey," Dean calls out, throwing a towel at his brother. "Shut it or else you can swim back."

Zeke pulls a face and flips him off, and I return to

my place next to Dean. Leaning into his side a little, I take his hand and place it on my lap.

The guys banter back and forth for a while, and I occasionally snort at whatever jab they're making. If I had a brother, I'd like the sort of relationship they have.

"What do you think?"

"Huh?" I glance at Dean, who's sporting an amused smile.

"The sun getting to you?"

"Not quite."

"I asked if we should head back in. Your grams was less than subtle about us paying her a visit today."

"I told Pops I'd help him work on the engine." Zeke blushes a little. He does every time he calls my grandad Pops, something both Grams and Pops insisted on. If I could love them any more for being so welcoming, I would. But my heart's already over-flowing.

I also don't have the heart to tell him the engine is a lost cause, as he's enjoying the time with Pops. Even if Dean hadn't whispered that to me one night when we were talking quietly in bed about everything and nothing, I would have known myself. Zeke's not the greatest at keeping his feelings locked down.

I know Dean loves that Zeke feels like he doesn't have to.

A quick look at the phone tells me it's almost lunchtime, and since Grams makes a mean sandwich, I'm keen to head on over. "We can go straight there rather than docking at my place." I glance at Zeke. "You want to stick with us, or are you going to jump back in the canoe?"

Zeke looks uncertain and glances at his brother.

"You don't have to canoe. You can stick with us."

Relief appears on Zeke's face, and I notice that while Zeke can be mouthy at times and appear like a confident kid, he also looks to Dean a lot. Whether it's reassurance or the go-ahead, I'm not sure.

"Cool." Zeke nods and eases back. We've been out for a few hours, the majority of time Zeke canoeing around the lake, usually within shouting distance. He's hung out with a couple of other kids who are a similar age to him from around the lake a few times, but he seems to like to spend time with his brother too.

It doesn't take long to head over to Grams and Pops's home. I'm mooring our boat when Pops steps out from his shed carrying something mechanical. Once again, he's covered in oil.

"Perfect timing," he says by way of greeting. "I could do with a pair of useful hands."

Knowing full well he's not talking about me, I sling an arm around Dean. "Come on. I know when I'm surplus to requirements."

Dean chuckles, and Zeke's smile is big. We leave them to it and make our way to the house. Grams is in the garden and stops what she's doing when she hears us approach.

"Hey, boys. Take these potatoes in and get them washed up. I'll make us a potato salad for lunch."

I take them from her and plant a kiss on her cheek. When I move away, she's tilting her face, expecting the same greeting from Dean. His smile is soft, and he sensibly doesn't leave Grams waiting.

"You need me to help you out here while Kieran takes those inside?" he asks.

That offer right there is one of many reasons why I love him and why a million times a day my heart skips a damn beat.

"You sure can, Dean."

I leave them to it and head inside, switching on the radio once I'm in the kitchen. As I'm scrubbing the potatoes, the news comes on. There's the usual old things—political bullshit, a visit from a foreign prime minister, and a raid resulting in multiple arrests. It's only when I hear the mention of Tim Delaware that I pause what I'm doing and pay proper attention.

As I'm listening, I grip the sink and frown. My frown morphs into horror as the story unfolds.

Tim Delaware's boyfriend, Jack Flemming, was attacked in a parking lot. Two people have been arrested, and Jack's in the hospital for non-life-threatening injuries.

"What—" One look at my face has Dean cutting himself off, and it's clear he's listening to the report. He pulls out his cell.

The report switches to another story, with no real details given. "Holy shit," I say, feeling invested in anything even mildly related to Tim Delaware. I have since last year when he came out.

Dean steps toward me, still focused on his phone. "This report says the attack is being treated as a hate crime." His gaze snaps to mine. "It was in the parking lot at his place of work. Apparently he was working late." Dean shakes his head, knowing I've taken an interest in Tim and his career. "Shit, did you know he's a social worker?"

I shake my head. While I knew Jack Flemming wasn't in the sporting world, just how much of an ordinary guy he is didn't really compute. A fucking social worker, so I'm assuming a half-decent guy at least. A man with an everyday job.

Not unlike Dean, especially when he graduates and pursues a teaching career.

"Why do they suspect a hate crime?" I swallow hard, not really wanting to know the answer but unable to help myself.

"Graffiti on his car, apparently." Tucking his phone away, he steps into my space and wraps his arms around me. I mirror his movements, savoring the connection and his warm body. "Why are people such hateful shits?" He holds me tighter.

Exhaling and taking a calming breath, I press my cheek against the top of his head before dotting a kiss there. "I don't know why some people have so much hate in their hearts." Sadness coats my words. I can't imagine how Jack Flemming is feeling, or Tim Delaware. All I know is if something like that happened to Dean, I'd lose my shit. And if it happened to Dean because of our relationship, I'd never forgive myself.

The door opens, and we part, Dean moving to my side. He doesn't fully let go. Instead, his arm snakes around my waist.

Paused in the open doorway is Grams. As always, she doesn't miss a thing or fail to read the room correctly. "Beer or hard liquor?"

God, I love her. Her words pull a smile from me, and Dean chuckles lightly at my side. "Beers would be great." I peer down at Dean, who must feel my movement so glances up. I ask him silently if that's okay with him, that he wants a beer. He nods, his smile tender.

Grams makes me sit my ass down, hands me a beer, and Dean reluctantly follows suit after a failed argument from him to finish preparing the potatoes.

"So, my boy, what's going on?" She sends me a pointed look before turning to the sink.

"Last year a baseball player came out that he's gay."

Grams nods, her back still to us. "That's very brave of him. 'Course, we all know it's absolutely bullshit that he has to be brave to do such a thing. The world needs to get over itself and let people simply be."

Dean squeezes my hand. "Maybe one day, Grams." A flush coats his cheeks, not dissimilar to his brother's reaction at calling my grams that. "The world's not quite there yet. It has its positive to being a twink and a little on the camp side."

I angle to look at him, and he shrugs, a bitter-sweet smile on his face.

"Sure, it means I feel vulnerable more than I like. I'm usually outed with one look. But I figure that comes with the pro of not having to contend with the weight of coming out or not. Most assumptions, about certain aspects of my sexuality at least, are usually correct. It makes being forced or feeling forced to stay in the closet all but impossible."

While my heart aches for Dean admitting he feels so vulnerable, I understand his version of the truth. Grams shifts, pulling our attention back to her.

"A twink? Is that like a Twinkie? What am I missing?"

It's impossible to not be amused by Grams. I leave this to Dean to answer, though. I'm a good boyfriend like that.

Amusement fills his voice when he says, "It's a term used fairly commonly in the LGBTQ+ community referring to a man, well, a man who looks like me."

My attention is completely on his face as I roam his expression. "So gorgeous."

Dean's grin is wide. "Well, obviously." He focuses back on Grams. "A gay guy who's smaller built, and slim, and looks… young, I suppose."

"Huh." Grams studies him. "Looking young should never be something to worry about."

"Oh, I'm not worried. Nor do I mind the term. I know some people do, but not me."

I stand and pull out a pan for Grams, to save her from bending, then fill it with water for her. She pats my hand when I'm done and indicates for me to leave her to it. Once my backside hits the chair, I take a pull of my beer, my mind drifting to the man beside me and his experiences as a gay man.

They're so very different to my own.

"And what is it about this baseball player that got you looking like it's the end of the world?"

My heavy sigh slips free. "The player's boyfriend was attacked yesterday and is in the hospital. There's not that much detail yet, but two men have been arrested and charged with committing a hate crime."

Grams stops placing the potatoes in the pan and stares at me, her eyes wide before they narrow. "For being gay?"

"Yeah, and I suspect for being in a relationship with a professional athlete."

"You don't know that," Dean says immediately. There's a sharpness in his voice that takes me by surprise. When I glance at him, he holds my gaze. "You don't. And either way, it doesn't matter. The men have been arrested, and I hope will receive more than a slap on the wrist."

"But it does matter." I shake my head. "The chances of Jack Flemming being targeted have got to be a shitload higher because his boyfriend is a pro baller, and fans don't like to be reminded players can like dick."

"Anyone who did this is not a fan." His voice is steady. "Whoever did this is a bigot and violent and hateful. Someone who's capable of that could just as well attack someone walking out of a queer club."

There's no room for negotiation in his words, but I don't believe them. I also know this is a conversation that won't get us anywhere but more frustrated.

The sound of a chair shifting at the table startles me. Worry creases Grams's lined brow. Hating the look on her face, I force a smile. "It's nothing to be concerned about, Grams." There's no need to build her anxiety by letting her know homophobic attacks are on the rise. What's the point?

She studies me, but whatever she's working out, I think she keeps to herself as she says, "Maybe we can send this Jack a gift basket."

Dean settles his palm on my forearm and squeezes. I know exactly what he's thinking.

"You know what, Grams, I think that's a great idea."

The smile she throws me was worth my agreement. Sure, it's strange sending someone we don't know a gift basket, but kindness matters, right?

"Perfect. You find out the best place to send it, and I'll get everything organized." And then she's off, standing again and picking up her iPad from the side table.

"Are you going to be okay?"

In response to Dean's quiet question, I take hold

of his hand and kiss his palm. "With you and Grams on my side, definitely."

A slow, tender smile lifts his lips. "I am at your side, on your side, and your grams is fucking amazing."

"She's the best," I answer. "And so are you."

CHAPTER 21
RULE 12: NO SUBSCRIPTION PORN

DEAN

WE ONLY HAVE A COUPLE OF DAYS LEFT BEFORE WE leave Vermont. The plan is to fly with Zeke home, then jump on a flight the following day to Mexico. Yes, that's a definite we.

After I spoke to Simone, who gushed like an awesome person, I then touched base with Lester and the other couple of friends who are heading to Simone's birthday celebration. Every single one of them promised to keep quiet about our relationship.

Did it suck asking them to do so? It should come as no surprise the answer is yes. This relationship I'm in breaks every promise I made myself. After high school and the jock who shall never be named, I was 100 percent determined to never be in a secret relationship. My experience with that is humiliating. At the time I thought I was heartbroken, but being in love with Kieran, I know now that's not the case.

But still, I'd been crushed.

Simone's been firing off texts most of the day about a couple of day trips, and I think I'm sending her the right emojis in response, but really I'm focused on the cost and hoping it doesn't break the bank.

"Why do you look like someone's kicked your puppy?" I snap my attention to Zeke. Armed with a huge bowl of popcorn and a soda, he sits beside me.

It's late afternoon, and we're just about to put on a movie. Kieran's gone to pick up a new boat engine with his dad and pops, his mom's out visiting her friends, so it's just the two of us. As it's been a while since we hung out, I'm more than happy for Zeke to pick the movie. I just want the time to chill with my brother.

"Do I?"

He crams a handful of popcorn in his mouth. "Uh-huh," he says around a mouthful. After swallowing, he lowers his brows. "You had this deep concentration thing going on. Are you constipated?"

He snorts out a laugh when I shove him. "No, asshole."

"Who are you messaging?"

"Simone."

He nods while munching away. "Mexico. You're so lucky." There's a note of envy in his voice that immediately makes me feel guilty.

"Yeah, I am."

Pausing midchew, he frowns at me. "You deserve to be lucky, though."

Warmth fills my chest. "I do, huh?"

"I can begrudgingly admit how hard you work. You deserve to have a break."

I lift my brows and indicate around the luxurious media room we're in. "This isn't a break?"

"Well, yeah, it's a break away from home, but you've still been working."

Zeke is such a good kid. Not to get me wrong, he can be a real pain in the ass, but I know more often than not he'll do things like cook dinner for Mom if she's working overtime, something he's been doing more of since I started spending virtually all my free time with Kieran.

Not wanting my mood to bring Zeke down, I ask, "And have you had a good summer?"

"Definitely." He grins. "A few degrees warmer would have been good, but it's been great." There's hesitation on his face when he stops talking.

"What is it?"

"Kieran's mom and dad said I'm welcome to spend next summer here too, if it's okay with Mom."

I'm not even surprised by their generous offer. Kieran's parents are incredible. They're kind and thoughtful, but hell, next year… My chest constricts a little. So much can happen in a year. And next summer Kieran should have been drafted. While he will have the summer off, I have no idea what that means for us. The last thing I want to do is put an expiry date on our relationship, not anymore. Not now I love the man.

"That's great of them. Perhaps we need to wait until next year to confirm."

His brow furrows. "Why? You think Mom will have a problem? She's FaceTimed Vanessa a heap now, and they seem to like each other."

"I think Mom will be fine with it."

He stares at me expectantly, but what the hell do I say?

"A lot can happen in a year," I settle on.

At my words he just seems more confused. "What's that mean?"

I sigh at the determination I hear in his voice. It's there in his eyes too. "It's… I don't know. Kieran may not be home next summer. He'll probably be moving to whatever League team he's going to be joining. It'll be a big move, and he'll be busy. Once he's in the

League, that's it. All his time and focus will be on the game and fitting in with the team."

Zeke scrunches his face up and angles back a little. "He won't be too busy for you or his family, and that won't mean I can't come here."

I hold back the pained sigh that's trying to break free. Between Kieran's reaction to the recent news report about the baseball player and me knowing full well he has no intention of coming out, all I want to do is snap or cry. But there's no way I'll do the latter.

"You don't know that." As soon as the words are out there, I slam my mouth shut. There was a bite to my words that should not have been directed at Zeke. I'm the one who keeps having internal freak-outs, and I know better than to let loose my inse-curities.

There are a few beats of silence. "I thought you guys were tight, all sickeningly loved up."

A sigh too heavy for my soul escapes. "We are, and I do love him."

"And he loves you, right?"

I bob my head and don't even try to hide the sadness from my voice when I say, "Yeah, but some-times love isn't enough."

Zeke seems to absorb those words as he looks away, staring blindly at the blank screen. "That's depressing as fuck."

His words are so deadpan that a loud snort tears from me. I don't even have the heart or energy to reprimand him for cussing. Instead, I offer, "Yeah, Zeke. It really is."

Despite some of my anxiety about Mexico and the cost, Simone's constant texts have successfully built my excitement. And when we finally arrive at the resort that can only be described as opulent as fuck, I have no drama relaxing.

"I could so get used to this." It's day two, and we're having a morning to ourselves. Not only because I need some quiet time, as it's been a manic and alcohol-infused trip so far, but Kieran's not been himself.

The plan is to finish this massage with a very happy ending, right here on our large private balcony. Then I'm going to get the truth out of him.

Kieran, on his stomach on the sun lounger, grunts his approval and sighs into my touch. Every inch of available skin is covered in coconut oil, and most of mine is too since I'm sitting on his thighs and period-ically gliding my dick through his butt cheeks.

Every time I do, I receive a delicious, needy moan from him.

Working my fingers over his skin, I glide them over his muscles and push my hands up toward his neck, leaning forward at the same time. My rock-hard dick wedges itself between his ass cheeks, my stomach flush with his back, and I rock a few times.

What I don't expect is for him to shift his ass, which locks on to my dick. I grunt. "Fuck. This is my show." I trail my fingers down his side and shift a little, rubbing over the globe of his perfect ass.

"In that case, fuck me already."

I nip at his shoulder. "You want me inside you?" With my words, I trace his rim. A shudder ripples over his body.

"Yes, so much."

I reward him with a finger, then two. I've already done a little work on prepping him. What can I say? A thirty-minute massage is too long for me to fully behave.

My fingers are slick, and there's virtually no resistance, so I enter a third.

Kieran shudders and angles his ass. "I love your fingers in me," he says with a groan. "But right now I really want your cock."

Clearly having enough of my teasing, Kieran uses those divine muscles of his to shuffle to his knees. This is after freeing my fingers from his tight channel.

Like the best boyfriend ever, his ass is high in the air, his head low on his arms.

"Holy fuck." That right there is awe in my voice. Every single time I see him like this, giving me his all and making himself so vulnerable, I hold on tight to the image and the memory. "You're so fucking perfect."

When he waggles his ass at me, I laugh, and he turns his head to look at me. Fire and amusement are in his gaze. "Perfect for you, and the most perfect ass you'll ever have," he sasses.

"That's the absolute truth," I say, repositioning myself and lining up against him. "How about me and my cock, the best you've ever had and will need?" I nudge against him, need rippling up my skin, while absolutely aware he's yet to answer me.

A little trepidation creeps into me when he remains quiet. I wish it didn't, as I know what we have is incredible. I'm also aware that we've never talked about this before and now isn't the perfect time.

"You're the only one I've ever had or will need."

His words are so quiet they take a moment to register, and when they do, I freeze, my breath whooshing out of me. It takes my mouth opening and closing a couple of times before I can form words. "I'm your first?" Breath, right alongside emotion, catches in my throat.

When he doesn't say anything, I tap his thigh and ease back.

"What?" he immediately says, and I can see enough of his profile to know he's embarrassed.

"Look at me."

For a moment, I don't think he will, but after a beat, he turns. His dick is still hard, his face bright red, and I just know it's taking everything in him to look me in the eyes. I stand and hold out my hand to him. Confused, he takes it, and when he does, I tug him, indicating I want him to stand.

"Where are we going?" He has a death grip on my hand, and that's okay.

When we're next to our oversized bed, I gently push him back and encourage him to scoot his ass up. While there's a glimmer of uncertainty in his gaze, he's totally on board with us being on the mattress.

I follow him and settle on my knees between his spread thighs.

"Your silence is freaking me out, Dean. I've never known you this quiet, ever."

I offer him a smirk but quickly sober. "I can't believe I didn't know."

The shrug he gives is a little too nonchalant. "That just means I'm a natural, right?"

Amusement bubbles in my chest, right alongside tenderness. "You absolutely are." I lean forward and kiss his chest, his neck, and then his mouth before pulling back. "I wish I'd known."

There's no longer an embarrassed flush in his cheeks, which I'm pleased about. "But why?"

"I would have like to take care of you better." I think back to our first time, but nothing in my memory screams his discomfort. All I remember is a bucketful of cum and my brain turning to mush.

A gentle smile lifts his lips, and he reaches up and cups my cheek. "You took care of me perfectly. You always do."

While it's a relief to hear, I don't know, I like to think I'd have savored it more or something, made sure I committed every breath, twitch, and groan to memory.

"Is it a problem, that you're my first?"

Surprise punches through me. "Hell no. I fucking love that I'm your first."

At my words, he sits up and manhandles me so I'm sitting on his lap, legs around his waist. "I love you." His breath fans across my mouth.

"I love you."

Just as I lean in to capture his mouth with mine,

his words steal my breath. "I'd like to think you're my last too."

There's no more thinking, no more analyzing, no worrying about us being too young, too naïve.

We're slippery with oil, and I want Kieran so badly that my hands shake as I reposition myself and slide inside him. Using every ounce of restraint I have, I move slowly, my gaze never shifting from his. Easing in and out of him, I try to pour everything I feel into every touch and every whisper.

Maybe this can be enough.

Love.

Unspoken words.

Declarations of forever.

I want to believe. Want so desperately to hold on to his words and this moment.

So I do.

"I want you to be my last too." The words come out on a jagged, whispered breath.

With his bottom lip pulled between his teeth, he nods, gaze earnest, and he pushes against me.

"Touch yourself," I plead, needing him to go over the edge. Heat coils inside me as I watch him jack himself off, and when he grunts, I focus on his face. His eyes are half mast, his bottom lip almost white, and I swear on all that is gay and magical, he's never looked more beautiful.

And then he's coming, and my brain stutters, body shaking, and I may black out as I all but collapse on top of him. Warm arms wrap around me, and he's petting my hair, dotting kisses over my head, and I'm sure this is it. The beginning of the rest of my life.

I don't even have the energy to laugh or scoff at my fanciful, romantic notion. How can I when I want it to happen so badly?

"That was…" I can't even finish, but it's enough to earn me a squeeze.

"I know."

Those simple words pull another content sigh out of me. "Shower?" I reluctantly ask, knowing I really need to ease out of him, but my dick is so happy where it is.

"Shower, then food."

Pressing my mouth on his coconut-scented skin, I ease out of Kieran. "Come on. I wouldn't want you to waste away."

"No chance of that with you filling me up three times a day."

My laugh is loud in the quiet room, covering the sound of the close-by waves. Still smiling, I stand and head for the bathroom to turn on the shower. A moment later, Kieran joins me.

We soap up and wash each other down, delaying

the likelihood of lunch anytime soon. When I'm working on cleansing his back and removing all traces of oil, I recall Kieran's quietness since being here.

"I know you've said you like my friends and are comfortable with them, but are you sure everything's okay?"

He angles to look at me. "Did it not just seem like everything was more than okay?"

He's got me there. It's only been the last half hour or so that the strange tension between us seems to have evaporated, though.

"More than." I follow up with a kiss on his shoulder. "But before that. You were quiet before we left Vermont."

Do you see that? There's a flicker of something, some sort of emotion on his face. I wait him out, wait for him to reach whatever decision he's trying to make.

When he turns around, I ease back a little so I don't have to angle my neck quite so much.

"I heard you talking to Zeke."

Puzzled, I shake my head. "About what?"

"A couple of days before we left, when I got back from picking up the outboard with Dad and Pops."

Oh. *Ooh.* I clamp down so I don't explain myself. I

absolutely will, but clearly what he heard me say has been weighing on him.

"You said love isn't enough."

Immediately, I shake my head. "No. I said *sometimes* love isn't enough."

"Isn't that just semantics?"

"No, it's not. It's literally sometimes it is and sometimes it isn't."

The expression on his face makes it obvious he's calling bullshit. "The way you spoke made it sound like you don't expect us to be together next year."

And there it is.

My gut tightens. This conversation is inevitable, but I kinda wish I could click my fingers and make it go away.

"Do you not think what we have is real?"

My brows shoot high. "Of course I do." I reach out for him and stand on my tiptoes. We're still not eye to eye, but we're a little closer. "I love you and want to be with you." I search his gaze. "And everything you just said while we were in bed, I want that so badly."

"Do you follow up that statement with a but?"

Unable to resist and hating the concern in his voice and his tense muscles, I wrap my arms around his neck. "Not a but exactly. More an…" I struggle for the right word. With no idea if I pick the right one, I offer, "…uncertainty. But not about my feelings for you," I'm quick to add. "More about what happens at the end of next year."

He must have known this was coming, as his understanding is immediate. And as we stand there under the spray, my toes aching and my heart bouncing around in my chest, I try not to hold my breath.

"You keep putting yourself last."

Shock has me falling flat on my feet and stepping out of his arms. I'm also seriously confused. "What?"

"You've told me enough about your one relationship in high school for me to know how much the guy hurt you. Not only did he refuse to step out of the closet, he proceeded to humiliate you in front of the whole school." He shakes his head and honestly, I have no idea how to feel. "You're worth so much more than that."

Tears spring into my eyes, emotion clogging my throat. I manage a shaky smile, saying, "I know I am." And fuck, I love that he knows it too.

"I've been asking you to do the same."

Fear turns the blood in my veins to ice.

"It's not okay. It's not fair. And it's so fucking wrong of me."

I frown. "But it's different." Isn't it? I'm not sure anymore. "Your family and friends know." That alone is a million miles apart from what I experienced with the asshole in high school.

"And when I join the League?"

Fuck. I can't do this here. The warm water is doing nothing to heat up my chilled body. Reaching out for the tap, I turn off the water. "Let's get dry." I step out, avoiding eye contact.

The huff that follows me is frustrated, but he follows me without saying a thing. We dry off, and as soon as I'm back in the room, I pull on my shorts. Already feeling vulnerable and uncertain, the last thing I want is to be naked.

"Will you let me finish?"

I cast a glance at Kieran as he ties a knot in his swim shorts. When my gaze meets his, I can't deny him, especially as he's right and this is something we should talk about. Taking a seat on the bed, I smile, letting him know I'm not pissed off at him.

The relieved expression he offers me helps settle my pounding heart.

He reaches out for my hand as he faces me, sitting on the mattress. "I think I'm going to take a job at Mom's company once school's finished up. She has an office in Atlanta."

So startled by his words, I forget to breathe. By the time I remember, I'm gasping for air and Kieran's gone a little pale. Despite my panic, I thread calm into each word when I ask, "What exactly are you saying? You mean over the summer?"

The alternative is not even conceivable. But when he shakes his head, a slow but firm no, my heart plummets, and that ice in my vein boils to fire.

"No." The word punches out of me with such power, I think we're both taken by surprise. "No fucking way are you giving up a chance to go pro. I just—" I shake my head, cutting myself off from the need to start shouting and swearing and maybe shaking him a little too. "I swear to all that is fucking holy, Kieran Kendall, no way in this lifetime will you pass up entering the draft. This is your future. Your dream. I will not now or ever stand in the way of that."

Red spreads like wildfire over his skin. "I know you won't stand in my way. I'd never expect you to. But I'm not prepared to lie about our relationship. I can't. Not anymore. Every time I can't do something as simple as hold your hand, I want to punch myself."

I have no choice but to slam my mouth shut. Everything in me is desperate to shout at him, demand he come out, which would mean the problem's solved, but I can't. Won't. That can never be my decision to make. If he wants to talk about it, I'm here for him, always. If he wants support to do it, I'll be there every step of the way.

That all has to be on his terms, though. He has to do it for him… maybe a little for us too, but this is his life.

"You not going pro is unacceptable," I simply say. Obviously, if there was a different reason he chose not to enter the draft, then he'd have my support. But not like this, for me.

Does the fact he's even saying this make me want to pounce on him, hold him tight, and make him promise to be mine forever? Of course it does. I've never been more certain that Kieran loves me with everything he has. But I can't allow him to make this decision because of me.

When he closes his eyes and leans in and presses his forehead to mine, my heart cracks open a little. I hate that he's hurting. Not only that, but he's shaking like a leaf. I wrap him up in my arms, and with his face pressed against my neck, he whispers, "If anything was ever to happen to you because you're dating a League player… if you were hurt… or fuck, even the thought of you being harassed…" His words fall away, and the realization of where all of this is coming from hits me.

He's frightened, and I think for the first time ever,

his fear of coming out is no longer for himself. No, it's his fear for me and my safety.

A tear slips down my cheek, and I hold him tightly. "Oh, Kieran." I sniff and shush him. "That's not going to happen, but if anything ever did happen"—his hold on me tightens and a sound of distress escapes him—"that would never ever be your fault. Ever." Angling away so I can see his face, I understand his agony, as I feel the same way. I attempt a small smile, saying. "While I never planned on falling in love with you, I've always known what I'm up against. And if that means we need to stay quiet for a little while until something changes, then I'll do that. Not just for you, but for us."

"No."

I huff out a laugh. There's only a touch of humor in the sound. His no sounds remarkably similar to mine. "But that's not your decision to make."

"Nor is me not entering the draft your decision to make." There's a stubborn set to his jaw that I've never seen before. It's seriously hot, and I wish it wasn't.

"Urgh." I fall back onto the bed. "You're impossible."

He follows suit but turns so he's on his side.

When he tugs my forearm away from my face, I don't resist. "You're impossible, and I love you."

The fucking, fuckety infuriating man…

"Just shut up and kiss me," I order. There's nothing I can do about any of this for the time being. Plus the draft deadline isn't till April. While Kieran knows I have a stubborn streak, I don't think he'll realize just how unbreakable that is.

How determined I can be.

But he will.

And with that final thought, I accept his heated kiss and wrap myself up in Kieran Kendall. This guy is an endearing fool, but he's mine.

CHAPTER 22
RULE 1 SECTION A: KEEP YOUR EYE ON THE PRIZE

KIERAN

"How's your tlayudas?"

Dean covers his mouth, still chewing. "Delicious."

"My mouth is having an orgasm," Simone says, and does this happy, humming dance in her seat.

"It's good, but not the best thing I've ever had in my mouth," Lester says, surprising the hell out of me. Out of the group of friends, he's the quietest. While his phone is constantly out and usually in use, he's not that talkative. It makes his response even funnier.

"No way I'm asking you to elaborate when you're wearing that smirk," Dean fires back, snickering and shaking his head at his friend.

It's been a couple of days since Dean and I pretty

much said forever while ironically coming to an impasse about how that future might look. For the time being, we've agreed on a truce. That means we're both ignoring the conversation ever happened and are instead focusing on soaking up the sea and relaxing in the resort.

And what a place to spend a vacation.

The hotel is exclusive. While I have no idea who Simone's family is, I have a feeling my family would appear like paupers in comparison. Last night at dinner, Tony Mason, a TV actor, sat just a couple of tables away. Apparently a big-time movie director was here last week too.

"So, plans tonight?" Simone rubs her hands together. It was her birthday yesterday. We had a night of dancing and so many drinks, Dean and I were competing for access to hug the toilet bowl. Yeah, it wasn't pretty, so be grateful I don't share the details with you.

It took most of this morning to recover. While I don't drink much due to training, I'm not usually this much of a lightweight. It may have something to do with the tequila, though.

"No tequila," I say quickly.

Dean snorts and reaches over to squeeze the back of my neck. "Put you off for life, huh?"

"Hasn't it you?"

He shrugs. "I'd say yes, but last night wasn't my first rodeo with tequila."

"Apparently there's some sort of cocktail party or something tonight," Lana suggests. "They've also got live music in the bar."

Sounds good to me.

Believe it or not, we have explored a little and ventured off the resort, but did I mention how nice this place is?

"I'm game for cocktail tasting and listening to music." Simone picks up her beer. "And maybe some dancing too." She clinks bottles with us all before taking a sip and returning to her food.

As I carry on eating, I keep casting my gaze over to the man by my side. He's grinning at something Lester said and tilts his head back in laughter. He's relaxed tonight, and the way the twinkling lights surrounding us and the flickering of candle flames on the table light up his features just so, he looks exceptionally sexy.

The place could easily be romantic… if it was just the two of us.

"I can feel your eyes on me."

Instead of glancing away, I offer a relaxed smile. "Is there a problem with that?"

The roll of his eyes doesn't remove his small smirk. "Nope. Take your fill."

I place my palm on his thigh, and he takes the cue and holds my hand. "We should definitely take a vacation at some point, but just the two of us."

"I'm more than okay with that as long as it's somewhere cheap."

Automatically, I scrunch up my face, but he shakes his head. "I'm just saying, you and me alone on vacation, all we'll need is a room and a decent-sized shower. Oh, and room service. Anything this fancy would be a waste of money."

"Well, I can't argue with that." Unable to resist, I steal a kiss. Dean hesitates a moment before I feel him relax, just enough for a lingering kiss.

A napkin thrown at our heads has us breaking apart, chuckling.

"No making out at the dinner table while there are single people present," Simone whines. "You guys are too hot for your own good, and together…" She shudders dramatically and fans herself.

Dean flips her off and throws the napkin back.

We continue eating, talking about going back to school. We're all going to be seniors, so it's going to be a full-on year.

It doesn't take long for us to clear our plates and head to the bar. Lana spots a high table, and we soon have enough high-backed stools to sit together comfortably. It's far enough away from the music that we can talk without shouting, but close enough that there's a fun ambience.

We're on our fourth cocktail, something sickly sweet and with a name that sounds like something I'd like to do to Dean. My lips a little looser than they were an hour ago, I lean in to tell him as much. "Cock sucking cowboy…" Startled eyes snap to mine. "How do you like it?"

"It's sweet." Dean doesn't quite pull off being unaffected. That may have something to do with me squeezing his thigh and my pinky brushing across his covered dick when I whispered the words to him.

"I think I could totally rock a Stetson. What do you think?"

By the way the browns of his eyes turn molten, I think he's imagining that in vivid detail. Just as he opens his mouth, Simone snort laughs and Lana pats her on the back.

Even though they've interrupted our sexy-talk time, I chuckle at their antics. It takes me a moment to realize that Dean has gone stiff at my side. Flipping my attention to him, concern beats at me at the expression on his face.

His eyes are wide, mouth a little open, and shit, if I didn't know any better, I'd think he'd clocked out. "What is it?"

His hand does this flapping thing, and he smacks my arm.

"Dean, you're freaking me the fuck out. Dean." The worried sharpness of his name drags his gaze to mine.

"Holy nuts. Ryan Broadwater." The grip he has on my arm is fierce.

"What?"

"Ryan Broadwater, Eagles player, is sitting right there."

I almost fall off my stool with how quickly I turn in the direction he's indicating. There's no subtleness to the move, and holy shit. He's right. Broadwater is right there. The League player. Holy shit. Sweat breaks out on my palms.

This guy is freakin' legendary. He's an amazing player. And he's here. Like thirty feet away.

"What the hell are you doing?" I wheeze out the words, panicked that Dean is already out of his seat. "Whatever you're thinking, no. You can't just go up—"

"Uhm, hello, sure I can."

"But he's clearly on vaca. You can't just go over and ruin his night."

"How will it be ruining it?"

I shrug. "Because he won't want to be hassled."

He eyes me a beat, lips pursed before it morphs

into a smile. "Hearing fans thinking you're awesome will not ruin his night. Trust me." And then he's walking over to where Broadwater is sitting with another guy. "Dean," I whisper hiss, but his back is straight, and I just know he's pretending not to hear me.

Dean loves the Eagles. Like hard-core follows the team. For me, on the other hand, it's Ryan Broadwater I could happily worship. While the Eagles aren't my team, I follow them enough to know almost everything about them. And Ryan Broadwater is one of my favorite players.

Simone catches my attention. "What's going on?"

I shoot a wide-eyed stare at her. "Ryan Broadwater."

Her brows dip in confusion. "Who?"

I gape, my voice weirdly high pitched when I say, "You don't know—" I shake my head. "Never mind. He plays for the Eagles."

"Eagles as in the basketball team?"

I nod, feeling a little unhinged.

"And what's Dean— Oh shit, he's heading this way, and has two men with him."

Heat rushes to my face, and I have no idea what to do.

"Kieran," Simone says pointedly and does an up nod, her eyes wide.

Fuck my life. I need to pull myself together. Wiping my hands, I knock back my cock sucker and stand, only to be greeted by Dean, who's worrying his lips and not looking at all as mesmerized as when he first left.

I stiffen. If either of these guys was an asshole to him, I don't give a shit who Broadwater is, I'll—

Dean takes me by surprise by stepping into my space, whispering, "I'm so fucking sorry."

"What?" I reach out and cup his cheek, wanting to comfort him.

His eyes widen at the contact, which I find even more concerning. "I outed you. I didn't think. I told them you were my boyfriend."

Understanding flutters to life, but since I'm here caressing his cheek and there's not enough space for a piece of paper to slide between us, my body as well as my heart already made my decision for me.

Ryan Broadwater, a League basketball legend, is going to know I'm a gay college student who has a sexy boyfriend. I smile, acceptance rather than terror rising to the surface. "You are my boyfriend, so I'm more than okay with that." For good measure, I press my lips against his and then ease away when I feel the presence of Ryan Broadwater.

And sure, while my nerves are regretting the spicy food mixed with cocktails, I relax my shoulders and reach out my hand to shake Ryan's. I can totally do this.

"BUT I'M NOT WILLING TO DO THAT TO YOU… TO US. I won't lie about loving you."

Am I a little embarrassed about that declaration? Maybe, but with the way we ended the night and how Dean keeps repeating those words, albeit in an amusing attempt at copying my voice, his smile is worth my flaming cheeks when I made the declaration in front of Ryan Broadwater.

And get this.

Ryan Broadwater and his *boyfriend*. Yeah… I know. I'm still reeling.

But when Dean and I got into it in front of our friends and Ryan and Nate, pretty much airing our laundry about me not entering the draft and Dean stubbornly arguing he wouldn't let me not and saying he'd keep our relationship secret, my heartfelt words had spilled free.

I meant every single word.

The shocker though was when Ryan made a similar declaration. Not only about his sexuality but also about his love for his boyfriend, along with his intention to marry the guy.

"Say it again." Dean is extra clingy this morning. It seems he likes it when I'm bold and confessing my love for him. That's more than okay with me. The epic blowie he woke me with this morning was an additional boon.

"Seriously?" Despite my groan, I glance down to where he's sprawled out half on top of me and smile.

In answer, he bats his eyelashes, which are currently mascara-free.

"Have you got something in your eye?"

He digs his fingers in my side, and I yelp and laugh and take hold of his hands to stop him. "Fine." I roll my eyes, but I give him what he wants. "I won't lie about loving you."

Bright, wide eyes peer up at me, and I have to admit, I like this whole breathless thing he has going on. "Fuck… hottest words ever." He plants a kiss on my chest, and while my cock valiantly stirs, there's no way I'm getting hard anytime soon.

So many orgasms in such a short amount of time are awesome, but I'm spent.

"What time is it?" I ask instead. We didn't arrange to have breakfast with our friends this morning, and I know that's a couple of times I've said "our" now, but it feels like they are. It's amazing what quality time and acceptance can do for accelerating a friendship.

Dean grabs his phone off the bedside table. "Just after eight."

"Do you want to go snorkeling or something today?"

He bobs his head, focus on his phone.

"What are you doing?" I ask when he shifts and sits up in bed. There's an expression on his face I can't read.

"I'm on Ryan's Instagram page."

That gets my attention, and I sit up too and lean in.

"He's posted a video… about an hour ago." And then he hits Play.

Ryan's on the beach, the early morning sun obvious in the wash of orange across the sky.

"Before I head back Stateside, I just wanted to share with you all that I'm gay. This is something I've wanted to say for a long time, and I'm in such a good place that it's a relief to be at this point that I can tell you the truth…"

"Holy shit," I say over the video, blanking out and not hearing anything else he has to say. "He's really done it." Energy vibrates under my skin, and I don't know if that's a good or bad thing. All I know is I need to do… something.

I clamber out of bed, tugging on my shorts.

"Kieran, what—"

My quick glance at him cuts him off, and understanding registers on his face. Shit, maybe I should ask him to explain this to me, as I have no idea what the hell is going on. What I'm feeling. Or even why it feels like I need to break out of my own skin.

"Why don't you go for a run? I'll grab us breakfast, and we'll eat here when you're done."

Dean's calm voice helps me breathe, and I'm so grateful he knows me so well.

With a nod, I tug on my running shoes and press my lips to his waiting mouth. "Thank you," I say, pulling away.

The gentle squeeze on my arm is just what I need. "I'll see you soon."

Exhaling, I nod, and head out, aiming for the beach.

As soon as my feet hit sand, I aim close to the shoreline where the grains have compacted, making it easier to run. With my head buzzing, I run until my loud pulse tries to drown out my thoughts. It doesn't work exactly, my thoughts persistent and almost shouting at me.

"Kieran Kendall. Next year I expect to see your name in the draft."

"I'll try my hardest."

When I responded to Ryan last night, emotion had slammed into me so hard, my knees had nearly buckled.

Fuck.

I slow down, breathing hard, and bend over, dragging in air. Falling back into the sand, my ass hitting the damp grains, I bend my knees, drawing in ragged breaths and staring out into the ocean.

Why is this all so hard?

Why the fuck am I so scared?

I still hate myself for it.

Focusing on the lapping waves and then farther away where the ocean meets the horizon, I attempt to get my head and my heart in order.

That Ryan's come out is incredible. Do I feel hopeful? Absolutely. Did I previously try to talk myself into being the second out League player? I did.

Ryan Broadwater is close to retirement. He has over ten years on me. Does it make me an asshole to know that next year could be his last, so where would that leave me?

Feeling my phone vibrate in my pocket, I remove it. Tyron is calling.

"Hey, Ty."

"Dude, Ryan Broadwater. You see it?"

"Yeah. I kinda saw him in the flesh too." I figure I can say that now considering his video is all over social media.

"For real? In Mexico?"

"Yeah. Last night was crazy. Actually had drinks with him and his boyfriend."

"No fucking way? Was he cool?"

"He was. They both were. His boyfriend's Australian too."

He's quiet for a beat, no doubt absorbing this new information. "And how are you?"

There's no point in acting clueless. Tyron has been my best friend for three years. Over that time we've talked about me coming out, and he knows my reasoning, my fears. I'm not sure he'll ever fully understand them since he's not queer, but his heart's in the best place imaginable.

Obviously now my fears have morphed to include Dean, wanting him safe and not touched by anything that could hurt him.

"Freaking out. Nervous. Excited. Fucking terrified."

"And what about Dean?"

"Supportive. Understanding. He's trying not to show his excitement and is failing miserably, but he hasn't asked me what my plan is." I also haven't shared with anyone, other than Dean—well, that was before yesterday's drink—my intention to not enter the draft.

And that's for all of the reasons you can imagine. It's also because, once I say it out loud to my teammates, the hollowness in my chest grows. Just the thought of changing the trajectory of my future fills me with an emptiness I can't fathom.

But to be without Dean would be like a black hole taking root in my chest.

Love… it's no wonder why so many songs and poems and stories are created as an ode. Before Dean, I had no clue what the big deal was. And not once did I think it would feel like this. Being in love, people's reaction to it, I don't know… it all felt like an overreaction. Something I'd roll my eyes at.

Oh, how naïve I was.

I wouldn't want it any other way, though.

"He's a good guy. I have no reservations in asking, though." I snort out a laugh as Tyron continues, "So what are you going to do, Key?" When I don't answer right away, he says, "Listen, I'm not even gonna pretend I know what you're going through, but the League is your future, and by the sounds of it, Dean is too. And whatever you decide, I've got your back. The whole team has."

"I know. Thanks, Ty."

"See you in two weeks, loser." He follows up with a chuckle and ends the call. Almost immediately, my cell rings. Admittedly, I sigh, but when I see it's Grams, I pick up.

"Grams, hey."

"Kieran, how's your vacation?"

Speaking to Grams always has the power to pull forth a smile. "Good, Grams. Hot, but perfect."

"And that man of yours?"

Like pretty much always, the mention of Dean helps me relax. "Enjoying himself. We think we're going to go snorkeling today."

"That sounds like fun. Make sure you wear sunscreen."

I chuckle. "I absolutely will."

"Sorry to be interrupting your vacation, but there's a reason I called."

While there's nothing off in her tone, I tense, hoping there's not a problem. "Is something wrong?"

"No, no. Nothing like that. It's just, I received a lovely phone call from that nice young man we sent a gift basket to in the hospital."

"Jack Flemming? Tim Delaware's boyfriend?"

"Yes, that's the one."

"Oh… wow."

"He called to say thank you."

I'm confused about how he got her number, but knowing Grams, she would have put it on the card.

"He also said he wanted to give us a couple of tickets to one of his boyfriend's games. I told him I have a wonderful grandson who'd really appreciate them, even though he's basketball obsessed."

I snorted. "I just bet you did."

"Anyway, I told him you were currently on vacation but would be heading straight back to Georgia for college. This is when he put our call on loudspeaker, and you know, Tim is also such a lovely young man. Once he heard you were in college and an athlete, he offered you tickets next week for their game."

"Holy… as in Philly?" While I wasn't a big baseball fan, I knew the game was coming up.

"The one and only. Apparently at next week's game, the one in Philly, they're going to do some sort of LGBTQ rally or cheer or something. Honestly, I'm not sure what they meant exactly. Anyway, I gave him your number. I knew you wouldn't mind, so expect a call."

My mind stumbles a little. The last twenty-four hours have been a serious whirlwind. "That's incredible. I forgot to ask, is he okay? Jack, I mean?"

Grams sighs. "He is. He's at home. He did need a few stitches, but he says there's no broken bones, and when I asked about the awful pissants who were responsible for his injuries, he said they hadn't been granted bail."

"That's a relief." I have to admit, I'm hella curious about the man. That he called my grams is wonderful.

"It is. I made sure to invite them both for a visit if they're ever passing through or needed to get off the grid."

Warmth sparks to life in my chest. Of course she invited them for a visit. "That's great, Grams. Thank you."

"Right. I'll leave you and Dean to it. Enjoy your last couple of days, and make sure you let me know when you've arrived back at school."

"Will do, Grams. Love to you and Pops."

A couple of loud kisses reach me, and the call ends. I stare at my cell, a growing flutter emerging in my stomach. And that flutter? I'm pretty certain it's growing hope, offset by a hit of bravery.

CHAPTER 23
RULE 3 SECTION A: NO DATING

DEAN

I'm not worried.

No, seriously, I'm not.

Honest.

Breakfast of pastries and fruit is covered and waiting to be eaten, and I'm sitting here, distracting myself with social media. Kieran went for a run an hour ago, so I know he'll be back soon, but shit, last night was surreal.

But I'm not worried.

Do you think I keep saying that to convince myself to feel that way?

I hate to agree with you if your answer is yes, but I'm mildly freaking out. Only mildly though, so that must count for something.

Kieran Kendall loves me. That's something I'm absolutely not concerned about. It's everything else that's so in the air that's making me itchy.

Heck, is it too early for another fabulous cocktail like I had last night?

I sigh and head out to the balcony. Maybe the ocean view will relax me. Five minutes in, and I'm back to watching mindless videos on TikTok. There's a couple from Zeke that make me snort, and I watch a few from some gay couples I only recently found. Since Kieran and I have been together, it's funny how even my TikTok algorithms have changed.

Let's not get carried away though and think I'm being all saintly. My feed is still chockful of hot guys, but there are noticeably more sweet and sometimes cutesy couple-y things I'm enjoying watching. I blame Kieran completely for putting love hearts in my eyes.

When I mentioned as much to him a few weeks back, he wasn't even apologetic. He did give me an incredible BJ, though, as recompense. These love hearts are totally worth it.

When I hear the door open, I almost fall off my chair in my haste to get up. Eager much? But, okay, I've been worried. I admit it.

My nerves are more shot than I've let on.

"Hey." I head back inside to greet him. The sweet

smile he shoots me whacks me in the chest. Not only does it constrict my heart, but a heavy rush of air leaves me. "You're looking delectably sweaty and lickable." It's easier to respond to the physical until I know where his head and emotions are at.

"I can promise my sweat is all kinds of gross." He chuckles. "But I'm happy to share." He's on me before I can even blink, wrapping his arms around me, kissing the ever-loving crap out of me and doing a magnificent job of sharing his sweat.

I don't even care that it's kinda gross. Not when his tongue is sweeping against mine.

Far too quickly, he breaks the kiss. Leaving me in a panting mess is unacceptable, but it seems he has other ideas when he says, "I'll let you shower me down if you can guess who I just spoke to on the phone." He waggles his brows, and there's a flush to his cheeks and a sparkle in his eyes that wasn't there when he left.

Is that something I should be jealous of, him reacting this way to someone else's phone call? But from the way he's still holding on to me and stroking his fingers up and down my back, I expect not.

"Tyron."

Kieran's face scrunches up. "Well, yeah, but that's not who else I spoke to."

"Well, since you didn't determine the rules, strip

naked and let me lather you up." When I start tugging on his shorts, he chuckles and clamps down on my hands.

"Guess again."

I huff out a breath. "You do like to change the rules, huh," I tease.

From the narrowing of his eyes, he knows I'm referring to so much more than this conversation. Those narrowed eyes quickly morph, and a cat-that-got-the-cream smirk appears instead. "Only where you're concerned."

I gasp, only slightly over the top. "Please tell me I'm the bad influence in this relationship." I grin so wide, I'm sure I look slightly unhinged, but amusement is sitting so heavily on my chest, I can't keep my emotions locked down. "Holy shit, am I a bad boy? Fuck, I've always wanted to be a bad boy."

The laughter that bursts free from Kieran is raucous and slams into my heart, making it difficult to contain my love for this man. When he's calmed down enough to speak, he says, "Please don't ever call yourself a bad boy."

My attempt at acting offended is ruined by my chuckle. "Does it not make you hard thinking about your boyfriend being a *bad boy*?" I aim for breathy, and even to my own ears it sounds gloriously ridiculous.

"New rule. You can say it, but in front of Tyron and the guys. Their reactions will be so worth it."

I pinch his muscular butt. "That's just mean."

"And you've distracted me so much my sweat's dried and I'm starting to stink."

My nose twitches, and I can't help but inhale, not when he says things like that. It's practically a challenge. "How can you smell so ripe so quickly?"

His mouth drops open, and a mischievous glint appears in his gaze. Then the asshole is dragging me close and rubbing his chest over my face. I splutter, cussing and shoving him away, all while laughing so much I get a mouthful of his sweat.

Eventually he sets me free and steps away quickly, hands up defensively in the air.

"Yeah, you better step away, ripe-ass." The twitching of my lips negates my nonexistent threat.

"So, this call."

I roll my eyes. "You think I still want to lather you up after that?"

"Well, since you stink now, maybe I'll lather you up instead."

This idea has merits I can totally get on board with. "Gale Sutton," I say randomly.

"What?" he says, laughing. "Why the hell would Gale Sutton call me?"

I totally grabbed on to the name of a League

player who I knew played with Ryan Broadwater, since the man is still on my mind. "So that's a no?"

"That's a no."

"Come on. Get your ass in the shower and you can tell me. I'm bored of this game." I head to the bathroom, pretty sure his gaze is on my backside.

Once we're in the shower, he shocks me silly when he says, "Tim Delaware."

"You're shitting me?"

"Nope."

I shake my head, wondering when this became my life. "I don't under… Oh, is this about his boyfriend. Shit, is he okay?"

"His boyfriend called Grams about the gift basket." My surprise must show, as Kieran chuckles, saying, "I know, I was surprised too. Just remember that the both of them spoke to Grams."

Just the reminder of that fact already makes everything so much clearer. White witch, remember?

"The Rams are playing in Philly next week. Tim's paying for our travel and an overnight stay in a hotel, as well as giving us two tickets to the baseball game."

"He is? But why?"

"I think they're just good guys. I think they were touched that Grams reached out to them, and I suspect Grams probably wrote them a letter or something. You know she has a lot to say and love to give."

Happiness bubbles in my chest. "She really does."

"Turn around so I can wash your back."

I do as instructed and drop my head when he massages my shoulders before working his fingers over my skin. Everything about Kieran's touch is perfect.

"So yeah, are you up for it? I said yes and thank you, but also said I needed to check with you."

My heart speeds up. While curious to know how he referred to me, I'm not going to ask. There's still a need for self-preservation. In truth, I'm still half expecting for the other shoe to drop. These emotions are on me, and I have no intention of laying them on his shoulders. Not to get me wrong, I could, and Kieran would do everything in his power to make it right.

He knows I want him to pick the both of us—me and a career as a pro basketball player. But I am adamant he has to make this decision when he knows in his heart it's the right one to make.

"That's incredible. I'd love to go."

"No arguing about not paying your way?"

I turn around and tap his perfect abs. "Don't be an asshole."

"I'm not. I promise." And from the widening of his eyes, I'm sure that wasn't what he intended.

"Good. Sometimes accepting a gift with grace and without fuss is the right thing to do."

As he tugs me close, his lips twitch. "You want me to give you a gift right now?"

Since my cock stirs and nudges him, it answers for me. And I'm happy trying to live in the moment and take each day as it comes. And speaking about coming, hell yeah, my boyfriend gives me one of the best gifts possible.

KIERAN'S BEEN IN CONTACT WITH TIM BY TEXT. THEY'VE messaged back and forth a few times, and it's nice to think that whatever he decides to do, he'll have connections who understand his perspective in some ways better than I ever will.

We flew into Philly a couple of hours ago and have since checked in to the hotel. Kieran's already told me it's the same hotel Tim and Jack are staying in, and we're going to meet them for drinks later.

It's weird but admittedly cool, and I'm happy to go along with it. When school starts, this next year is going to be manic, especially with my role as mascot for the season. I also need to make sure my GPA doesn't drop, and sometime soon, I need to decide if I want to go to grad school to train to be a teacher.

I'm still on the fence, and that worries me a little. To teach well, to be effective in the classroom, I need to be both sure and passionate, right? I'm not quite sure I'm feeling it. Perhaps my tutoring has warped my experience a little. Either way, I've still got some time.

Kieran scoots past a few people to reach me. He's laden down with beer and hot dogs. I reach quickly for the dogs before he drops them, and my stomach grumbles happily at the scent of stadium food.

"Thanks."

He gifts me a smile before sitting next to me. "Great seats."

"They really are." We're a few rows back between the dugout and third base. I know enough about baseball to know the rules, but it's never grabbed my attention. "You ever played?" I indicate toward the field.

"A few times as a kid. It never stuck."

"A bit too slow, huh?"

Kieran chuckles. "You know it, but we best not say that too loud."

"This is pretty awesome, though, right?" A glance

around the ballpark shows more than a scattering of rainbow flags and other LGBTQ paraphernalia on display. That the game organizers and I'm sure the management and players, and looking around, lots of the spectators, are making this very visual show of solidarity is remarkable.

When we first entered and took in the sight, I'm not gonna lie, emotion hit me square in the chest, and from the look of awe on Kieran's face, he felt it too.

"It is." He peers over at me. "I'm pleased we came." His smile is endearingly sweet, so much so my fingers twitch to reach out to him. Instead, I subtly tuck my hand under my thigh.

We don't have to wait long for the players to enter the field. When they do, I immediately grin. Both teams are wearing pride colors— The Rams logo on their caps and their right sleeve, and the Panthers have a rainbow stripe at the front of their jerseys.

They're not the first team to do anything like this, which is awesome, but everyone in the crowd understands the significance of why they're doing this today—Tim's first game after his boyfriend's attack.

Emotion grips me, and I want nothing more than to reach out to Kieran. Tension thrums through me as I struggle to contain the push of feeling.

"Hey." And his hand is on mine, squeezing, his

voice soft, concerned. And holy rainbow hearts, I needed his touch, his comfort.

I can't look at him, though. If I do, I'll become a blubbery mess. There's no way I'm ruining my mascara. I chuckle lightly at the thought and press my arm against his.

"You okay?"

I bob my head, still refusing to make eye contact with him. "Yeah." I squeeze his hand for good measure.

We settle into the game, enjoying the atmosphere, cheering extra loudly when Tim pitches. But damn, it's a slow-ass game. I'm enjoying it because of what today's game represents, but I make two trips to the concession stand, once for chips and once for beers. Kieran goes a couple of times too.

I consider pulling out my cell, but figure that'd be rude considering Tim's generosity. Kieran's taking it all in, but since the last inning, he's been jittery. A couple of times I nearly put my hand on his leg. It's weird.

"Do you need to pee?" I finally ask.

"What?" Wide-eyed, he peers back at me. "No, why?"

"You're all, I don't know, not exactly on edge but you keep bouncing your leg."

Once again the announcer is saying something

and music is playing. Honestly, I've switched off; it's all sounding pretty much like white noise.

"I'm okay."

Not convinced, I study him. It's only when he offers me a smile that I return my attention to the field. While I don't expect I missed anything, you never know. It seems we're at the end of an inning.

"Do you want an ice cream sundae?" It's a warm evening, but at least the lowering sun means it shouldn't melt too quickly. When Kieran doesn't respond, I look at him, but the question dies before I can ask again.

He's pink-cheeked and a little wild-eyed.

"What is it?" As I ask the question, I'm aware of hollers and whistles around the stadium. Curious, I glance around and notice the large screen. Graphic love hearts decorate it, along with the words "Kiss Cam." Sweet. I love the kiss cam. I freeze when my face appears on the screen, right alongside Kieran's.

Holy shit.

Almost giving myself whiplash from how quickly I jerk to look at him, I lose the ability to breathe. There's no doubt Kieran's focus is solely on me. As if in slow motion, he leans forward, never losing eye contact, and I swear my heart is going to beat out of my chest.

And then he smiles, and I know this is all okay.

His mouth captures mine. It's sweet and little more than a long peck, but I get the message loud and clear.

Kieran Kendall is all in. Not only that, but he's absolutely mine.

CHAPTER 24
SECTION C: REMEMBER YOUR TEAM

KIERAN

"It was worth it, then?" By Tim's smirk, he seems to already know the answer.

"Yeah. I made the right call. Thanks for setting it up."

We're in the hotel bar, not long having dinner. I'm not sure where the rest of his team is, but I appreciate Tim Delaware taking the time out to spend with me and Dean. Both him and Jack.

"The power of the kiss cam, right?" He lifts his beer up to me and then takes a healthy swig. For a moment, his attention drifts to Jack, who's at the bar with Dean, talking animatedly. We're sitting a short distance away.

"It meant a lot to Dean," I admit. It should be

strange talking to Tim about shit like this, but over the past handful of days, I've opened up to him by text, something that surprised the hell out of me. It doesn't take a genius to understand why, though.

What Tim's been going through are my worst fears wrapped up in an ugly bow.

He's also the only other person I've opened up to about next year. Back in Mexico doesn't count, since it was Dean who spilled those beans.

When Tim returns his focus to me, he says, "I know I'm pissing Jack off, but I can't take my eyes off him."

"Understandable."

He bobs his head. "I need to be able to move on, though." The words don't seem to match his tone.

"How are you going to do that?"

A huff of breath precedes him rubbing his hand over his face. "Well, if I had my way, he'd quit his job and have a bodyguard." I go to laugh but stop myself when I realize he's absolutely serious.

"And, uhm… I'm assuming you're not getting your way?"

"That'd be a no. I have to trust that he knows what he's doing and believe that the homophobes of this world stay out of our way. It's a hard pill to swallow, but I'll do it because that's what Jack wants."

"Shit, man. I can't imagine." The tightening in my gut is unpleasant.

"I hope you never have to," he says. "Have you made any decisions about next year? Talked about it with Dean?"

"The kiss cam," I admit, "was about narrowing my options. That video is out there now. It always will be."

Tim surprises me by grinning and sitting forward, holding his beer bottle out for me to tap. "Here's to stepping out of the closet for good, Kieran. It's one hell of a thing."

With a huff of a shaky laugh, I tap my bottle with his and take two large gulps.

"I'm out." I shake my head. "Like, I knew that and that was the plan, but holy shit, I'm really out."

"Let me know if you shit yourself and need to go and change."

My laugh is immediate. "Is that what you did?" While I'm jesting, I'm also curious. He came out while already pro.

"Fuck yeah. I had a week of interviews and dealing with bullshit and coming out a million times. You would have thought the Tweet would have done the job for me, but apparently not." Going quiet, he studies me. "But your situation is different. Going pro as an openly gay man, and already in a relationship, there's no major surprises, you know? No coming out to your tea— Actually, does your college team know?"

"Yeah. They have from the beginning."

"And how'd that go?"

"They took me to a gay bar when we were freshmen so I could get my dick sucked."

Loud laughter bursts free from the both of us. He's not quite got control of himself when he says, "You see, man, you've already done the hard stuff." A glance at the bar makes him sober. "And what happened to Jack shouldn't stop you."

I want to call bullshit, but I don't think I can without being disrespectful or without getting my ass kicked. Something in my expression must give me away, though.

"You don't believe me?"

I settle on, "I want to."

"Listen," he sounds tired, "when I found out what had happened to Jack, for a moment there my world imploded, and I swear my heart cracked wide open. But it was Jack who kept me grounded, helped make me think more clearly. Does that mean I'm not scared?" He grimaces and my gut tightens. "I'm freakin' terrified at times, but I can't and won't let hateful assholes ruin my life or Jack's. That means I fight and will continue to fight, every single day if I have to, by calling out hate and homophobia and all the bullshit. And I have the voice and the standing to do so." His gaze doesn't waver when he continues, "And considering I know full well you're in the running to be in the top three draft picks, I figure you'll have a pretty powerful voice too, Kieran Kendall."

Of course he's right—about my voice, that is. It's something I've always known, even if I refused to admit it to myself before.

"The question is, are you willing to fight to make a change?"

The urge to scream "yes" rides me, but it's caught in my throat. Fighting every fucking day sounds exhausting. But isn't that something I'll have to contend with anyway? Fuck if I know. I've never been in a relationship before, let alone lived as a completely out gay man.

"Even if it means I have to make shit up as I go along to do it?" The sound of my pulse is loud in my head. "Because I have to tell you, Tim, I have no clue what I'm doing."

He tilts his head, the intensity in his gaze difficult to look away from. "And that's why you surround yourself with good people, allies, and those of us waving our rainbow flag right beside you. We're all making this shit up, paving the way, Kieran."

He stands abruptly. "Come on. Let's go see what they're up to and grab a shot. I think we need to celebrate our being all profound and shit with something that's going to set our throats on fire."

Laughing, I stand and follow him over to the bar. Unable to resist, I say, "There are much more fun ways to set throats on fire."

He snorts and claps me on the back. Shifting his focus to his boyfriend, he steps up to Jack's side. "We doing shots or what?"

"We are?" Dean's wide eyes are on me, and I shrug. "Anything but tequila."

I chuckle as I join him. "What Dean said. Not everything on our trip to Mexico agreed with us."

"In that case, let's have four fireballs." Jack orders for us, and before we know it, we've had three shots and I'm talking Dean out of going dancing.

"But I need the practice."

"Do you dance?" Jack asks.

"Super-secret insider info here," Dean whisper hisses, not doing a great job of keeping it down. "I'm the team mascot."

"No shit." Both Jack and Tim laugh. "How long have you been doing that for? Is that how you guys met?" Jack asks.

"Just since January—"

"And no, we met last year on a group project, and

if you listen to Dean tell it, I was a complete asshole." I follow up with a wink at my boyfriend. His cheeks are flushed, and he seems absolutely in the mood to party.

"It's true. He was," Dean confirms. "He was so uptight and had all these rules." I quirk my brow at him, but he simply grins at me. "Rules, schmules, though, right, Kieran?" He tries to haul me close, so I go willingly to press against his side.

"That's right. If they're not in the game book, they're definitely meant to be bent."

"Or obliterated," he says, pressing a small kiss on the corner of my mouth.

"And on that note," Tim interrupts, "we're going to head on up."

"Is there a nightclub upstairs?" Dean's eyes are wide, his voice eager.

"Hell no. Just a king-size bed with my and Jack's names on it."

At those words, I turn to Dean, remembering us having a similar exchange what feels like years ago rather than a few months. He's already watching me, a look in his eyes that makes me feel like I'm at the center of his world. "Upstairs?"

"Definitely." And then he's tugging me up, urgency in his movements, Tim and Jack laughing loudly beside us. And while it's a struggle to contain

Dean in his tipsy, lust-fueled state, we manage to get to our room without being arrested.

Once I have him backed against the wall, spreading kisses across his neck as though I need the taste of him as much as I need air, I try to ignore Tim's words.

But it's impossible.

What exactly am I prepared to do to have it all?

CHAPTER 25
RULE 4: SMILE AT ASSHOLES AND KILL THE BASTARDS WITH KINDNESS

DEAN

Thankfully I was able to pick up a couple of shifts a week at the diner. It's less than last year, but with my mascot gig, I no longer have time for more. The full scholarship is totally worth it, though, an amendment to last year's since apparently I'm kicking ass dressing up as a bear.

School doesn't start back until tomorrow, but town is already busy with students, as is college. And as I've been milling around the place, organizing books, and using the campus's general facilities, it's obvious that the kiss-cam moment really did go viral.

It's hard keeping my cool and ignoring the stares, but the extra smiles I receive kinda balance things out.

I've almost finished my afternoon shift, and about to deliver an order, when I notice Danny Lloyd sitting in a booth. He's with a couple of other guys, ones I don't recognize. As I'm looking over, his gaze connects with mine. He sends me a friendly smile, so I respond in kind and carry on my way.

"Here's your order. Does anyone need a refill while I'm here?" I ask the table of four.

All four indicate no, so I leave them to it and pull out my order pad as I make my way over to Danny. It's been a long time since I saw him. It was actually that party when he behaved like a dickhead, but his smile was friendly, so I'll do my job.

"How's it going over here?"

"Great." Danny angles back a little so he's not having to crane his neck. "You have a good summer?"

My smile is instant. "It was the best, thanks. You?"

"Yeah, it was good. I didn't get jetted off around the country or to any place that serves umbrellas in cocktails, but I got some surf in." His tone is nothing but pleasant, but his words get my attention. Is he talking about me?

Rather than ask and get into anything, I simply nod. You're impressed that I don't call him out, huh?

Yeah, me too. But who has time for bullshit? "Right, what can I get you?"

There's a flash of something in Danny's gaze, and I flick my attention to the two guys he's with, who are smirking in a way that could easily get my back up if I think too hard about it.

Pen poised, I wait expectantly and lift my brows, indicating I'm waiting.

"Vanilla milkshake, burger and fries," Danny finally says.

I jot it down and look at his friends. They order the same, and I fight to contain my eye roll. Like the champion I am, I simply offer a tight smile and let them know they won't have to wait too long.

I walk away, half expecting some additional commentary, but there's none. Once in the kitchen, I let Jeff know the order, ask Lucy for the drinks, then check the time. Fifteen minutes and I'm out of here. Tonight I'm staying over at Kieran's, and I kinda wish I'd accepted his offer for him to pick me up.

My feet ache. It's been a long eight-hour shift and has been busier than I expected. The long summer break has made me soft, I think, or at least not used to waiting tables for eight hours.

Lucy lets me know the shakes are ready to go, so I carry them over and place them in front of the guys.

"Here you go. I'm just about to clock out, but Tammy will look after you."

"Oh, you're going already?" Danny asks.

My brows draw low. "It's been a long shift, so it doesn't feel like 'already' to me," I offer with a polite smile.

He nods, though I don't know, I have a pretty decent bullshit radar, and I'm not buying the expression of understanding on his face. "Well, if you're going now, let me give you this." He winks and passes me a card… yep, a legit business card.

A quick glance shows me his number is printed on it. That's all. Absolutely nothing else. Can you believe this guy?

I hold the card in front of me, my brows furrowed. "What's this?"

"My number." The weird wink is back.

"Why'd I want your number?" It's time to call him out. "Haven't we had a similar conversation to this before?"

His careless shrug is annoying. "Just thought you might get lonely."

"I'm fine, thanks." I place the card on the table and freeze when his hand clamps down on my wrist.

There's nothing more that I hate than being underestimated. You'd be surprised how many times

I've been manhandled over the years by people thinking I'm a pushover because I'm not five ten or something. Hell, maybe you wouldn't, because like me, you know how many entitled assholes there are in the world.

"Take it. You think that because you kissed on video he's going to stick around for you? You know come two months he's going to be away so often he'll forget you and go looking elsewhere."

Tensing my jaw, I narrow my eyes and give his hand a pointed look. I don't pull away, don't wrench it back. Whatever he sees in my expression works, as he releases me and lifts his hand in surrender.

"Why don't you just keep the card and think about it?"

Anger vibrates under my skin. "Why don't you enjoy your milkshake, try not to choke on it, and don't think about approaching me again." It's an absolute directive.

The smile he's been aiming my way morphs into a sneer. "Whatever you say. I'm just trying to offer some friendly advice here. Kieran Kendall is dedicated to the game. If you think for one second you'll ever come first, you're a bigger fool than I thought. But hey, maybe that's what he likes about you."

Fuck, I want to punch him. Maybe throw his

shake over his head for being a prize prick. It takes every ounce of self-control I have to walk away. Each step is painful and loud with the sound of my pulse throbbing in my ears.

There's so much I can say to him. Tearing apart his words could be so easy. At the top of the list is the obvious of him being a jealous prick. But fuck, I need this job.

His words grate at me as I finish up and finally clock out. Did anything he said scrape at some of my insecurities? I hate that they do, but I'm also certain enough about my feelings for Kieran and his for me that I refuse to spiral.

I leave work out the back, even though I need to return to the front of the building where I'm parked on the street. But there's no way I want to be anywhere in the vicinity of Danny.

I shake my head, thinking how people can hide their real intentions and hate so well. I don't know if it's worse or not that Danny is gay. Am I naïve to expect an unspoken solidarity among queers? Snorting humorlessly, I can only believe the answer is yes.

Head high, I walk past the diner and keep my hands by my side so I don't flip Danny off. When I focus properly on the path in front of me, my heart flips over itself, pushing aside the anger taking hold of it.

Kieran's leaning against my rust bucket, arms folded, smile aimed my way, gaze roaming over me from head to toe before settling on my face.

I can't imagine never reacting this way when I see him. Between his styled brown hair, which I love to run my fingers through, the scruff on his face that I love the feel of, and the piercing intensity of his deep brown eyes, he's the image of perfection.

"Hey." I step into his arms and savor pressing my lips against his. Just two weeks ago, I didn't dream this was possible. Hoped, for sure, but now, while still at college... I sigh against his mouth before hugging him hard.

He squeezes me back and dips his head so his mouth his close to my ear. "Is something wrong?"

I shake my head. "Not anymore."

"You sure?"

I angle back and smile. "I'm absolutely positive. You came to surprise me?"

"Kinda figured I should grab every moment I can get with you."

"And that includes a short car ride?" My chest warms at the thought.

"Car ride, lunch, high fives on the basketball court." He waggles his brows, drawing a laugh from me. "As many nights as possible I can steal you away."

I'm more than okay with that. "Where's your car?"

"Back at your house."

"Shall we get going?"

He angles for another brief kiss, not giving a shit about the foot traffic. When he pulls away, I look over my shoulder, my brows shooting high when I see Danny standing in the doorway.

"What the fuck's he doing here?" My gaze snaps to Kieran's, my ear-splitting grin immediate when I see his narrowed gaze matches his disgruntled tone.

"Get your ass in the car." I unlock it and hold the door open for him, indicating for him to plant his ass down.

After a beat, Kieran looks at me, amusement clear on his features. "I could get used to you being all chivalrous."

I snort and push the door closed once he's sitting. I chuckle immediately. My car is tiny, and Kieran's huge frame in it always tickles me. The seat's already back, though. Something he did a while ago and I've never corrected.

When I turn, I once more glance at the doorway of the diner. I raise my hand and send Danny a finger wave. Well, that's before I turn my hand around and flip him off and mouth, "Fuck you."

"What was that all about?" Kieran asks once I'm settled by his side.

"Just finding the best way to handle jealous pricks." I side-eye him and take maybe a little too much delight in the way his eyes widen before he angles to peer over at the diner, then back at me.

"Should I be worried that mouth of yours is going to get us in trouble?"

"My mouth only gives you the best kind of trouble." I quirk my brow and start the engine.

"There's no arguing with that."

As I pull out, I fight a smirk. "That's probably the smartest thing you've ever said."

He snorts and shakes his head. "Yet all these brilliant smarts of mine are going to hit pause come the end of the school year and be diverted to me pulling off brilliant games."

I jerk in his direction so fast, I oversteer.

"Fuck." He reaches out and grabs the wheel, and wide-eyed I stare back at the road. Thank fuck there was no oncoming traffic.

"Shit. Fuck." My chest constricts and I have no choice but to pull over. As soon as I do, I unclip my belt and spin in the seat. "Explain." It's all I can manage with my mind whirling around and hope trying to break free.

"In the new year, I'm going to apply for the draft."

"You are?" Emotion punches against my chest and jams itself in my throat.

"I am. I wa—" He grunts when I launch myself at him. Clambering over the shift, I've never been so grateful for his long legs ensuring his seat's as far back as possible.

And then my mouth is on his. I swipe against his lips, seeking entry, needing this moment, desperate to show him how proud I am of him. There's no holding back as he wraps me up in his arms and we do a fucking epic job of devouring each other.

"Fuck," I groan when I realize how hard he is and exactly where we are. Rust bucket, remember? No fancy blacked-out windows for me. I angle away to see his face properly. "You're entering the draft."

"I'm entering the draft."

I'm sure my grin matches his, and it's fucking beautiful. "I'm so proud of you."

There's a shift in his expression, a softening. "Thank you."

"You're going to be amazing."

He chuckles. "Hopefully." He shifts in his seat. "As much as I love feeling your cock against my stomach, you best move before a cop pulls over and charges us with lewd behavior or something."

I move away, grumbling, "If we do, it'll all be your fault. Why would you tell me while I'm driving?" My brows shoot high. "I nearly crashed the car!"

"Because I haven't seen you all day, and I was going to wait till tonight, but when I saw you flipping off that wankstain, I just, I don't know, couldn't hold it in anymore."

Amused, I shake my head and pull away from the curb once it's safe to do so. "He is a wankstain." I sniff, trying to sound indignant. "And holy shit, you're going to be a League player."

"If I make the cut."

"It's adorable that you're being all modest. Don't. It doesn't suit you," I jest, darting away from him as best as I can when strapped in. "Hey, driving, remember!"

When his palm settles on my leg, I relax under his touch, and as we drive to collect his car, I can't help but think about those checkboxes I always compared Kieran to when I pretended I wasn't affected by him.

Finally, amazingly, every single one is checked off. Right alongside so many other traits I'd never considered. Feeling a rush of love, I gather his hand

and pull it to my mouth, planting a kiss on his warm skin.

I don't need to look to know he's focusing on me. Nor do I ever need to doubt that we're the center of each other's worlds. There's more than enough room for careers and chasing dreams.

He really is my unicorn jock.

EPILOGUE
RULE 1 REVISED: PLAY HARD, LOVE FIERCELY

KIERAN

Five Years Later

"Are you about ready?"

I quirk my brow at Dean. This whole innocent act he's attempting with that question is cute.

"What?" he says when I don't respond. There's nothing innocent about this man or his wide-eyed stare. Even the tone of his "what" makes my lips twitch.

"Am *I* ready?" I stand from the sectional and stalk toward him, enjoying his flush and how his gaze eats up my every movement.

"Well, you look presentable enough." Another slow trail of his gaze over my suit-covered body follows.

"I do, huh?" I step into his space, grabbing handfuls of ass cheeks as reward.

The truth is, for an hour and a half I've been trying to coax him out of the home office so he can get his ass into gear. The new literacy content developer contract he's recently secured is stealing away too many hours. But that's Dean. He's a perfectionist, and he gets such a buzz out of literature and all things grammar.

And since it means he works from home, I'm all for it, especially as it makes him so damn happy.

"I'll *do* you when we get home to show you how much, but right now you're making us late." He angles up, presses an all-too-brief kiss on my lips, then steps away chuckling.

"You're such a smart-ass," I say as he walks to the sideboard to grab his keys and wallet.

"And never forget it," he throws over his shoulder. My stare is stuck to his ass, though. He fills out the suit pants to perfection. I can't help but wonder if anyone would really miss us if we give tonight's event a miss.

"Don't even think about it."

My attention snaps to Dean's face. Yeah, totally

busted, and the asshole is a total mind reader, but in my defense, he knows I get all hot and horny when he's wearing a suit.

"The guys are relying on you—"

"On us," I correct, because as much as he tries to brush away any recognition or praise, Dean had a big role to play in the creation and growth of the annual Sporting Pride Auction.

Every single time, he blushes. This time is no different. Neither is the warmth that settles in my chest when I see his heated cheeks.

"—on us," he says gently, "to get those bids up."

I take hold of his hand. "We best get to it then."

Tonight we arranged a car so we could both kick back after the auction and indulge in a few beers. It's not often we can get together with Tim and Jack, and even rarer are we able to hang out with Ryan and Nate, since they moved back to Australia a few years ago.

Sometimes I can hardly believe this is our life, and we're richer because of the people we've met along the way. And no, I'm not talking about the tidy sum of money my recent contract or endorsements created. Though admittedly, they're pretty sweet deals.

"Are you prepared for the LA game on Tuesday?"

Dean asks once we're in the car and on the way to the hotel.

"Yeah, definitely. With Miles out with his injury, we've had to change a few plays, but Carlton is stepping up." At least the flight to LA isn't a long one. We moved to Phoenix a couple of years back when I transferred, and while it sucks to have to pull up sticks after three years, I don't feel guilty that I'm happy Dean stepped away from pursuing teaching.

His job means he can travel and be anywhere. It's made life and both our careers so much easier to manage.

"And you're not flying out with the team, right?"

He snorts. "That'll be a hell no."

"We're not that bad."

His brows fly high. "When I see you with your team, especially in a confined space, it's like we're back at college, spending hours on a bus together."

"You saying my teammates are immature?"

"No." He shakes his head. "I'm saying *all* of you are immature and still act like you're in college."

With swift moves, I attack, my fingers at his waist. He laughs loudly and attempts to push me away. "You see. Like this. Nothing's changed."

Taking pity on him and knowing he'll get pissy if he's too rumpled, I let him go, instead holding his hand. "Absolutely nothing's changed. You wouldn't want it any other way, right?"

I swear he melts in front of me, and I know he's going to treat me extra carefully later when he takes my ass. "I definitely wouldn't want it any other way."

He accepts my kiss, and we continue the journey with small talk and chatting about the items our committee arranged for tonight.

There's a sparkle of humor evident when Dean asks, "Who do you think will bid on Ty's contribution?"

"I'll bid to not win or take it home." I'm not even joking. Tyron still has very much the same personality as when we were at college. He has that whole conundrum thing going. You know, the one of appearing a little mean and grumpy, but he also has the most ridiculous and kind soul. But yeah, an oil painting of himself is something so brilliantly grotesque, I can afford to never see it again.

"I think Charlie was hoping he was joking when Ty commissioned it."

I snort. "Charlie should have known better."

"The Mexico trip that Ryan and Nate put in…" Dean's smile is soft when he speaks, like it is every time we talk about that time in our lives. Ryan Broadwater helped me start to believe this life we have now was possible. Sure, Dean and I are responsible for every decision we made, but it doesn't mean I don't recognize the helping hands we had.

"You want to go back to the resort?"

"Privacy, few prying eyes, and you getting your ass tanned, hell yes."

"Naked sunbathing, huh?"

"I'll even apply the lotion." His brows waggle, and this conversation is getting ridiculous as well as leading into the territory where I'm going to get a stiffy. Not a good look in the tight-fitting suit pants I'm wearing.

"Change of subject."

The grin he shoots me is far too smug. He's such an adorable asshole.

"But seriously, if you want us to bid on the resort, we can. Though we can go anytime you want us to in the off-season."

"Let's win the auction version. It'll mean more considering the good the donations make."

"We can do that."

He squeezes my hand. In response, I stroke my thumb over his soft skin, grateful for every touch.

The past five years have been interesting. There have been a few bumps and scrapes, but we're stronger for it. And though I want to kick my younger self for hesitating and nearly running from the best thing that ever happened to me, I know this is the way things were meant to happen.

Just as we're pulling up to the hotel, I focus on the man at my side, appreciating just how incredible he is.

"What?" he says after a few seconds of me staring.

We're both pointedly ignoring the cameras and flashes. Sure, we hate them, but at least tonight, the press being here will help raise awareness for a good cause.

"You wanna break a few rules tonight?" I drop my gaze to his mouth, making my intentions clear.

"With you?" His gaze darts around my face, a small smile curving his lips. "Always."

Go Bears! Want a cheeky bonus scene with a dance-off and Dean and Kieran's first on-court kiss? You can get the link in my Facebook group, RoMMance with Becca & Louisa or by subscribing to my newsletter. GET READY for book two, Facts, Smacts! Yet to meet Ryan Broadwater? Now is the perfect time to check out No Take Backs.

ALSO BY BECCA SEYMOUR

Zone Defense

No Take Backs | No More Secrets | No Wrong Moves

Fast Break

Rules, Schmules! | Facts, Smacts!

True-Blue

Let Me Show You | I've Got You | Becoming Us | Thinking It Over | Always For You | It's Not You | Our First & Last

Outback Boys

Stumble | Bounce | Wobble

Stand-Alone Contemporary

Not Used To Cute | High Alert | Realigned | Amalgamated

Urban Fantasy Romance

Thicker Than Water

ACKNOWLEDGMENTS

I can't thank you, my readers, enough for your support and encouragement to keep going and to continue creating stories. This writing gig is as wonderful as it is challenging. It's your faith in me that keeps me going.

As always, my team of editors, Liv, Donna, and Kim, deserve so much thanks and credit. You really are incredible.

Claire from BookSmith Designs reads my mind every single time. I'm so blessed to have your support.

A special thanks to Barb and Arden who work tirelessly behind the scenes supporting me. And a special thanks to the fabulous team of reviewers who took on my ridiculously adorable guys.

A HUGE thanks to my group, RoMMance with Becca and Louisa, for your fun interactions and daily support, and obviously my bestie Louisa for keeping me entertained.

ABOUT THE AUTHOR

I live and breathe all things book related. Usually with at least three books being read and two WiPs being written at the same time, life is merrily hectic. I tend to do nothing by halves, so I happily seek the craziness and busyness life offers.

Living on my small property in Queensland with my human family as well as my animal family of cows, chooks, and dogs, I really do appreciate the beauty of the world around me and am a believer that love truly is love.

To check for updates head to my website:

HTTPS://BECCASEYMOUR.COM

HTTPS://LANDING.MAILERLITE.COM/WEBFORMS/LANDING/R9F0I4

Plus, join my Facebook group.

HTTPS://WWW.FACEBOOK.COM/GROUPS/ROMMANCEWITHBECCALOUISA/

On TikTok, follow me here: HTTPS://WWW.TIKTOK.COM/@BECCASEYMOURWRITES

facebook.com/beccaseymourauthor

twitter.com/beccaseymour_

instagram.com/authorbeccaseymour

bookbub.com/authors/becca-seymour

www.ingramcontent.com/pod-product-compliance
Lightning Source LLC
Chambersburg PA
CBHW030955190726
48285CB00004BB/1323